Hopeless

P. ROSE

I love hearing from my readers! If you would like to chat with me, please follow me on Facebook at https://www.facebook.com/AuthorPatriciaRose/ or email me at patricia_rose.author@aol.com. I also have a newsletter, published periodically. I'll be glad to add you to the mailing list if you request by email.

Editing by Heather Osborne
Cover by Amanda Walker

ISBN-13: 978-1543164879

ISBN-10: 1543164870

CreateSpace Independent Publishing Platform, North Charleston, SC

Printed in the United States of America

First Edition
Printed March, 2017

Dedication

This book is dedicated to the two closest friends I've never met. Colin Rutherford and Heather Anne Osborne, both writers, took me under their wings a year and a half ago when I first stepped into the arena of dedicated Indie publishing. Their assistance, both personal and profession, has been inestimable. Thank you, my friends.

Prologue

This is not happening.
This is not happening.
This is not happening.

I mouthed the words silently, my lips barely moving, one word for each step I took, one for each breath. The hallway was institutional, harshly lit and silent, except for the slight squeak of my sneakers and the solid, measured steps of the man beside me. He was wearing boots. Not cowboy boots...motorcycle boots, with harness straps. They were black, slightly creased, but shiny and clean. His gray dress slacks covered most of them, but I'd been looking down, staring at my own feet and his, as we walked down the long hallway.

This is not happening.

We were in the basement of the building, just like they show on television. The silence echoed around me, pressing in on me, threatening to take the air from my lungs. I glanced up once, to see how much further we had to go, and the fluorescent light fixture above me spun in my peripheral vision. I breathed in and out, and then again, concentrating on the simple act as if my life depended on it.

1

This is not happening.

We stopped in the middle of the hallway, in front of a long window, and he tapped lightly on the glass. I paid attention to my breathing, and I stared at my shoes, noticing the scuff of reddish mud on my left sneaker. I heard a noise on the other side of the glass, and my eyes shot up of their own accord. My heartbeat accelerated and my breathing quickened, the fluorescents hazy in my eyes from the sudden tears blurring my vision.

I was relieved we weren't going inside the room…ashamed of my sense of relief, but relieved anyway. There was a gurney on the other side of the window, close enough I could have reached through the glass and touched the motionless form of the woman under the green hospital sheet. I felt myself shaking violently, and the bile in my stomach soured, threatening to rise. I felt the man waiting for me, and I didn't know why. Finally, I nodded once, sharply, lying to tell him I was ready.

Inside the room, the morgue attendant in surgical scrubs carefully folded the sheet down off the woman's face, uncovering her to below her neck. His movements were precise but respectful, and he smoothed the sheet neatly before stepping away from her. She was beautiful…or she had been. She had short, curly red hair, smooth features, full, bloodless blue lips…and she was so very pale.

I didn't realize I was holding my breath. I heard the man's voice from far away, gentle, but insistent. "Miss Pendleton? Is this your friend?"

The tears spilled over, and the window swam in front of me. My knees turned to gelatin, and the man with the gray suit and the motorcycle boots caught me, as the institutional tile floor suddenly came up to meet my face.

Hope Pendleton
Two Weeks Earlier

"I kid thee not!" Callie exclaimed, her green eyes dancing at me from across the table. "I swear to *god,* Hope, you should have seen his face! His eyes got *this* big!" She gestured widely with her hands, clearly exaggerating, but her laughter was contagious. As always, she was on warp speed ten, talking way too fast, gesturing wildly for emphasis, and as animatedly involved in the telling of her story as I was in the listening. She should have been the investigative reporter—we'd both said so a number of times.

"Cal, that is so gross!" I wrinkled my nose in mock disgust, stabbing another forkful of my chicken salad. "So, come on, don't leave me hanging here. What happened next?"

"You should have seen Dr. Monroe—you just made a joke, by the way—you know, Gross Room, gross—

3

when she stepped out of the path lab and saw it on the floor. I actually felt sorry for Jason." Callie mimicked the prim, British doctor I'd met only once. She pursed her lips in a prissy way, as if she were delicately sucking a lemon, and arched an imperious eyebrow. "'And *what* is going on out *here,* Mr. Winston?' And everyone was just standing there, frozen, you know, because nobody was going to be the first one to say anything."

I nodded, caught up in the story, envisioning the scene as my best friend described it. "What did Jason do?"

Callie grinned and took a quick gulp of her iced tea, drawing out the suspense. "He just looked at her, threw his hands up in the air, and said, 'Ya know, Doc Monroe, any day you come in to work and drop a patient's brain on the floor is bound to be a shitty day!'"

Cal subsided into a fit of laughter, and I laughed with her, imagining her geeky co-worker saying exactly that.

"Oh, my god, poor Jason!" I gasped, when I'd finally caught my breath. "Who does that, though, Cal? How in the world did he drop a *brain?* Nobody does that—nobody!"

"I know, right?" Callie agreed, motioning our waitress for the check and digging into her purse for her wallet. "And you know nobody in the Gross Room is ever going to let him forget it, of course. It went through pathology in ten seconds flat, so I'm sure it's already all over the hospital!"

I nodded, well acquainted with the gossip mill serving as Chatham Hills Medical Center, one of the major corporate employers in Chatham Hills, Tennessee. I'd done enough stories about the hospital during my internship to know more dirt than most, but Callie had the real inside scoop.

My best friend since fifth grade—cute, freckle-faced, red-headed Patricia Callahan—had always dreamed of being a surgeon. Her dream got waylaid when her parents were killed in a car accident, leaving her to finish raising her angry, rebellious brother. Instead of pursuing her own goals of college and medical school, Callie had taken the first decent-paying job she could get straight out of high school. Now, it was ten years later. Callie's brother, Rory, was completely absent from her life, and she still worked in the same position as a data entry technician in our small hometown hospital's pathology department.

I'd been the lucky one. I earned my B.A. in Journalism and moved away from Chatham Hills to Louisville, Kentucky. Even though Louisville was a traditional southern city in its own right, it was a four-hour drive and a century forward in time from my tight-knit, incestuously conservative hometown. I had a job I loved with the *Louisville Metro-Tribune,* a minor local newspaper, and if my nightlife wasn't so much to speak of, that was by my own choosing. After a long work week, I usually wanted nothing more than to cuddle up with a great book, a hot cup of tea, and the one man in my life, Mr. Wuzzles, my small, four-year-old orange tabby cat.

"I'm getting this," I told Callie, pulling out cash and snatching the ticket from her hand. She opened her mouth to object, and I preempted her sternly. "I have more money than you do."

Callie wrinkled her freckled nose and stuck her tongue out, looking for all the world like she had the first day I'd met her in middle school. "Bitch," she accused cheerfully.

I grinned, putting money on the table, and we both

stood.

"God, Hopeless, I wish you could stay longer!" Cal moaned, hugging me fiercely.

"We'll do a weekend before the end of summer," I promised, as we walked toward our cars.

"Weekend!" she exclaimed, her face brightening. "Yes! With Midori Sours and Cosmos and chick flicks!" Her face suddenly took on a strange, wary expression. "That reminds me…I have plans this weekend. Can you be my safe call?"

I stopped in the hot July parking lot, an icy chill suddenly rolling up my back. My good mood was gone. I hated that Callie could tell immediately, even though I fought to keep my expression neutral.

"So…what's going on this weekend?" I asked cautiously.

Callie looked away from me, and, when she looked back, her reply was equally cautious, her voice subdued but determined. "I'm going to meet a guy, Hope. If everything's cool, I'm going to have a play date with him."

I sagged against Callie's red Impala and studied my tennis shoes while I absorbed her answer. The first time she had asked me to be a 'safe call' for her, I'd envisioned 'play date' to mean tennis or handball, or even *Magic: The Gathering*. Whips and chains had been the last thing to enter my mind, and I had been horrified when Callie explained to me what she had meant by 'playing.' Still…she was a consenting adult, and I loved her more than anyone in the world. Who was I to judge?

"Is it someone from your local…umm, group?" I asked finally.

"No," she replied. "He isn't in the local community, honey. He's not from Nashville at all—just here for a few months for work. We've been talking online, and his closest references are in Australia. That's why I need the safe call. I can have Michelle do it, if you're not comfortable. It's just…I trust you more."

She knew how to get to me. She always had. I'd been her safe call before—this would be my fourth time, actually. Everything had always been fine, and the sharp pang of fear I felt for her was just me, overreacting.

"God…Cal," I groaned. I looked at her, really studying her face. She was smiling at me, but it was tremulous. She knew how hard this was for me to do. But…I knew how hard it was for her to ask.

"What…" I faltered, remembering the last time, and the bruises she had covered so carefully with concealer makeup. She could see what I was thinking, and she reached out for both of my hands. I squeezed hers tightly, as I asked the question. "What are you going to let him do to you?"

"I know this is hard for you, Hope," she told me, echoing my thoughts from earlier. "I really understand how…disturbing it must be. But, I *need* this. I promise you. It makes me happy."

Her words were quiet and sincere, and she had me, even though she had deliberately dodged my question. "Of course, I will," I told her, swallowing the lump in my throat and blinking my eyes quickly. "Honey, I'm all for anything that makes you happy, you know that!"

Her face was full of joy again, and she hugged me tightly. "I *always* know that, Hopeless!" She grinned. "I'll be fine, I promise. He's a really nice guy."

I bit back my first response and glared at her fiercely. "You send me *everything* you have on him. Everything! You got that? I want his driver's license number, his passport I.D. number, I want his fucking *fingerprints!*"

Callie saluted me sharply, her eyes dancing. "Ma'am, yes, ma'am! It'll be in your email by tonight, I promise!"

I couldn't help myself. I smiled back at her. I was completely confused by her life choices, but, as always, willing to support her and be her friend, as much without judgment as was possible. "When are you meeting him? And where?"

"Friday at 1900, in Nashville," she told me, and then frowned, switching from military time for my benefit. "I'll make my calls at 7:30, 10:00, and whenever I'm home safely."

I nodded, acknowledging the times. "Tomatoes?" I asked.

She confirmed her code word, squeezing my hands happily. "Thank you *so* much, Hope! I love you! Thank you for not judging me, sweetie."

I swallowed hard, and this time, my smile quavered. "You be careful," I told her. "Don't let him hurt you … so much."

She nodded soberly, but she was too happy now, too excited at the prospect of her weekend play date. I knew she wasn't really hearing my warnings. I bit my judgmental tongue and reminded myself, yet again, she was an adult. The sex games she played were consensual. *I was overreacting,* I told myself. The Irish in her made her naturally fair-skinned, and she bruised so easily…I tore my mind away from those thoughts, before I could open my mouth to say something negative.

I pulled my car keys and sunglasses from my purse, putting the glasses on quickly to cover the doubt in my eyes. Callie and I hugged goodbye again, and she got into her beat-up red Impala, buckling herself in, while I walked over to my new Prius and the four-hour drive home.

Callie was good to her word. The next morning, I sat at my dinette table and spooned coffee into a saucer, blowing on it carefully to cool before passing it to my caffeine-addicted cat. I read her email. *'He's Wonderful!'* was the subject line. I fought the impulse to stick my finger down my throat and gag, deciding the gesture would be wasted on Mr. Wuzzles.

The email wasn't as detailed as I had hoped it would be, but at least there was a small photograph attachment. Daniel Fletcher, AKA Mr. Wonderful, looked to be in his late thirties or early forties. *He was handsome*, I admitted grudgingly, *but not in a pretty-boy way*. He had dark hair and brown eyes, a strong, square jawline, lips too thin for my taste. His face wore an expression somewhere between surliness and amusement, as though he had not wanted his picture taken. He wore— what else?— a plain black t-shirt and a silver rope necklace. His upper arms were muscled, but not overly so. He was admittedly a man I would have looked at twice, and I felt an empathetic ping of Callie's attraction.

Her email gave me his name and his internet pseudonym of 'Painman.' I allowed myself the satisfaction of gagging over that one. It also included his birthdate and the note, 'Dominant, HIV-, drug/disease free. Light smoker, social drinker. Jack and coke with ice, served flat on the palm of your hand, with your eyes *down*.'

I swallowed my sense of revulsion, reminding myself, for the millionth time, Callie's choices were her own. With a sigh, I closed the email and shut down the laptop, drinking the last of my coffee and carrying the cup and saucer to the dishwasher. There was nothing more I could do. I could ensure Callie's safety, as I had done on her previous 'play dates,' by being her safe call, but that was the limit of my power. I couldn't protect Cal from herself. I couldn't stop her from degrading herself, or allowing herself to be beaten. I could just be her friend, and hope like crazy she got bored with her 'alternative lifestyle' sooner rather than later.

I turned the water on in the shower and stripped, my mind still grappling. I'd known Cal since fifth grade, but I still didn't understand this part of who she was. She was my closest friend, and we told each other *everything*. Almost a year ago, she had eagerly confided in me, telling me she had 'found herself' in submission, and she was happier and freer than she'd ever been. I truly tried to understand and be happy for her, but I balked at her invitation to attend a sadomasochistic party. I was positively horrified the next day when she proudly showed me the bruises and welts—whip marks!—on her back and legs. For the first time in my life, Callie felt like a stranger to me. I simply couldn't understand her, and I was at a loss for my inability to share her apparent joy. Cal had gone someplace sinister and dark, and I couldn't follow. All I could do was watch, wait by the telephone, and pray she was being careful.

I spent most of my workdays, both Thursday and Friday, in the Jefferson County Clerk's Office, researching the property purchases and sales of a certain member of the Jefferson County Chamber of Commerce, whom, my editor suspected, had accepted some cushy graft payments. Investigative reporting at its finest hour—buried in deed books and registries too old to be digitalized. Friday evening couldn't come (and go!) quickly enough for me.

I arrived home around five o'clock Friday afternoon,

carrying the three bags of groceries I'd picked up from the local market on my way. Mr. Wuzzles had made it quite clear to me he required more cat treats as sustenance, or he would waste away to a mere shadow of himself. I set the grocery bags on the counter in my kitchen and caught up my cat, who suffered politely while I snuggled him.

"I love you *best,* Mr. Wuzzles!" I told him, enjoying my silly ritual. When he had enough, he meowed disdainfully, and I set him down. I quickly put my groceries into the pantry and refrigerator. My cell phone rang, as I expected, around 5:20 p.m.

"Oh, god, Hope, I wish you were here!" Callie wailed pitifully. "I don't know what to *wear!"*

I laughed. Some things, apparently, never change— not since middle school, in any case. "Okay, Cal, one step at a time. What have you got it narrowed down to?" I pulled a Diet Coke from the fridge and settled into my spot on the sofa. Mr. Wuzzles promptly plopped down next to me and began kneading my thigh.

Callie and I talked for the next twenty minutes, finally settling on her green silk cami, with matching jacket, and a just-above-the-knee black skirt. She was going for 'demure' instead of 'slutty,' and I heartily approved her choice. I didn't think Mr. Wonderful would need much encouragement. According to Cal, he had been a 'Dominant' in the 'lifestyle' for five years, and he worked in an import/export firm based out of Australia, with a corporate office in Nashville. Cal had spoken to him several times on the telephone since Wednesday afternoon, and she seemed beside herself with anticipation at the thought of actually meeting him.

I agreed he seemed attractive enough, and we had the same old conversation we always had about how looks don't make the man. Before I knew it, Callie was signing off and heading out the door for her thirty-minute drive to Nashville, and the small Italian restaurant where she would be meeting him. I wasn't even half-joking when I suggested she meet him at Green Hills Mall or the Grand Ole Opry instead...the more public, the better! I reminded her to call me promptly on her agreed marks, and she teased me about being a mother hen. I threatened to call her every five minutes, and she counter-threatened to give me *way too much* information. We laughed, said we loved each other, and hung up shortly before six.

I settled in to wait.

My Friday night routine was *not* set in stone, thank you very much. I sometimes went out to dinner with friends, and I had even suffered the occasional blind date here and there. But, my weekend evenings were habitual enough that Mr. Wuzzles had my number, at least. I had changed into my summer sleepwear—an oversized t-shirt and red bedroom slippers, with pom-poms on the ends of false laces. Those, of course, were for Mr. Wuzzles. He adored my bedroom slippers, his adoration surpassing normalcy and actually approaching the zone of 'foot fetish.' He knew as soon as my cup of tea had brewed, and I'd settled on the couch with my dinner *de nuit* (a Lean Cuisine frozen meal), found my place in my newest novel (Anne Bishop's *Written in Red*), and pulled my feet up onto the sofa, the pom-poms were *his!*

He was lying on his back next to my foot, a pom-pom held lazily in one paw and a deep, contented purr rumbling through his chest. He was half-asleep, so he startled slightly at 7:30 when my cell phone chirped, and I moved to answer it.

"Hey, honey," I greeted. "So, how's it going?"

Callie's laughter came through loud and clear. "So far, great!" she told me, her voice warm, but less gushy than normal. Callie was in her 'mature mode, ' I knew. She was a woman who flirted now, not a 'bestie' with a fan-girl squeal. I smiled, feeling happy for her, while the knot in my stomach started to dissolve.

"So, dish," I ordered. "What's he like?"

"He is very, very *fine,"* she told me, her words directed both at me and the man who was sitting near her. "Very much a gentleman. We're at Stefano's now, and I'm thinking about either the veal or chicken parmigiana and a summer salad, with tomatoes, of course."

Tomatoes. Excellent. I breathed fully, relief flooding into places I hadn't even realized had been tight with apprehension.

"I'm so glad, honey," I told her sincerely. "Does he look like his picture?"

"Not so much," Callie admitted. "He's older than his picture, his hair is different, and he's as—"

"Enough, *cher.* Hang up, now." I heard his voice, the words quiet, yet the tone of command unmistakable. Callie's sharp intake of breath told me the tone had not escaped her notice, either. I bristled in resentment, but I still wasn't ready for Cal's immediate compliance.

"Gotta go, Hope—love ya, bye!" she said, and she hung up, before I could even voice my protest.

Well. Crap.

I glared at my cell phone for a moment, and then down at Mr. Wuzzles, who was now gripping my pom-pom, his claws lazily flexing into the soft cotton.

"I guess I've been dumped," I told Mr. Wuzzles crossly, as I found my place in my novel again. "It's pretty clear she doesn't need me tonight!"

13

I was annoyed. I loved Callie like a sister, but she could be an inconsiderate ass sometimes, especially when there was a man involved.

I sighed, turning back a page in my book, knowing I'd have to re-read a few passages. It wasn't like it hadn't happened before—on *both* our parts, actually. When I'd been all wrapped up in *Braaaaaad* in college, I'd been pretty beastly to Cal…and she had put up with my bitchy, petty-assed self, her only retribution being to poly-syllabize his name and punctuate it with an eye roll every time she said it. *God, he had turned out to be such a jerk!*

I smiled, feeling my anger soften at the memory. All women did stupid shit when men were involved. God only knew why.

"I much prefer *your* company, Mr. Wuzzles," I told my cat, with conviction. He *mrrrphed* his agreement and batted ferociously at the evil pom-pom which had slipped through his grasp.

I read until shortly before ten, then put the book down for a while. I turned on the television and headed into the kitchen to put on another kettle of tea. *I was going to give Callie a curfew,* I thought, as I checked the time on my microwave. 9:58 p.m. She was going to have to dump Mr. Wonderful in time to give me her final safe call by midnight. Well, okay, by one. I wasn't going to sit up waiting until three in the morning, like I'd done the last couple of times she had 'played.'

9:59 p.m. I played with my teabag while it steeped, then took my phone over to the dinette table and sat. Mr. Wuzzles came over to investigate, so I removed my cup from the saucer and put a few spoonsful of tea into it for him. I'd chosen a non-caffeinated herbal blend, so Mr. Wuzzles sniffed it politely and decided to wash his ears instead.

14

10:00. I listened to the drone of the CNN anchor and waited. Callie usually called a minute or two before her prearranged time, but it wasn't like we'd synchronized our watches or anything. I really needed to lighten up, and stop overreacting so much to her…lifestyle.

10:04. I refused to think about whatever Callie was doing that had her so distracted. Well, okay, I did think about it, but not in detail. All right, maybe a bit of detail about the sex part, at least—*it had been awhile, okay?*— but definitely not about the other stuff.

10:06. My irritation flared up again. It was bad enough Callie was exhorting my indirect participation in her activities, but the least she could do was be considerate of the fact I was using my Friday night waiting by the telephone for her call!

10:07. Not that I'd been doing anything else with my Friday night, anyway. Reading. Playing with Mr. Wuzzles.

10:10. Enough. I picked up my cellphone and speed-dialed, hitting the send button. I breathed in deeply, determined my irritation with Callie would not show itself in my voice. The phone rang. And rang. On ring number six, it clicked over to Callie's voicemail. "Hi!" her cheerful voice greeted. "You've reached Trish Callahan's cell phone, and I'm not answering it. You know what to do at the beep."

I hung up and stared at the phone for a moment, stunned. I hit send again. Again, six rings and voicemail. I hung up and hit send immediately, getting a busy signal as I crossed the circuits. I waited almost a minute before dialing again. Voicemail.

I paced. Now, I was pissed. And scared.

10:13. Voicemail.

15

Okay, stop and breathe. Real life happened. She could have left her phone in her purse and gone into another room. Maybe she was in the bathroom. I needed to chill a little bit, and give her a few minutes.

I waited. I breathed. I chilled. For seven, unbearably long minutes, I chilled.

10:20. Voicemail. I was frantic now, and ready to admit it. I dialed repeatedly, hanging up the moment I didn't get through, then immediately dialing again. Voicemail. All circuits busy. Voicemail. And voicemail again.

I stared numbly at my phone, shocked and disbelieving. Not even Callie would be twenty minutes late for her safe call, for fuck's sake—she was the one who had taught me about them, stressed to me how important they were. I was going to have to call the police. Oh, my god, I was going to have to report this, and I didn't know one fucking thing about Mr. Wonderful that would help them find Callie! I fought down my panic, as my thumb automatically hit send again. I needed to boot up the laptop and get that email—

"Hello?"

10:24 p.m., and Callie answered, sounding sleepy. My breathing roared in my own ears, and I felt my face flush with anger. I was going to *kill* her myself!

"What happened to ten o'clock?" I snapped, not caring a bit if my irritation was showing in my voice. I wanted it to show. I wanted to scare the hell out of Callie, like she had just scared me, to hurt her and shock her, and to let her know her best friend was *furious* with her!

"Ohhh...heyyyy, Hope. How're you doing?" Callie's voice was still sleepy, and it had a dreamy, happy quality to it that set my teeth on edge. She had explained it to me—or she had tried. I knew all about 'subspace' and the 'endorphin high' she got from letting some pervert asshole beat the crap out of her, until, in defense, her brain flooded her bloodstream with chemicals like dopamine, serotonin, and adrenaline. I knew, intellectually, how good it was supposed to feel, just like a long-distance runner's 'high' when he finally broke through the wall and hit his pace. At the moment, I didn't give a shit.

"I'm just fucking peachy!" I growled at Cal, my voice hard and angry. "How are *you,* is the question."

"I'm wonderful," Callie replied dreamily. "I'm having a good time, Hope. We're in a … I guess, a hotel, and man, it's schwanky!"

"Why the hell didn't you call me when you were supposed to?"

"What?" Cal asked, as though she'd missed the question. "Oh, dinner? Yeah, dinner was great, Hopey. I had the veal."

'Hopey.' My mind froze, and the blood rushed in my ears, making it seem as though the word echoed in my skull.

"What are you talking about, Cal?" I asked slowly.

"No, I didn't eat the salad," Callie said, and then, inappropriately, she giggled. "No tomatoes at all."

I swallowed, the phrase 'no tomatoes' ringing in my brain, just as the word 'Hopey' had. We had worked out the code phrase months ago, when she had gone on her first 'play date.' If everything were okay, she would somehow work the word 'tomatoes' into the conversation. Callie was a health freak, and she ate salad with every meal except breakfast, which was why we had chosen the code…simple, easy to remember, consistent.

Callie had just told me she had had 'no tomatoes'; in

17

itself, that was enough to make me panic. But, she also called me 'Hopey.' Callie never, *ever* called me that, and I knew she had said it intentionally, to let me know something was *very* wrong.

In ninth grade, I was crushing hard on cute-but-dumb JV football jock, Tom Quinn. The Sadie Hawkins dance was coming up, and it was the girls' turn to invite the boys to the dance. I was terrified, but for two weeks, Callie worked to convince me I was beautiful enough, funny enough, and smart enough Tom would be crazy not to go with me! With Callie's encouragement, I finally worked up the nerve to ask him, just before last period, the week before the dance.

Apparently, I was beautiful, funny, and smart, but I wasn't a cheerleader, and I wasn't blonde. Tom had openly laughed at me and called me 'Dopey Hopey.' It was the cruelty of the laughter more than the nickname that sent me, mortified, to the girls' bathroom to sob with the angst only an adolescent girl could understand.

Callie did not suffer jerks lightly. She'd been so enraged on my behalf, she had somehow gotten hold of a handful of gay porn magazines, which she stashed in Tom's gym bag, leaving it partially unzipped. It was all over school Wednesday morning that the magazines had spilled out of Tom's bag before P.E. class. Not even his status as uber-jock could stand up to that. Copies of *Butt Boys, Jock,* and *In Touch for Men* had been bandied around the boys' locker room to hoots of cruel laughter.

Even then, I had thought the punishment exceeded the crime, but Cal had glared at me and told me fiercely you did *not* mess with her BFF. She never told me how she'd gotten her hands on those magazines, either. But…she would *never* have called me, 'Hopey.'

"Where are you, Callie?" I asked gently. I waited

several long moments for a reply.

"I told you, in a hotel with my friend, Daniel," she told me, her voice a stoned purr. I listened closely, comparing her voice to other times she'd been riding the endorphins. This wasn't the same. Callie was drugged, and I knew it. I heard a rustling, as though she had adjusted the phone, and when she continued, her voice was slightly muffled. "Thanks for calling, though, okay? I love you, Hope."

She disconnected, and I started trembling. If this was a prank, or some kind of test of the 'emergency safe call system,' I would never speak to Callie again. But I knew in my gut, it wasn't a joke. When she had said, 'I love you,' she had been saying, 'Goodbye.' I could hear it in her voice, and I could feel it in my heart. My hands shook violently, as I pressed the three digits and hit send. I had just stepped into my worst nightmare.

"Louisville Metro 911. Please state your emergency," the slightly nasal, tinny female voice asked.

"Please, I need help," I choked out. "My best friend's been kidnapped."

Gerard
The Spy

Jimmy Lau, a Red Pole Enforcer for the Chinese mafia, sat at the head of the table, leading the late-night business meeting. It was the position of power, which meant a great deal to Lau. Two Asian businessmen and a white man, each in their sixties, sat along the left side of the table, and a dark-skinned woman in her forties sat on the right. I sat at the foot, closest to the only exit. Lau was the only person in the room I knew, and I wasn't there to socialize. I kept my mouth shut and my eyes and ears open, as both of my employers expected.

I worked for Jimmy Lau, in the capacity of one of dozens of security specialists in his massive criminal enterprise, and the chief of his Nashville area security operations. Unknown to Lau, I also worked for the Central Intelligence Agency. I was a member of an international drug enforcement task force, and we were looking to put Lau's massive criminal enterprise out of business.

My supervisors were practically drooling at the prospect of getting Lau in on something that could stick; when we brought him in, they were going to push him hard to give up his superiors, hoping to work their way as far up the chain of command as they could go. They were following the drugs; the human trafficking operation was secondary. Personally, I had no interest in seeing Jimmy Lau behind bars. I wanted the son-of-a-bitch in the ground.

I'd spent four years 'running' for Lau, and I'd risen in his organization to a position of power and trust almost unheard of for a non-Asian in the Triad Society. Lau liked my work. I had no conscience, as far as he knew, and I didn't lose the contents of my stomach easily. I had seen Lau torture three women, and then indifferently order their executions. The risk to the integrity of the case, and to my own life, had prevented me from acting. I'd been powerless to stop his heinous crimes, but that didn't make it one bit easier to sleep at night. We needed Lau—and his organization—under the Racketeer Influenced and Corrupt Organization Act, or the arrest would be useless.

We were closing in on the bastard now, though. No more women would die—all I needed was one more piece of the puzzle, and we would shut down Lau's entire sordid operation.

RICO was key. Arrest under any other grounds would be more damaging than nothing at all. The necessity of getting a RICO arrest had made it impossible for me to interfere with Lau's contemptible acts of sadism, when he'd realized his beautiful prisoners were trying to escape. RICO was why the dying screams

21

of those three young women would haunt me for the rest of my life.

My orders were clear. We couldn't settle for just Jimmy Lau. He was merely the tail of the lizard; if we took Lau down, without killing the entire beast, that tail would merely re-grow. Another Red Pole Enforcer would simply move in to handle the southeastern U.S. territory. That wasn't going to happen; not if I had anything to say about it.

I brought my thoughts back to the meeting I was attending. For several frustrating minutes, three of the men in the conference room spoke in Chinese, while the rest of us simply looked at each other.

Finally, Lau switched to English.

"So, the medication is a carefully controlled mixture of Rohypnol, cocaine, and OxyContin," he said, nodding to the English-only speakers in the room. "It's a specialized 'blend,' a designer drug, if you will. It has been shown to keep the merchandise placid and relaxed, yet still in a semi-conscious condition for feeding and cleaning. It allows the merchandise to be cared for, so it is still of value when delivered to its new owner."

I thought of the pretty, mocha-skinned girl in Lau's 'care' right now, and deliberately blanked my face to conceal my thoughts. There was too much riding on this for me to get qualms. The girl was overly-sensitive to the drug, but Lau's physician—yes, his own *personal* physician, bought and paid for like a box of condoms—was monitoring her closely. Hippocratic Oath to the contrary, Dr. Albrecht Meier had the fringe benefit of being allowed to fuck her, so he was motivated to keep her healthy.

"What is the practical application?" the black woman asked. Her voice was a husky contralto…it would have been lovely to listen to, had circumstances been different. "Our US clients aren't part of your 'export trade,' Mr. Lau. They aren't interested in being docile—they simply want to feel good."

Lau nodded with a polite smile, but I saw the snake-like coldness behind his eyes. He was king of his world, and he didn't like being challenged. I knew the African-American woman somehow supplied Lau with the leads he needed to find slim, beautiful, young women with no family or social ties, but I would bet a week's pay she had just overestimated her own importance in Lau's operation.

"My scientists are adjusting the formulas, 'tweaking' them a bit, if you will pardon the pun, *cher*." Lau's soft Cajun accent contrasted enough with his Asian features to seem exotically foreign, and the woman clearly missed the hint of anger in his tone. "They are reducing the amount of Rohypnol and increasing the OxyContin. Their protocols are very specific, and all of their testing procedures are well beyond my own understanding…but, essentially, I am given to understand the end product will produce a euphoria rivaling both MDMA and heroin, yet not inducing loss of consciousness. My science team is very certain the drug will be popular among the recreational crowd."

Lau's 'science team' consisted solely of Dr. Meier, a closet Aryan, unlicensed medical quack, and sadistic rapist. His 'protocols' consisted of shooting the girls up with different cocktails before fucking them. If he remembered, he even wrote the formulas down.

"How will the product get to our distributors?" the white guy asked, and I snapped to full alert, knowing I was up next.

"Ah, a good question, my friend," Lau said, his voice

much warmer than when he had addressed the woman. "It is the reason I have invited Mr. Gerard, my security chief, to attend our meeting today."

I pulled up the PowerPoint presentation and stood. "Thank you, Mr. Lau," I said, and indicated the screen with no further pleasantries.

"As you all know, Lau Enterprises is a vast corporation, with multiple avenues of revenue," I said, my voice as toneless as that of any other white-collar drone in corporate America. "Mr. Lau has purchased the cooperation of several politicians, as well as ranking officials in the DEA, FBI, and local police. The Nashville law enforcement will not be a problem, except for one or two trouble-makers. Now, further out..."

The meeting lasted an hour and a half. At the end of it, Jimmy Lau came out on top, just like always.

Some days, I really hated my job.

Hope
The Nightmare Begins

The good news was they believed me. I'd had a horrifying vision of being told something along the lines of, 'We can't even take a report until she's been gone twenty-four hours,' and then having to drive down to the Nashville police station by 9:00 Saturday morning to bash somebody's brains in.

It was nothing like that. I censored what I told the dispatcher, of course, to make it seem as though Callie had just planned a normal date, with a normal guy. Since it was an online relationship, she and I watched each other's backs. When I explained about the 'safe call' we used, the dispatcher told me it was good thinking. She also told me calling the police immediately upon learning of a 'suspicious situation' was a smart move; it could make their job easier, and it could make a difference to Callie.

The dispatcher set me somewhat at ease. She was reassuring, but professional enough to calm my panic, and she helped bring my own professional persona out. She told me her name was Karen, and that was the moment I started breathing again. I felt like there might be some hope after all, because she was a *person*. She was *Karen,* and she was taking this as seriously as I was. I was impressed with how thoroughly she interviewed me over the phone, asking questions that made me remember details I would not have thought of mentioning.

Of course, I'd already intended to tell them what Callie and I had planned for her to wear, but Karen also helped me remember other facts. 'Daniel' was older than in the picture he'd sent Callie. He had a deep, somewhat husky-hoarse voice and a slight, but unusual, accent. He had called her *'cher.'* The name of the restaurant they'd met at was Stefano's Italian Ristorante, and by 7:30 p.m., they had not yet ordered their meal. By 10:00, they were in a hotel, and it was one of the more luxurious hotels in Nashville, for Callie to consider it swanky. I was impressed with how many details I actually did know. I took diligent notes throughout our conversation, jotting down my answers, and any other thoughts I had, so I could review them later.

When Karen had the answers she needed, she transferred me to the police department in Chatham Hills. I waited on hold for several minutes, while she relayed the information I'd given her. I was then asked exactly the same questions by Sgt. Brooks of the Chatham Hills Police Department. Brooks was less personable, but he was just as efficient, perhaps more so, than Karen had been. He told me to forward him a copy of the email Callie had sent, with the photo attachment, and assured me it would be sent to the FBI. He warned me not to get my hopes up; the probability of immediate identification, even with the FBI's fancy facial recognition software, was very low. These things took time.

I agreed to forward the email. I edited it and sent it to him, while I addressed his other questions. I was torn between the need to protect Callie's privacy (and job), and the need to tell the police everything that could possibly help them find her. At the moment, I didn't see why they needed to know about her lifestyle choices. They might later...but I would protect her privacy, for as long as it was an option.

Callie had no living relatives, except an aunt with Alzheimer's, who lived in a Chatham Hills nursing home, and her younger brother, Rory. Rory had dropped out of her life almost four years ago, and, last I heard, was living in New York City. I promised to look for any contact information for Rory, but also agreed to sign their documents as Callie's next-of-kin. It was only when Sgt. Brooks told me he could fax the paperwork up to Louisville Metro PD for my convenience that I realized what I'd intended to do from the moment Callie hung up the phone.

"Thank you, Sergeant, but I'm coming down to Chatham Hills," I told him. "I'll come into the station tomorrow and sign whatever you like, and I'll bring some current pictures of Callie.

"Any information you can give us will be helpful, Miss Pendleton," Brooks told me, "and it's certainly your choice to complete the documents in person. You might consider it a waste of your time and resources, though. Nowadays, a faxed signature is just as legal as the real thing."

His voice was pleasant, but it was a subtle deterrent,

a gentle suggestion to keep my buttinsky butt up in Kentucky, where it belonged, and let him do his job. I understood his position, and I respected it. This wasn't television, and I was neither Cagney nor Lacey. However, in the moment I'd made the decision to keep Callie's private life private—for now—I also decided I was going to put some of my own investigative journalism training to use.

It *wasn't* television, and I was jaded enough to realize police resources were limited, especially in a three-stoplight town. In most of the adult missing persons' cases in the United States, the 'vanished' simply came back home a day or two later and picked up their lives. In a case like Callie's, though, they would investigate. The police would do what they could. And when that had run its course, and they came up empty, they would add Callie's file to a big stack of other people's files. They would recommend I contact a private investigator, if I were still insistent on answers. I was skipping that step. I would find out everything I could, above and beyond what the police would uncover in their investigation. I would, of course, immediately turn over anything I found that could help Callie. I had no intention of interfering with their investigation; I was simply adding my own resources to it.

I finally hung up the telephone, just before midnight. I had three pages of notes on my steno pad, including an extensive to-do list. Sgt. Brooks had told me the CHPD would be sending a unit to the restaurant where Callie had last been and also to her home. He didn't tell me when, and I crossed my fingers, hoping the fact it was late on a weekend would buy me just a little extra time. I wanted to search Callie's house myself, before the police officially stuck their noses into my best friend's sex life.

With that thought in mind, I went online and found a Holiday Inn near Cal's house. I reserved a room for the night, with a very late arrival hold. I packed one large suitcase, my overnight bag with personal items, and my laptop as quickly as I could, moving in a fear-induced state of panicked autopilot. I stopped moving only once…to call Callie's cellphone again in the desperate hope it wouldn't go straight to voicemail.

It did.

I hung up. My hands were shaking, but I didn't have time for that. I would permit myself to have the mother of all meltdowns, but not until Callie was home safely. She could cry with me, and we would both get smashed senseless on Midori Sours and Cosmos.

It was almost 12:30 when I gathered Mr. Wuzzles up for a goodbye kiss, loaded my bags into the car, and pulled out of my apartment parking lot. I had forty dollars in cash, two credit cards, and a full tank of gas. I was good.

Traffic was light, and I exceeded my normal five-miles-over by quite a bit more than was cautious. I pulled into the check-in driveway of the hotel at 3:55 a.m., feeling exhaustion crawl through my body like a sudden onset of the flu. On check-in, I smiled perfunctorily and even laughed at the hotel desk clerk's flirty, early-morning witticisms. I handled all of the pleasantries of registration without batting an eye, got the key card for my room, and managed to drive around the side of the hotel to my room's entrance. I even managed to bring my bags and laptop inside.

Then, I sat down on the edge of the bed, and had the mother of all meltdowns. It started with blurry eyes when I again got Callie's voicemail. It ended with me completely bawled out, splotchy-faced and snotty-nosed, utterly exhausted, but, somehow, also feeling cleaned out and reinvigorated. I needed to sleep, if I wanted to be able to function. I also needed to go to Callie's house and dig through every single love letter, email, photograph, journal entry, calendar, computer log, or anything else I could find, until I found something that would help! I had to find out about Callie's 'lifestyle' acquaintances and play partners. I had to find Rory, wherever the hell he was, and determine if he even gave a damn about his sister's well-being anymore.

I needed to do all of that *now*.

I think I had known that already. I hadn't stripped out of my travel clothes or even taken my sneakers off, while I sat and sobbed. As comfortable as the bed might be, there was no way I would be able to sleep until I at least got a good start on the investigation. The first forty-eight hours after a kidnapping were crucial—I knew that much from television. We were on hour number six.

I grabbed my laptop and left the room, stopping at the vending machine halfway between my room and the hotel exit to buy a Diet Coke and a Snickers. I devoured the candy bar in the car, telling myself it was for the energy boost, not because of nerves.

Fifteen minutes later, I was in the flower bed next to Callie's front porch, looking for a gnome. I wished I'd thought to bring a flashlight. Her bushes had grown significantly since I'd been to her house last, but still— *ah, yes! There he was.* David, the concrete garden gnome with the pointy red hat, was sitting atop a concrete mushroom. And beneath David's mushroom, as it had been since I could remember, rested the spare key to the Callahan family home. I picked it up, wiping the dirt onto my jeans.

Cal's parents died intestate, never expecting to be t-boned on a sleety February night, just three months before their daughter's high school graduation. The family home, a modest, two-story Cape Cod in an upper middle class neighborhood in Chatham Hills, belonged to Callie now...or, actually, to Callie and Rory. Mr. and Mrs. Callahan had not had to foresight to plan for the disposition of their material goods, but they had apparently been big believers in mortgage protection insurance, and that had saved Callie and her brother from homelessness. With the mortgage paid in full, and the additional life insurance Ryan Callahan carried through his employer, Callie and Rory had been able to live comfortably, though not extravagantly, long enough for each to finish high school.

For one, terrifying second before I unlocked the door, I allowed myself to imagine never stepping foot into this house again. *What would happen to this wonderful old home, with so many of my childhood memories inside it, if Callie didn't come back safely?* The thought soured my stomach immediately, and I had to struggle to keep the candy and soda down.

I stepped into the foyer, hitting the light switch with ease of habit. I set my keys and purse on the credenza beneath the stairs and looked into the living room on the right. Callie had changed the furniture after her parents' deaths, and she'd added a large flat-screen television. The paintings and family photos on the walls remained the same.

I automatically walked through the foyer into the kitchen, halfway tempted to open the pantry door and go digging for cookies, as I'd done so many times in the past. The range was new. It was nice. I shrugged my

31

laptop carrier onto the kitchen table, fighting the desire to sit down and cry again. I'd already done that. I needed to get to work now.

I opened the cabinet next to the refrigerator where the Callahans kept their medication. I pulled out three acetaminophen tablets and helped myself to another Diet Coke from Callie's fridge. Yeah, boy, nothing like two shots of caffeine at 4:30 in the morning!

I was stalling, and I knew it. With a determined sigh, I stepped into the dining room, which I would make my working space. It was out of the kitchen but close to the necessities of coffee, soda, bathroom, and Tylenol. The lighting was also good; Callie used this room to pay her monthly bills, apparently, so the china cabinet served as her work center, as well as a place to stack the dishware her mom had been so proud of. It was a disorganized mess.

I turned away from the china cabinet and back to the dining room table. Setting my laptop down on one of the chairs, I stacked the dusty, permanently-placed dinner settings and removed them, knowing my detritus would spread as I gained information. I tore the sheets from my steno pad and set them on the table, putting my laptop beside them.

I picked up my steno pad, heading back through the foyer and up the stairs. I was going to have to start in Callie's room, looking through all of her personal belongings. I felt like an interloper, but…if not me, who? Nobody else had the responsibility, nor the right, to be here doing this…not Rory, and definitely not the police! It was on me.

I was curious to know if Callie had taken over the master bedroom after her parents' death. She hadn't; it was a fairly well-appointed home gym, with a treadmill, an elliptical, a stationary bike, and a Bowflex. A small stereo system and a flat-screen television were mounted on the wall. She'd been very frugal with her money to be able to build her home gym. *Nice.* Even nicer, though, Callie actually *used* her gym equipment; unlike me, she was not allergic to exercise, and she kept up a daily regimen. She was in excellent physical condition; that should help her survive whatever was happening to her. I yanked my thoughts away from that direction.

I opened the door to Rory's bedroom, not sure what changes I was expecting. There were none. Literally, the room looked as though it had been untouched since Rory left home, four years prior. It had been dusted occasionally, but everything else—including the pile of dirty laundry on the floor at the foot of his unmade bed—was exactly as he had left it.

"That's creepy, Callahan," I muttered to myself. "Really creepy, girl."

Walking into Callie's bedroom felt as familiar as walking into my own, even though I hadn't been inside her home in several years. She had rearranged her furniture from what I remembered; the double bed no longer abutted the wall, and her dresser was on the left, instead of the right, but everything else was still Callie. Perfectly, wonderfully Callie.

Her bed was made, but haphazardly—sheets and blankets pulled up but not tucked. The headboard, as always, was so stuffed with books, she couldn't possibly fit another one into the shelves. A few stuffed animals and several additional stacks of books topped the headboard. She had a makeup vanity she'd gotten in our sophomore year, and her cosmetics were scattered all over it. I walked over, smiling, feeling somehow better than I had in hours, as I twisted her mascara closed. I'd

33

told her for years it would dry out, but she was always in such a hurry, she forgot to close the damn things. The girl went through mascara as quickly as I went through toilet paper.

Next to the small vanity was her desk, with, thank god, her laptop. Callie sometimes took her laptop in to work, and I had worried she might have had it in her car when she met Mr. Wonderful. I was happy to see it sitting there; I fully expected to be reading her personal documents before the sun rose. I needed to make that a priority; I was pretty sure the police would take the laptop for evidence.

It could wait for a few minutes, though. I looked at the other items on Callie's desk. A planning calendar—I would definitely be looking through that. A framed picture of Callie and me during the summer before our senior year of high school, our arms flung around each other, wearing matching green bikinis and enormous smiles. I lingered over the picture, smiling at the memory. We'd had so much fun that summer! Callie had bemoaned the extra freckles the constant exposure to the sun had given her, but she was still stunningly beautiful. Her curly red hair, Irish green eyes, and sunburned face contrasted sharply with my long brown hair, dark eyes and deep tan, but our happiness, friendship, and innocence made us look like sisters…and the matching green bikinis didn't hurt, of course.

Next to the picture was a digital camera, which I would snoop through, once I figured out how to work it. Beside that was an index-card holder, which Callie had used as a place to store her thumb drives. I groaned inwardly. There were at least a dozen flash drives in the box, and I was positive I knew my friend's organizational system: none. I would find anything and everything on

34

those flash drives, and there would be absolutely no classification system to differentiate photos from documents from .mp3 downloads. It would take hours to go through. Maybe I would get lucky, and she would have stored a last-minute IM from Mr. Wonderful, telling me exactly where she was.

I sighed, and looked away. *Sure. Maybe it would have the fingerprints I'd told her to get, too.*

It wasn't going to be that easy, of course. Between the police and me, we needed to find Callie *fast.* Every moment she was gone was another moment something terrible could be happening to her, another moment of her life she could never reclaim.

I shook those thoughts off. I didn't have time for self-pity. I needed to find her address book, or something else with Rory's contact information. I also needed a more recent photograph of Callie to give to the police. There was a good chance she'd have a photograph of herself on her digital camera, one of the flash drives, or perhaps, on the computer itself. I knew she sent photos of herself to prospective play partners...hopefully, I could find something suitably PG-13 for the cops.

I also needed to prepare a flyer to take into Office Max, after going to the police station. I intended to plaster Chatham Hills and downtown Nashville with her face and my contact number. I would offer a substantial reward for any information leading to her safe return; Callie and I could argue about that when she was home safely.

I scanned the room again, wondering what I was missing. I'd have to contact the hospital on Monday, but I didn't know what to tell them. I was sure the police would be interviewing Callie's co-workers, but somehow it felt disloyal to tell them she was missing.

I was tired. It was almost five in the morning, and my brain was moving in circles. There were still things I needed to get done before I went to the police station—or worse, before they sent their investigators here. I knew as soon as that happened, it would kill any chance I had at keeping Callie's secrets. I planned to move some of her more personal possessions into the trunk of my car…once I found them.

With grim determination, I sat at Callie's desk, turned on the small lamp, and powered up her ancient laptop.

It was password protected. *Shit!*

I bit back a groan of frustration. I lifted the laptop and looked beneath it, hoping the password was taped on the bottom. No such luck. Rummaging through the papers on her desk didn't yield it either; only an errant electric bill, showing she was late on her payment. I flipped open my steno pad and added 'pay electric bill' to my list of things to do later in the morning.

Okay, I could do this. Callie's password wouldn't be something she would write down, anyway. We'd argued over password security several times since I had written a feature on identity theft. I had lectured her on the importance of mixing numerals, symbols, and letters into any password she used. She had laughed at me and told me it didn't matter—she used the same password for everything. She always had, always would, but to make me feel better, she would add 'an underscore and a one' behind it from now on.

So…that was something, right? Knowing Callie, her password would be a person's name, because names were important to her, and they were easy to remember.

I thought for a moment, then typed:

hope_1
Password not recognized.

Okay.

hopependleton_1
Password not recognized.

Hmm. So, okay, maybe I wasn't the be-all and end-all of her universe after all. With a wry smile, I thought about it a bit more. Callie had adored her father; she had always been a 'daddy's girl,' and his death had devastated her even more than her mother's.

daddy_1
Password not recognized.

ryancallahan_1
Password not recognized.

ryanmichaelcallahan_1
Password not recognized.

Over the next twenty minutes, I entered every possible combination of every person, or pet, in Callie's life I could recall. Coworkers, past and present. Old high school crushes and teachers. The name of every Dominant she'd mentioned to me, then, on impulse, 'Mr. Wonderful_1' and 'Mr. Wuzzles_1.' The message came up with infuriating consistency.

Password not recognized.

"God, this is hopeless!" I groaned, rubbing the grit from my eyes. I rested my head on her desk, closing my eyes for just a moment. *Hopeless.*

hopeless_1

The laptop made its funny whirring noises, and then Callie's desktop background appeared on the screen. The moment was anticlimactic. I had no desire to whoop with joy at my victory. I didn't have a victory. I didn't have *anything*, except maybe some access to some of the things Callie kept private, and, maybe, within them, a clue to where she was.

The sun had risen, and I'd added, 'buy ink cartridge' to my to-do list. My eyes burned, and my heart ached. I had several excellent color photos of Callie and seven more pages of notes to sort through. I was overwhelmed at everything I had learned about my best friend, and discouraged at everything I had not. I felt dirty, as though I'd spent the time digging through her underwear drawer. Psychologically, I suppose I had. Physically, it was still on my to-do list.

It was 6:20 a.m. I wanted to be at the police station promptly at nine, but I *had* to get at least two hours' sleep. It was ridiculous to even think about going back to the hotel. I set the alarm on the headboard of Callie's bed, stripped, and crawled in without a second thought. As I drifted off to sleep, I smiled, remembering dozens of other times I had slept in this bed, albeit wearing pajamas. "I'll find you, Cal," I murmured, my eyes already closing. "I promise."

To my chagrin, I overslept the alarm.

Eric Grayson
Frisson

I pulled into the lot of the station house in Chatham Hills, Tennessee, just before ten, and sat in my government-issued Crown Victoria, finishing a stale 7-11 coffee. I struggled one-handedly into my tie. I hated tying the goddamned things so I always left them in a noose and pulled them on over my head. It was Saturday morning, a beautiful, sunny, blisteringly *hot* day in July. Nobody should have to wear a tie on a day like this.

"Federal Bureau of Idiots, at your service," I grumbled, tipping an imaginary fedora to my reflection in the rearview mirror. In truth, I was excited, even more than I wanted to admit to myself. This call from Louisville might be the break I needed. I had a lot of time, effort, and resources invested in the Jimmy Lau investigation, and I'd been sitting on empty for a while. I was hoping that was about to change.

One of my instructors at Quantico had said something along the lines of, 'A good detective can feel when he's getting close. There's an undeniable *frisson* when the pieces start falling into place.' There wasn't much to go on in the Louisville report, but I had a feeling in my gut. I'm not the *frisson* kind of guy, so a gut feeling was about as close as it was going to get.

I was, however, a damned good detective, and I was getting close.

I continued ruminating as I got out of the car and walked into the station house. It was a modern brick and glass affair, with a sweet central air conditioning system already running at full blast.

The reporting party had used the term, 'safe call.' Yeah, it was thin. Vanillas were starting to pick up on the use of safe calls, especially with online hookups. But, still…it wasn't a term used often by the non-kink crowd. Even more, the RP had called the cops immediately after hanging up with her friend; she and the missing person had an actual code word pre-established. *That* gave me a *frisson!*

My badge was familiar to the small town's duty officer, so I barely flashed it before he waved me around the metal detector. He buzzed me in, and I poked my head into his glass-enclosed office. "Good morning," I said, adding a benign smile. "Sgt. Brooks in the house?"

"He's in his office, second floor, third on the right," the officer replied, his eyes going right back to the report he was reading. Call me jaded, but I had the feeling he was going to uncover the porn or the sports section the second I turned away.

Brooks' office was tiny—even smaller than mine in D.C.—and he didn't have a window. I congratulated myself on winning the 'whose-is-bigger?' contest that always hangs there between the locals and the Feds, and then tapped politely on Brooks' open door. He'd been aware of my presence, I was sure of it. The difference between Brooks and the OD was his porn was probably right there on the computer screen. I didn't allow myself to smile at the thought, but when Brooks looked up at me, I smiled a polite greeting as I stepped in.

"Eric Grayson," I said, extending my hand. "We spoke last night."

He rose and shook my hand, and in those milliseconds, we appraised each other. I had about two inches on him; he had about thirty pounds on me. He was a black man, late forties, balding but not shaved, with sharp, intelligent eyes. He'd been a house mouse long enough he'd gotten a bit of a beer gut, but he kept in shape overall.

"Welcome to Chatham Hills, Special Agent," he said, indicating one of the two chairs opposite his desk. "You got here fast."

"Eric," I said, as I maneuvered myself into the chair. Like I said, mine was bigger.

Brooks considered me, lifting an eyebrow in surprise. I was being courteous and respectful, and he wasn't sure how to handle that. I got the impression he didn't hold much affection for the Feds, as a rule.

"Joshua," he replied, responding to my courtesy with his own. I was pleased. It never hurt to have a solid working relationship with the locals. "Can I get you some coffee?"

I grimaced and shook my head, putting my hand to my stomach in mock pain. "No, thanks. I just survived one bad cup of coffee, it's too soon for another."

His chuckle was rich and deep, and I smirked in response. He handed me the file. I had been polite as I played the game, and I hadn't allowed my eyes to wander his desk overmuch. He knew what I wanted, and I knew he knew. He wasn't making me jump through hoops to get it—score one for the good guys.

"Thank you, Joshua," I said, taking the thin folder from him, and resisting the urge to open it immediately.

"I had Central copy it for you, so that one's yours," he offered.

I raised my eyebrows, nodding in appreciation. Score two for the good guys. I opened the file then, scanning the first page quickly. "You spoke with the RP – Hope Pendleton," I read from the file, "personally, right?"

"Yes. I took the call straight from Louisville dispatch."

"What was your impression?"

"The lady's scared," Brooks told me. "Right or wrong, she believes her friend is in deep shit."

I nodded. I believed that, too. "She seem on the level to you, or a flake job?"

"Oh, very much on the level," Brooks replied, leaning forward in his chair and handing me another sheet of paper, one that had not been in the file. I don't think he would have given me that extra sheet of paper, if I hadn't played nice. "In fact, I expected her to be sitting on my desk at 8:30 this morning. I even got here on time, just to make a good impression."

Brooks grinned sardonically. "I ran her through NCIC, and she's clean. I also did a superficial background check, which you've got right there. She's a reporter for one of the Louisville papers. Nothing major league, but she's observant and smart, and she's familiar with the concept of objectivity. She has an apartment in a decent part of town, pays her bills, nothing outstanding with the DMV."

42

I looked up at Brooks, genuinely appreciative. "Thanks very much. You saved me a bit of phone work."

He shrugged. "I like to know what's going on in my backyard, Eric. You have a pretty wide range of flags out there, so I got curious."

"It's an interesting case. My daddy always said you have to cast a wide net to catch the big fish."

"Your daddy really say that?" Brooks asked, eyeing me skeptically, as I stood to leave.

"No," I replied honestly. "My daddy was a CPA, and he couldn't have caught a fish if his life depended on it."

Brooks laughed, and I joined him.

"Well, if there's anything else I can do to help...?"

I shook my head, giving a wistful thought to my former partner on this case. "Unfortunately not, Joshua. Not unless you can morph into a hot, white, five-foot-nothing sex kitten, with a thing for whips and chains."

His laughter followed me into the hallway.

***

I started the engine and cranked up the air conditioning, entering Patricia Callahan's address into the GPS. I opened the thin file, which I would soon be incorporating into the seven boxes of paper data in the Knoxville office already accumulated in the Lau matter. I skimmed quickly, fighting off a sense of letdown. There was even less here than I'd hoped, and I hadn't been hoping for much. There was no mention of the missing person's involvement in BDSM, and the photograph of her 'date' was clearly not one of Lau's boys. That wasn't racial profiling on my part; I knew the face of every man in Lau's lower echelon—Chinese, white, and black – as well as I knew my own. This alleged perp – Daniel Fletcher—was not on Lau's payroll.

Still, there was the safe call itself, and the code phrase. That was not something girlfriends normally did for each other in the vanilla dating world.

"It's way too thin," I admitted to myself, wondering if I should head back to the Knoxville office, or just call it a day and go to my hotel room in Nashville. I had just made the four-hour drive from Knoxville to Chatham Hills, and I wasn't eager to turn around and do it again. Nashville was only a forty-minute drive, tops. "Patricia Callahan is probably home right now, feeding her cat and blogging about the great sex she had last night."

I felt a childish twinge of resentment. I'd like the chance to blog about the great sex I'd had…well, anytime in the past six months.

There was a description, but no photo of Callahan in the file, not yet. She lived on Creekside Lane, Chatham Hills, Tennessee, which the GPS said was about ten minutes north. Screw it. I'd go by the house, maybe canvass a few of her neighbors, and then I'd go back to my hotel in Nashville for the weekend. I'd head into Knoxville on Monday morning. Lau's monthly shindig was a week from today; that would give me more than enough time to catch up on my paperwork in Knoxville and kiss my ASAC's ass before I needed to be back in Nashville.

I pulled up in front of Callahan's house at about 11:00 a.m. There was a vehicle in the driveway, a white Prius. I quashed my disappointment, but it took a herculean effort of will. Any LEO knows the vast majority of mispers weren't actually 'missing persons' at all—most walked away from their lives voluntarily. Most also returned … usually within three days of being reported missing. Dollars to donuts, Callahan was safely inside her home. Good for her. Good for Jimmy Lau.

Sucked for me.

Son of a motherless goat.

I got out of the car anyway, my own sense of perfectionism not allowing me to leave it unfinished now that I was actually at the woman's home. At least, I could call it in to Brooks, and we could both cross it off our lists. Maybe I'd catch a break next Saturday at Lau's play party.

Eric
Ground Rules

I was just raising my hand to ring the doorbell, when the front door opened. The woman standing there was more startled than I was; I, at least, had been expecting to see someone on the other side of the door. She stepped back defensively, closing the heavy door halfway, and positioning herself behind it. I took a half-step back at the same time. I could almost feel the apprehension radiating off her. She was jumpy, her reactions similar to those of a violent crime victim. My immediate instinct was to soothe her. Calm victims were cooperative; relaxed witnesses were more reliable.

"Miss Callahan?" I asked. I kept my voice courteous, professional, and non-threatening, while I mentally scrambled over the details in the slim file, trying to make the missing person's description match the woman in the doorway. No way, not even close. Callahan was of Irish descent, light-skinned, short curly red hair, five-foot-two or three, with green eyes. This woman was about five-foot-seven, long honey-brown hair, and eyes the color of pecan shells basking in sunshine. She wore a plain white blouse and jeans, and had a black leather briefcase slung over her shoulder. She was attractive—not airbrushed, movie-star beautiful, but girl-next-door-who's-always-been-hot beautiful.

Since when had I gotten so poetic? Yeah, she was striking—so what? *Keep your dick in your pants and your mind on the case, Grayson,* I chided myself.

"Who are you?" she asked, distrust evident in her voice. She looked like she hadn't slept much ... hair still damp from the shower, slight darkness under her eyes, no makeup. It clicked, and I knew who she was, although I still wasn't sure why she would be coming out of Callahan's house.

"I could ask you the same question." I reached with slow, deliberate movements into the breast pocket of my suit jacket, and pulled out my wallet, flipping it open to my credentials. "I'm Eric Grayson, a special agent with the Federal Bureau of Investigation, ma'am." Score another one for me for not using my friendly sobriquet for the Bureau. Professional, polite, personable. My daddy *had* taught me that.

I've been in the Bureau for eight years, and I long ago lost count of the number of times I've flashed or shown my I.D. In eight years, this was the first time anyone actually took my I.D. from my hand to inspect it. I waited patiently while Miss Pendleton read my credentials and compared my face to the official photo. I had been on a DEA co-op assignment the last time I'd had my creds updated. My hair had been long enough for a ponytail, and I had almost a week's worth of black stubble on my face, but I was still recognizable.

Miss Pendleton surprised me further, shifting slightly and removing a spiral notepad from her shoulder bag. She flipped it open one-handedly and wrote information down from my I.D. I arched an eyebrow, but didn't comment.

"Who is your supervisor, Agent, and what's the telephone number for your office, please?" she asked me.

"Eric is fine. Which office number would you like, ma'am? I'm stationed in D.C., but I'm currently working out of the Knoxville field office. My ASAC—Assistant Special Agent in Charge—is Peter Zewicke in Knoxville."

She glanced down at her notepad, and then back at me. "I have plenty of paper," she told me. "I'll check both."

I managed to not grin at her, but it was tough. *I liked this woman!* I gave the name of my D.C. ASAC and both switchboard numbers and watched as she dutifully wrote everything down, her handwriting neat and precise.

"You won't be able to speak to either supervisor," I warned her.

She looked up at me warily.

"They're Monday to Friday guys. The switchboard can confirm my active status, and then, they'll put you through to voicemail."

She almost smiled at that. I felt an intense, unprofessional desire to see what her smile would look like.

"I'll verify this, and be right back," she told me, starting to withdraw into the house. I made an abrupt sound to stop her and gestured toward my wallet. She'd written the information down, so she had no reason to hold on to my credentials. Not that I was suspicious, but I felt better with my I.D. in my pocket just the same. She handed it to me and then closed the heavy door in my face. I bit back a chuckle at the sound of a deadbolt lock turning and a chain being pulled.

Son of a motherless goat! Alert, smart, sexy, and suspicious as hell! Now, why couldn't I find a girl like that?

I dismissed the thought, studying the tidy porch and the surrounding houses while I cooled my heels. It was a nice, middle-class neighborhood, quiet on a hot Saturday afternoon. I heard somebody mowing grass a few houses down, and an older woman walked a schnauzer on the sidewalk across the street. He strained at the end of the leash to sniff the blades of grass just beyond his limit, and then he urinated decisively. Apparently satisfied with himself, he scratched his feet on the grass, walking in place and kicking up a little Kentucky 31 and topsoil. I mentally saluted the dog and continued my observations. Callahan's flowerbeds were well-tended, and her grass was appropriately cut and edged. Her home fit right in with the neighborhood, *exemplar* of the American Dream in a neat, well-trimmed package. This was no crime scene—the crime had happened far away from this serene little 'burb. Still, this was where the victim lived, and there was evidence to be found here.

A few minutes later, I heard the chain slide and the deadbolt unlock. A slightly chagrined, but friendlier, woman greeted me. "It's been a difficult night, Agent Grayson," she told me, holding the door open. "I apologize if I was rude, but I'm a bit hypervigilant right now. Please, will you come in?"

I smiled at her, as I stepped inside Callahan's house. "Miss Pendleton, I can't tell you how much I wished

49

every woman in America had your instincts and your sense of caution."

I had said her name. I saw it register on her face, and I quickly held up the slim folder I was carrying. "I got a copy of the file from Sgt. Brooks," I explained. "You're listed as the reporting party."

"Oh, of course," she acknowledged, shaking her head and smiling wanly. "This way."

She led me through a foyer with a maple sideboard on the left and a formal living room on the right. A short hallway opened up to a large, comfortable kitchen, separated by an open pass-through from a smaller dining room. I quickly scoped the dining room; it had apparently been set up as Pendleton's command center. Two laptops, a printer, and several neatly labeled files occupied half the table. My own notes on the Lau file had looked much like this…two years ago.

"Coffee?" she offered.

I nodded, and she poured a mug from the half-full pot warming on the coffee maker. She gestured toward the sugar and quart of milk on the countertop, and I shook my head. She picked up her own mug and moved toward the kitchen table.

I hesitated when she indicated a seat, and I glanced toward the dining area. "To the trained eye, Miss Pendleton, it looks like you've started an investigation."

She met my gaze levelly. "I'm an investigative reporter, Agent. It's what I do."

I nodded slowly, proceeding with extreme caution. I had an ally here, and I didn't want to alienate her. On the other hand, I couldn't condone her interference in an FBI operation—*my* operation. With the Triad Society involved, she would get herself killed.

"I'm not questioning your skill, as either a reporter

or an investigator, ma'am. On the other hand, I am concerned about the poss—no, the probability—you could interfere with an ongoing investigation."

Pendleton shot me an incredulous look. "Ongoing?" she questioned. "Callie's disappearance was reported…" she looked over at the microwave's time display, "…fourteen hours ago." She took a deep breath, as if to rein in her temper. "Agent Grayson, there's no point in fooling around here, because we both know what's going to happen with Callie's case. Your people will come out, ask her neighbors if they heard or saw anything suspicious, and you'll hand out some business cards. You'll go to the restaurant where she was last seen—maybe—and talk to the manager. He'll get a business card, too. You'll put out an APB with Callie's photograph and the description of the guy she was with. You'll ask Callie's coworkers if she's been depressed or out-of-sorts lately, and you'll hand out more business cards.

"When nobody calls you back, or when the calls are from crackpots, you'll add Callie's case to the hundreds of other cases you already have overflowing on your desk. When I continue to be a pain in the ass—and I promise you, Agent Grayson, I will—you'll suggest I hire a private investigator and put up 'Missing Persons' posters, preferably offering a large reward. Am I right so far?"

If Jimmy Lau weren't involved, she would have nailed it. "In most missing persons' cases, you would be correct," I evaded.

"So, why is Callie's case any different?" she challenged.

"Miss Pendleton—"

"Hope."

51

"Hope. Thank you. Hope, you want me to be direct and cut right to the chase, yes?" At her nod, I continued. "Let me ask you a question about your friend that might help put us on the same page here. To your knowledge, has she been involved in any kind of unusual sexual activity? Anything related to sadomasochism?"

She was very good, but I was watching for it. If I hadn't been watching, I would have completely missed it. Her left eye twitched, almost imperceptibly.

"Not that I'm aware of," she lied smoothly. *Too* smoothly. There was no incredulity, no outrage I would dare suggest such a thing about her upstanding friend. "I really believe this concludes our business, Agent." She rose, expecting me to do the same.

I remained seated and nodded toward my mug. "Mind if I finish my coffee?" I asked politely.

She stiffened, not expecting the question, but inclined her head. "Suit yourself," she said. *Ah, the courtesy card.* Not very effective with men, but it worked on women every time. It's sexist, but it's true.

I took a deliberate sip of my coffee, watching her silently. She turned away from me and walked over to the sink, where she rinsed her cup. She had lied. Patricia Callahan *was* involved in BDSM, which upped the probability of her being one of Jimmy Lau's girls exponentially! I had my *frisson* back, and it was *frissing* its ass off!

I let the silence between us become uncomfortable before I spoke again, and when I did, I deliberately kept my voice casual. "If it were me, Hope…if I had a friend I cared about, who had gone missing…I'd be asking myself why the Feds were involved, not even twenty-four hours after my friend was gone. I'd be wondering what they knew that had any bearing on my friend's case, maybe on her safety."

My words hit home. Hope's back was still turned, but she had stiffened, her posture rigid.

"I'd also be a lot more interested in my friend's welfare than in either my pride, or hers. I wouldn't really care who knew jack about my friend's personal life, not if it mattered to the investigation. I'd want the best possible shot for her safe return, and if that meant relying on the resources available to the federal government, that's what I'd lean toward."

She didn't respond. Maybe she would, in time, but if I pushed too hard now, I'd lose her. I stood. "Thank you for the coffee, Hope."

She turned then, and her face was a raw mixture of anger, fear, and determination. "It doesn't work that way, Agent," she accused.

"Eric."

"Fine. It doesn't work that way, *Eric.* I've been told too many times in my career to stand back and let the boys do their job, and they *don't.* The police don't do *anything.* This time, it's not about my career, Eric. This time, it matters."

Her words hit home, too, but I remained calm. "This time you're not talking about the police, Hope, or even the FBI. You're talking about *me.* It matters to me, too."

I saw the thoughts warring in her mind, and I waited silently, willing her to trust me, to tell me what she knew. The unprofessional part of me that had wanted to see her smile and hadn't had sex in six months kind of liked watching her think. She bit her lower lip, apparently unaware she was doing it. It was cute. I was pretty sure she'd aim a knee at my balls if I told her that, so I waited, letting her break the silence.

"I want to be involved."

That didn't sound good. "In what way?" I hedged.

"I want to help with the legwork. I want to be kept informed, and I will keep you informed. I want to actively work on finding Callie."

I was already shaking my head. *No way in hell.*

"That's not an option, Hope. I'm sorry. We can't risk endangering you. If the perpetrator I suspect is involved, this situation can go from bad to deadly in two seconds flat." I paused and hardened my voice. "On the other hand, if there's anything you know, and you're not telling me, you're obstructing justice, and you can go to jail. You already know that."

"Then charge me based on your assumptions, or get the hell out."

Well, that had backfired. Her voice was flat, uncompromising. She either knew the law well enough to walk the line, or she had *mucho* big *cajones*. It was most likely a combination of both.

I took another swallow of the coffee, now cold, and grimaced in distaste. I set the mug back on the table. "If I could let you help me, I would," I told her honestly. "God knows, I'll take all the help I can get. But it's not a reasonable request, Hope. It's too dangerous to involve a civilian." I stood, picking up my file and making my way into the foyer.

She was right on my heels. "For whom, Eric? For me, or for you? Is it my safety, or is it your *job* that worries you?"

Her words hit a nerve I didn't know was so raw, and I turned on her, my voice icy with anger. "Lady, you don't know jack about my job," I said coldly. "I have lived and breathed my job for the past twenty-two months, and I mean 24/7. Your friend went missing last night, and I am very sincerely sorry about that, but there are fourteen other Patricia Callahans who have gone missing over the past two years.

"Those are the ones we know about, anyway. And I think there's a connection, but I don't know because you're busy playing games, and won't verify anything I suspect. Without verification, I'm in exactly the same place I was before Patricia Callahan was taken – *nowhere!* I've worked this case well past the point of obsession, taken time from my dau—" I stopped abruptly and exhaled. I'd said a lot more than I'd intended to say. "Good day, Miss Pendleton."

She touched my arm. The gesture, as much as her words, stopped me from slamming the door.

"I was out of line," she said quietly. "I'm sorry."

I nodded stiffly, but my voice was a bit more civil. "Good day, Hope," I said, turning again to leave.

"Wait," she said. "I'll give you a copy of the information I found on Callie's computer."

Son of a motherless goat! What was it I'd said about not letting pride get in the way? I turned back, still angry, but categorically unwilling to let this lead slip by. The team would confiscate that computer when they got out here. *Who knew what garbage—or gold—Hope had dug up?*

"I took notes on everything I thought would be useful," Hope said, walking back through the kitchen into the dining room. She opened a manila folder on top of a small stack of files. I saw her neat, precise handwriting on the papers, before she turned the printer on and placed them in the feeder to make copies. "I'll do my best not to obstruct justice as I carry out my investigation, Eric," she promised, with a wan smile.

She reached into a second folder and withdrew several more pieces of paper, clearly already extra copies. The top sheet had several color photographs of a woman

55

with red hair. Hope handed that stack of documents to me as well and walked me back to the front door.

"I won't—I can't—let this go, though. I'm sorry. Callie and I have been best friends for years … we have shared everything with each other since we were twelve years old. I don't have a sister, but if I did, I would love Callie more."

I hesitated at the doorway, looking down at the photographs. I suppressed a groan. I recognized the girl immediately. I knew her as 'fet,' not Callie, and I'd seen her at several munches, although I hadn't spoken to her more than briefly. The description in my folder from Brooks did no justice to the face I looked at in the photograph. Callahan had bright, happy green eyes, a small, freckled nose, and short, curly, carrot-red hair. A brilliant, vivacious smile consummated the picture of a face far too young, innocent, and alive to be where she had to be at this moment.

"Don't go in as a reporter," I said finally. I looked directly at Hope, trying to hammer the importance of my words into her brain with the force of my will. "Don't do *anything* to draw attention specifically to Callahan…Callie. He picks girls with no family for a reason. Don't do anything to make him suspect someone is looking for her. I promise…you don't want him to move her out of Nashville before we can get inside. If you even *think* you've been noticed, run for your life. You will be."

She paled but nodded her understanding. It was all I could give her, and it was a lot more than I had any business saying. I reached into my breast pocket and withdrew one of my business cards, handing it to her with a sardonic smile. "Please call me if you find out anything further."

Hope
Meet & Greet

Well, that had sucked dirt. I locked the deadbolt and security chain after the FBI agent left, allowing myself to sag against the door. Agent Grayson had thrown me off my game; I hadn't expected him to be at the door, and I had not handled him well. He was certainly professional enough, but something about him shook me badly. He was in his mid-thirties, tall, well-built, with short brown hair, a straight nose, square chin, perfect lips, and incredible, piercing blue-gray eyes.

I could admit it to myself; he was well past sexy. That wasn't what shook me up so much, though. It was more the way he carried himself...he seemed so confident and controlled, as if he had every step of the path outlined in front of him. I'd deliberately provoked him into anger. I would never admit that, though of course, not to him or anyone else...well, except maybe Callie. I had wanted to see his confidence waver. I didn't know why—and *that* was what shook me so much!

I had reacted to the FBI agent on a personal, not professional, level, and *I didn't know why.* Yeah, he was hot. A lot of the guys I dealt with on a regular basis were hot, and not one of them had been able to put even a crack in my façade of expert investigative journalist.

He, annoyingly, had remained completely professional, even in his anger. *I promise...you don't want him to move her out of Nashville.* Dear god, that thought had never even occurred to me, and it should have! I was way too close to the case. I was losing my objectivity.

"Shake it off, girl," I told myself sternly. "Of course, you're not going to be objective—this is Callie! That doesn't mean you're going to screw up. Just get your head together!"

The pep talk helped. Agent Grayson...Eric...had been an unexpected element, and he had caught me at less than my best moment. Okay, I could move past that. At least, he was working on Callie's case, and he seemed dedicated and resolute. I believed him when he told me he lived his job, and I trusted he would do everything he could to get Callie back safely. I just didn't know if it would be enough. Eric had confirmed my worst fear, the one thought I had skirted around but not even allowed myself to think. Whether intentionally, to bait me into turning over my notes, or by mistake, he had told me Callie's disappearance was not unique. He was involved in her case already, because there were *fourteen* other missing women!

"Sweet Jesus," I muttered, suddenly nauseated. This was a bigger playing field than anything I'd ever been on, and I was so far out of my league, it was daunting. Eric had been worried about my life, not his job. I had known that, even when I hurled the accusation at him. I was simply trying to bait him into anger, and getting nothing…just a colder tone of voice—one I really didn't want to hear again—and the assertion he was doing his job.

If a visit from the FBI was 'unexpected' enough to throw me completely off my game, what would it be like to meet the bad guy? Was I ready to find out? What if there was more than one bad guy? That was a very real possibility, and it sent a shot of liquid fear into my gut. I swallowed hard. This wasn't a TV show or one of my crime novels. It also wasn't my run-of-the-mill investigative work for the *Tribune*. I wasn't digging around in the trash cans of white-collar criminals, looking to find the paper trails to expose graft or corruption in hopes of a front-page byline. This was real. It was dangerous. Deadly, if Agent Grayson wasn't exaggerating.

I promise…you don't want him to move her out of Nashville. I wouldn't—couldn't—allow myself to consider what that meant. Fourteen girls…and Callie! There was a criminal component at work in Cal's disappearance, one much more complicated than a bad blind date or a guy looking for a kinky good time. I finally said the words to myself. This was either serial murder or human sex trafficking. Mr. Wonderful was a killer or a slave trader…and he had my best friend.

For now, I promised myself. *Only for now.*

I moved on autopilot. I went into the kitchen, rinsed Eric's coffee mug, and set it next to mine in the dishwasher. I called my neighbor, Debi, who had my spare key, and I arranged for her to pull my mail for the next several days, feed Mr. Wuzzles, and water Gertrude the Philodendron, my only houseplant. I left a message on my editor's voicemail, taking the week as vacation leave, due to a family emergency. Then, I went into the dining room and pulled out my to-do list, which I'd accidentally photocopied to Eric. The list of tasks, which had grown from the information I'd culled from Callie's desk calendar and computer, was intimidating:

- meet Sgt. Brooks and sign next-of-kin documents
- interview waiter at Stefano's
- pay Cal's electric bill
- continue researching BDSM
- find Rory
- 500 copies of Missing Person flyer
- buy ink cartridge
- Saturday night—Meet & Greet, Belle Meade Warren's Steakhouse
- Sunday—Google map and attend Cal's UU service – talk to youth group pastor
- Monday—call hospital and tell she needs leave of absence, Dr. Monroe
- Monday—go to Cal's shrink appt, Dr. Rouchard
- keep digging through Callie's stuff

It was almost one in the afternoon. My stomach growled at me crankily, reminding me I hadn't eaten today. Okay, so it would be McDonald's on the way to the CHPD, and after that, I would handle it as it came at me. I double-checked I had my cell phone and wallet, grabbed my keys, and started to leave. At the front door, I paused, considering. The FBI was involved. That meant an almost certain expedition of this investigation. I went back upstairs and grabbed Callie's laptop and the index card box full of thumb drives. I carried it out with me to my car, glancing around guiltily while opening my trunk. I pulled up the carpet, and hid the laptop and flash drives in the wheel well with the spare tire. It formed a lump when I replaced the carpet, but it was as good as I could get at the moment.

I got into the car and headed for the CHPD.

***

The afternoon sun was broiling when I left the police station at 3:10 p.m. Sgt. Brooks struck me as competent, but realistic. He was significantly less committed than Eric, although his case load probably had more to do with that than his personal preference. He'd informed me Daniel Fletcher's photograph had already been circulated via the Tennessee State Police intranet, and he would add Callie's photos to her description, which had also been circulated. The Chatham Hills PD, the State Police, and the FBI were all working together, with the FBI holding jurisdiction over the file. I'd already met the lead agent assigned to Callie's case.

I learned some very grim statistics from Sgt. Brooks. In the last year alone, Tennessee law enforcement had dealt with almost 40,000 violent crimes, from simple assault to rape and murder. There were currently more than 1,300 open missing persons' files in the state of Tennessee, and more than *seven hundred thousand* in the nation! Many adults vanished voluntarily, for reasons of their own choosing. They could certainly do so easily enough—it is not a crime for an adult to abandon his or her life voluntarily. Unless there is clear indication of endangerment or criminal activity, law enforcement agencies simply don't have the manpower or resources to investigate every call they receive. Additionally, most adults who are reported missing either return to their homes or are located, usually before an investigation even gets started.

However, there were still tens of thousands of people in the United States who were never found, and that number included only cases properly reported to the authorities. Who knew how many of the disenfranchised were never even reported missing? There was no way to estimate how many of the unreported missing people were victims of violent crime, or how many had been given new identities of 'John or Jane Doe' in morgues far from their home. Only the bizarre circumstances surrounding Callie's disappearance had prompted the immediate response I had received from the authorities in Louisville and Chatham Hills. I found myself oddly grateful to the BDSM community for teaching Callie about safe calls, even though I knew someone in that community – or someone using that community as a hunting ground – was responsible for her kidnapping.

My head ached, and I felt discouraged. Based on Eric's remark about not drawing attention specifically to Callie, I decided against putting up posters. That meant I didn't have to stop by Office Max. There wouldn't be enough time to interview the staff at Stefano's, so I would do that after Callie's church service on Sunday. For today, I would check out of my hotel and bring my bags to Callie's house, and then I would dig through her closet to find something appropriate to wear to the Saturday night 'munch' meeting in Nashville. *Yay! I was going to meet and greet a bunch of perverts.*

***

I brought Callie's laptop back inside and spent more than two hours searching through it when I got back to her place. I found a few of the chat logs she'd saved (none, unfortunately, with 'Painman'), and learned Callie used a 'scene name' to protect her identity. I heartily approved

62

that decision. Apparently, it was an accepted custom in many BDSM communities. Callie's scene name was 'fetishgirl.' The linguistics of BDSM were, in themselves, a convoluted topic. Apparently, since Callie was submissive, she referred to herself in lower case, and she always addressed the Dominant as 'Sir' or 'Ma'am' – upper-cased. That seemed to be the accepted standard. There were a minority of BDSM participants who stylized themselves Lords, Lieges, Dukes, Demigods, Exalted Grand Poohbahs, or other nonsensical hogen-mogens, but, fortunately, it was a small minority.

Both 'submissive' and 'Dominant' were *nouns* as well as adjectives, which completely offended my inner grammarian. When used as nouns, 'Dominant' was capitalized; 'submissive' was not. Callie was a submissive; she would obey a Dominant. A Dominant would dominate a submissive. 'Dominate' was a verb and only a verb, thank goodness. Apparently, there was a good deal of snarkiness from both submissive and dominant BDSM participants on that point, which would have provided some amusing and educational reading, if I'd had more time.

I was surprised to find many Dominants in the Nashville community were women. I hadn't expected that, although it seemed obvious, once I thought about it. It didn't make any of this insanity seem less…deviant to me, but it did take most of the wind out of my gender-based indignation sails. Since Callie had always talked to me about male Dominants, I had assumed it to be requisite the men were dominant and the women submissive. That wasn't true at all; while most BDSM participants in the 'pansexual' community seemed to follow that model, there appeared to be very little discrimination based on gender. Nor, surprisingly, on size, appearance, handicap, race, or sexual orientation. Shamefully, one of the very few truly accepting communities in America was a fringe element in our society.

In its own weird way, the research into BDSM was fascinating to me. Googling 'BDSM' yielded *millions* of hits and googling 'rules for new submissives' was equally daunting. Apparently, the only absolutely consistent rule throughout the world of BDSM was there were no absolutely consistent rules. The concepts of safe calls and safe words seemed to be well accepted as the norm, and the phrase 'safe, sane, and consensual' was bandied around quite often. SSC was not the only standard of play, though. There was also RACK, for 'risk-aware consensual kink' and 'edgeplay,' for play that actually held legitimate risks of injury or even death. 'Breathplay' was a popular form of edgeplay, which led into an entire segment on erotic asphyxiation. I shuddered when I read that; *no, thank you!*

There were even different *kinds* of BDSM—pansexual, polyamorous, Leather, Old Guard, Next Generation, and even asexual. There were casual weekend 'players,' like Callie, and there were people who lived their daily lives in 24/7 Master/slave relationships! I found that one hard to believe in 21st century America, but it was, apparently, more common than anyone could imagine.

As my kinky vocabulary increased, I found myself becoming less sensitive to some of the terminology. I decided that was a good thing, and I practiced saying some 'trigger' words out loud in different imaginary contexts. It would probably blow my cover, if I slapped some dominant Exalted High Poobah across the face for calling me 'bitch,' when it wasn't necessarily intended as a pejorative term.

I made myself stop reading at 6:30 p.m. so I could put on some light makeup and choose a costume from Callie's selection of kinky clothing. I had already put the most damning of her kinky items into the trunk of my car, relieved there wasn't a larger selection. I left her remaining clothes alone; any Goth girl could be found clubbing in most of the same getups.

I wanted an outfit to help me fit in quickly, something that said, 'new, but totally non-threatening, submissive person.' I'd considered taking on the role of a 'Domme,' but realized almost immediately I would be unable to pull it off. I had no experience bossing anyone around – I couldn't even get Mr. Wuzzles to leave my tilapia alone! After that annoying realization, I decided taking the role of a new submissive was my best chance of finding Callie. I needed to follow in her path, either by befriending somebody she had befriended or by baiting somebody she had attracted.

I laid several outfits on Callie's bed to see how they looked. I was about four inches taller than her, so one of her miniskirts would be absolutely out of the question. We were roughly the same proportions otherwise. I usually wore a size 8, but was most comfortable in a baggy size 10. I could sometimes pull off a 6, depending on the cut of the outfit. I wore a B-cup and Callie was a generously-filled C. She owned three absolutely *gorgeous* corsets, and I intended to bitch her out mercilessly for not sharing! A cursory attempt, though, had shown me I would never be able to get one on by myself. I wondered how Callie had managed it.

I finally settled on a black leather skirt, with laces going up both sides...*all* the way up both sides! That necessitated wearing a thong, which sent me figuratively screaming out of my comfort zone, but it worked. The skirt would have been an inch or two above knee-length on Callie, so it hit me at mid-thigh. It looked good. Slutty, but good. I chose a comparatively demure cream-colored blouse with a scooped neckline, and my own black pumps I'd had the foresight to toss into my suitcase. They were conservative, three-inch heels, but they were comfortable, and the thong more than made up for my lack of 'come-fuck-me' shoes.

I couldn't decide if I wanted to wear jewelry, so I went scrounging around in Callie's jewelry box for ideas. Perversely, the only thing which appealed to me was the gold crucifix her father had given her for her sixteenth birthday. The cross was unusual; it appeared to be shaped out of thorns, the beams twisting slightly and ending in sharp points. I wasn't religious, but Callie was, so I fastened it around my neck defiantly. It nestled in the scoop of the blouse, and it looked perfect. I took a last critical look at myself in the full-length mirror on the back of Callie's closet door. Good god, I did not look like myself at all! I felt a flutter of fear and excitement in my stomach. It was time to do this. I grabbed Callie's laptop to re-secure it in my car trunk and headed out.

***

The hostess at the Warren's Steakhouse in Belle Meade greeted me with a cheerful, welcoming smile. "You're with the internet group, right?" she asked, and it wasn't really a question.

"Um…yes?" I replied, and it wasn't really an answer.

"They have the back meeting room," she said, her smile warm and friendly. She grabbed a menu, and indicated I should follow her.

That seemed incredibly … easy.

The smell of searing meat made me hungry. I'd eaten a pack of cheese nabs for lunch earlier, but they were long gone. Warren's had an amazing salad bar and delicious steaks, but their real killer was the three-billion calorie bloomin' onion, a deep-fried, artery-clogging slice of herbaceous heaven! Cal and I split one every time we came to Warren's…which is why we usually celebrated our special occasions at Red Lobster or Applebee's.

The hostess stopped just outside a closed door and handed me the menu. "Tommy and Verlaine will be your servers tonight. Enjoy!"

She left me then, holding my menu. I seriously considered running along after her and then jumping right into my car. I took a deep, deliberate breath. I could do this for Callie. *For Callie,* I told myself again, screwing my courage to the sticking place à la Lady Macbeth. I opened the door.

There were about forty people in the room, some already seated at tables, but most clustered in small groups, laughing and talking. At first glance, they seemed disappointingly…normal. There were certainly a lot more piercings and tattoos (or in one case, neon pink hair) than I was accustomed to seeing, but that was the only immediately discernible difference. The group was predominantly white, with three African-American women and one man, one Hispanic man, and one Asian woman. They were all ages, all sizes. Most of them were wearing jeans and t-shirts, but several, like me, were in costume. I saw several people—both men and women—with collars on their necks, and several with black leather jackets or vests. One older man, probably in his seventies, was wearing leather boots, chaps over black jeans, a vest, and a leather biker's hat with chrome chain around the brim.

I stood there for a moment, undecided. There were more people than I'd anticipated, and I was early! I was about to turn around and find a bathroom to hide in, when an overweight woman in her forties, clustered with a small group standing near the entrance, looked over at me and smiled. "Ahh, there's that deer-in-the-headlights look I love so much!" she called. "Well, come on it, honey. We don't bite."

From a table halfway across the room, a man called out, "I do, but only if you ask nicely!"

There was some half-hearted laughter at what was obviously an old joke. I smiled nervously and stepped in, walking over to the woman who had greeted me. "Hi," I said, my sudden shyness only partially feigned. She stepped back to invite me into the cluster of four women and three men.

"Hey, sweetie. I'm Celia. Welcome to the Nashville munch."

Celia was wearing jeans, a t-shirt, and a black leather collar with a small, heart-shaped charm dangling from it. I froze, forgetting my cover story completely. Thankfully, Celia didn't notice my hesitation but started right in introducing the others in the group. "This is Adele and Nymphette, Master Stephen and his boy, Tim, Miss Tracy and her boy, Blade, and Linda H. I'm Celia, of course, the big mouth, and I belong to Sir Nightwind. He's around here somewhere—I keep misplacing him."

I chuckled, starting to relax a little bit. "I hope there's not going to be a quiz," I smiled. They smiled with me, which was good. "I'm Chloe," I said. It was my middle name—hopefully, I could remember it. "I…um, found this group on a website…"

"Most people do nowadays," Miss Tracy said. She had a slightly northern accent…definitely not a

Tennessee native. She was a Dominant; I had picked up on that much. I wasn't sure how to address her, so I just smiled and nodded.

"Yes, Ma'am, either the web or Bubba's," the girl called Nymphette said. The honorific came out of her mouth easily; apparently, the sticking point was my ears...or, more appropriately, my brain. The door opened, and several more people entered the room, immediately greeting and merging with another group. I'd been born and mostly raised in the South, the only child of a career politician. I could 'Ma'am' and 'Sir' with the best of them. As long as no one expected me to address them as 'Master' or 'Mistress,' I might survive the night.

"This is a pretty informal group, Chloe," Miss Tracy told me, almost as though she had read my thoughts. "It's an opportunity to meet people who have been involved in the lifestyle for a while, and to ask any questions you might have."

"Yes, Ma'am, thank you," I said politely. To my surprise, I felt my face heating slightly. There was something definitely...different...about addressing a Dominant as 'Ma'am,' something that resonated more deeply than the mere social courtesy. I didn't like it a bit.

I was beginning to be able to tell who was who, at least. Most of the Dominants carried themselves with a certain posture...body language, facial expression...emanating confidence and power. The Dominants made and held eye contact, whereas the submissives often looked down or away. I found myself emulating submissive behavior, not only because it was what I had decided for my 'cover story,' but because it did come a bit more easily to me in this nerve-wracking setting. That annoyed me. When this was over, and

69

Callie was home safely, I was going to spend a month reading nothing but feminist literature to scrub out my brain!

For now, I stood quietly and listened. My group resumed a conversation they'd been having about—of all things!—the *Harry Potter* movies. I could have participated, had I been so inclined. Like Blade, I believed the books were better, and the movies didn't do the series justice. Like Nymphette, I believed no movies *could* have done the series justice. And like Miss Tracy, I acknowledged Rowling's books had taught an entire generation of children about the magic of reading, and she deserved accolades for that, if nothing else.

I was still feeling out of place, but much more comfortable. This was just another social gathering, honestly. When people started moving toward seats at various tables, I followed along with Celia. She nodded to a seat next to hers at the large round table. I could see most of the people in the room from this vantage point; only a few tables toward the back of the room were obscured.

"All right, folks, settle down." A male Dominant, a good-looking man in his late thirties with short blond hair and a neatly trimmed beard, walked down the middle of the rows of tables, trying to get everyone's attention. There were a few random 'Shhh!'s, and then the room settled down enough for him to continue. "Welcome to the Saturday night munch. Tommy and Verlaine are our wait staff tonight—" he waited patiently through appreciative hoots and whistles "—and, as always, you'd better tip them big for putting up with our shit! I'm Kernan, and I'm your President for another four months, two weeks, and a day. Not that I'm counting. After that, someone else is taking the gavel, even if I have to ram it up their ass!"

"Better use a condom, Kernan!" Celia called out.

I smiled, biting back a nervous giggle, as the Dominant glanced our way.

"I hear you, Celia. Watch your mouth, girl, or I'll nominate Nightwind myself."

Celia shook her head wildly but kept her mouth shut.

When Kernan began speaking again, his voice held the well-polished sound of long practice. "Okay, the first order of business. Welcome to NAMTA—the Nashville Area Munch Group and Tennessee Fetish Alliance. If you are a law enforcement officer, you are requested to identify yourself, and please leave the premises. This is a private gathering of like-minded individuals. Second, our purpose is to meet and greet, and that is our *only* purpose. There will be no nudity, no pornography—and yes, Velvet, the pictures on your cell phone do count—no solicitation, and no illegal drug use of any kind on these premises at any time. If you're in fetish wear, you must be street-legal before you leave this room. Warren's has gone out of their way to treat us well, so do *not* piss me off. Again, tip your servers very well, and keep your goddamned hands to yourselves. Any questions so far?"

There were none. To my surprise, I found I liked Kernan. As silly as so much of this stuff sounded when I was reading about it online, it didn't actually feel silly at the moment. I could admit to myself I appreciated the no-nonsense, genuine approach Kernan had; it was a bit harder to admit, but I also liked the…swagger. The ultra-confident, alpha male arrogance was intriguing. It was even kind of hot, in a completely unrealistic, romance-novel fantasy sort of way. I found myself thinking when Callie was home safely, I might talk to my editor about a series of articles on the underground community;

71

perhaps even attend a few of Cal's events with her. I was beginning to feel comfortable, and I enjoyed the people-watching as Kernan went through a fairly lengthy list of announcements.

My feeling of comfort vanished abruptly with Kernan's next sentence. "Okay, so we're going around the room introducing ourselves, because we have several newbies tonight. All you have to do is stand up so we can see you, give us your first name or preferred scene name, and how you identify—Top, bottom, switch, Master, slave, submissive, Daddy, boy, girl, pet, puppy…whatever the hell you label yourself.

"Everyone got that? Your name and how you identify. Anything else you want to add is welcome, but not mandatory. Boydton, you are limited to one minute of speaking time, because I've had too many complaints about having to listen to your shit. Everyone else, take as long as you like. If you go on too long, I guarantee, we'll let you know."

There was laughter and some catcalling. I felt like I was going to throw up. I did *not* want to speak in front of this entire group—*I was doing quite well with my little clique of seven, thank you very much!* I glanced at the door, wondering if I could slip out, unnoticed.

Luckily, Kernan started with the row of tables opposite my own. Introductions would travel to the back of the room and then back up on this side. My table would be last.

My desire to sneak out ebbed slightly, as people stood up and started speaking. I desperately wanted my spiral notebook and a pen to take notes, but I quelled the urge, and just listened closely. As each person stood and introduced themselves, there were murmured greetings and quiet words of welcome from others in the room. It had the feel of an AA meeting, but friendlier. These people knew each other. Newbies were welcomed warmly.

"Hi, I'm Mandi, and I live with my Owner, Mistress Carolyn. We've been in the lifestyle for about a year now, and we're really getting into puppy play."

"Hey, everyone. Master K from the House of Rope. My slave is Eileen and subs are Whipgirl, Kitten, and Velvet. I've been into bondage and rope play, especially shibari, for about seven years, and I've taught classes in Tennessee, Kentucky, and Virginia. I'm presenting next month at Fetish Camp in Atlanta—hope to see some of y'all there."

"Hi, I'm Carl. I'm a switch."

"I'm Pleasure. I'm a Top, and I'm looking for a girl or boy to train."

"I'm Sir Cougar, and I'm a Dominant. I'm new, glad to be here, and hope to be learning a lot."

"Hey, peeps! I'm Kitten, and I belong to Master K and Eileen."

There were subtle groans when the next speaker stood, so I craned my neck to see him near the back of the room. The man immediately reminded me of Jabba the Hutt. He was about that size, with greasy, slicked-back hair and a ridiculous, slightly comical Hitler mustache.

"Well, you all know me," he announced, his booming voice carrying easily through the room. "I'm Master Boydton, Gorean Lord, and Master of the House of the Firm Hand. If any of you newbies are hungry for training, you can petition me, and I will consider your plea for collar. You'll find I'm a strict, but fair, Master, which is why I'm known as the Firm Hand." He paused, as though waiting for applause, then continued, "I've

73

been a Master all of my life. I've been practicing sadism for twenty years before there even was a 'lifestyle,' and I've owned at least thirty girls. I'm an expert in all types of edgeplay, including knifeplay, breathplay, and, of course, the bullwhip." Boydton chuckled, clearly expecting others in the room to react in some positive manner. Apparently, no one else had gotten that memo, and I wasn't about to draw his attention my way. Finally, he moved on. "Well, let's see, what else about me? I started in S&M long before the internet even existed. I can teach the Gorean positions of submission, as well as how to find your slave heart and how to beg for release. If you want the mentoring of a true Dom—"

"Okay, Boyd, time." Kernan's interruption was met with a few murmurs of relief.

Celia leaned in close to me, and whispered, "In case you didn't catch the Obvious Ball, Boyd's a real ass. You'll want to steer clear of him, especially when you're new."

I nodded agreement, preparing to answer her, but my mouth went dry when the next man stood.

"I'm Falcon," Eric Grayson said. He looked directly at me when he spoke, his lips curved slightly upward. "I'm a Dominant, and I've been in the lifestyle for six years. If you want to know more, ask."

Boyd scowled as Eric sat down, as though irritated at the simple legitimacy 'Falcon's' words carried, especially in contrast to his own self-aggrandizing articulation. I stared at Eric, taking in the tight black t-shirt, well-worn leather vest, comfortable blue jeans and the leather boots. *What the hell was Eric doing at* my *munch? Had he come because he'd seen it on my to-do list?*

The man beside Eric stood, and I barely heard him announce, "Hi, I'm Dale, a submissive, currently

74

uncollared. Been in the lifestyle about ten years now." A woman stood and spoke, and two other men. I tuned them all out, my eyes still locked on Eric's. He lifted an eyebrow at me. He was…amused!

I broke eye contact, a mixture of emotions roiling in my stomach. I felt angry he was here, and embarrassed, but I didn't know why. I wanted to be indignant because he was stepping on my investigation…but he *was* the Federal agent. And, I had to admit, he looked a lot more comfortable in his costume than I felt in mine. *Damn him! He could have told me he'd be here!* I fumed for another moment, and then determined my course of action for the night: I would ignore Eric completely.

I felt Celia stand up next to me. "Hey, everyone. I'm Celia, or Soft Iris online," she said, "and, to a lot of you, I'm just Merry Fucking Sunshine! My Master is Sir Nightwind, and no disrespect intended, Sir Kernan, but even if I have to safe word in public, he is *not* getting back on the board!"

There was laughter, and then it was my turn. I stood, suddenly shaking again. "I'm …" I wasn't speaking loudly enough, so I cleared my throat and restarted. "Hello, everyone. I'm Chloe, and I'm submissive…I think." I glanced around the room quickly, smiling at everyone, except Eric, and then sat down, relieved the ordeal was over.

Across the room, Boydton stood back up. "Welcome, little one," he said. To my horror, he was looking directly at *me!* "I'm Lord Boydton, as you may recall, and I am the Owner of the largest House in Tennessee. I have five girls in service to me now, but there is always room in my stables for more. Chloe, is it? If you'd like—"

"That's it, Boyd," Kernan said sharply. "You already

had your time. If you want to pimp your—"

"I was merely offering my mentorsh—"

"Enough!" Kernan's voice was a whip crack of anger.

"Of course," Boydton said, easing his weight back onto his chair. "I yield the floor," he stated, with pompous gravity.

Celia met my eyes, and we spoke volumes to each other in that moment. I was relieved when Nymphette was the last to stand and make her introduction.

Almost immediately, as if they had been awaiting a signal, Warren's waiters or waitresses appeared at every table, taking people's orders. I was stunned. *What had happened to the two servers I was told about?* I voiced that to Celia, and she grinned.

"Oh, they love us here," she explained. "They'll send almost the whole crew to take our orders all at once, and then Tommy and Verlaine will bring food out as it comes up. We'll keep them hopping for the next two hours, but Kernan always makes sure we tip well, so I don't think they mind."

"They don't," Blade added. "A few months ago, I overheard one of the waiters tell Miss Tracy they actually have to draw names to see who gets our room for that week, or they wouldn't have any wait staff at all to cover the front rooms."

I nodded my understanding, privately amazed. The wait staff certainly seemed friendlier than most others I'd encountered. I placed my order, proud of myself for not getting the bloomin' onion. A six-ounce sirloin and baked potato would about do me in.

I touched Callie's crucifix, reassuring myself silently. I didn't know how much I could learn about Callie tonight, but I had to get to know this entire group of people *very* quickly. The evening was going well so far,

Eric's presence excepted. I was fitting into the role of 'new submissive,' and I'd already been accepted by a small group within the group.

"So, um…what is Lord Boydton's deal?" I asked Celia.

She rolled her eyes. "Oh, jeez, Chloe. Every group has to have one, right? He's ours. He's Gorean, so he thinks that makes him God's gift to the world of kink."

I frowned. "He doesn't look Korean," I noted.

Seven faces turned my way.

"What did you say, dear?" Miss Tracy asked. She looked as if she were trying to swallow an uncooperative goldfish.

"I don't mean to sound racist," I clarified, glancing warily at the others at the table. I suddenly had everyone's complete attention, but I wasn't sure why. "I just said I don't think he looks Korean…or Asian at all, really, but he made such a point of it. I mean…"

There was a moment of silence at the table, which Blade finally broke with whoops of gleeful laughter. Everyone roared then, and I smiled, confused.

"Oh, my god, I *love* this girl!" Blade squealed, grinning at Miss Tracy. "Can we keep her, Ma'am? Please? I've always wanted a little sister!"

I wasn't sure what had gained me instant approval, but I was willing to go with it. I had apparently tickled the entire group. Celia had mascara tears rolling down her face but seemed helpless to stop laughing. I smiled along, figuring there would be an explanation forthcoming soon.

"Chloe, you just made my night," Blade grinned at me.

"Gorean," Celia emphasized the pronunciation when she was able to talk, "is a type of BDSM lifestyle, kind of

like a lifestyle-within-a-lifestyle."

I stared at her blankly, which sent Blade into another fit of giggles.

"It's this way, Chloe," Blade explained. "There was a series of these lame-assed science fiction novels, written back in the sixties and seventies, about a world called Gor. Every man was a natural-born Master, every woman was a slave, yadda-yadda. The books gained a cult following, and now, it seems every BDSM community in America gets stuck with some pompous-assed wannabe who claims he is a 'Great Master of the Gorean way.'" Blade made the air quotes around his words and snorted. "Boydton is ours…but from now on, that bitch is Korean!"

I mouthed an apologetic, 'Oops!' which sent the table into more gales of laughter. Okay, so I had just learned about *another* type of BDSM to add to my research work. *Sheesh—subgenres within subgenres!*

Our food arrived while my tablemates were still explaining Gorean slave positions to me. Miss Tracy finally put an end to the topic when Blade pulled out his cell phone, intending to Google *sensei* in Korean.

"Put that away!" Miss Tracy snapped sharply to Blade. "For vanillas, what we do is just as silly to them as Gor seems to most of us. There is authentic beauty in some of the positions and ideals of service John Norman created, and some people do legitimately choose that model in their D and s lives. Just because you don't respect Boydton is no reason to disparage the entire construct."

I watched a few of the others at the table nod, agreeing with her in principle.

"And *you,*" she continued, stabbing Blade with a withering glare, "had better watch it, boy. Boyd is still a

Dominant in our community, and if you don't cool your jets, I will have you at his table licking his boots in apology."

Blade sobered immediately and spent the next several minutes eating his steak with single-minded precision. *Jesus!* I felt bad for him; he wouldn't have gotten scolded if I hadn't misunderstood. *Talk about a bitch! Or...not?* I glanced surreptitiously at the others seated at the table. Nobody seemed particularly shocked at Miss Tracy's harshness, and Blade himself didn't appear angry, just very...sincere...in his desire to avoid additional chastisement. I was confused as hell.

"Well, um...what Boyd said about needing a mentor...?" I asked, leaving the question open-ended.

"It's not mandatory, but it is recommended," Master Stephen said, to nods around the table. "Of course, you'll want a submissive for that, hon, not a Dom."

"Dale mentored me," Adele said shyly. It was the first time I'd heard her speak all night.

"Dale is awesome!" Celia seconded. "Finish up, and I'll introduce you to him."

I nodded and turned back to my steak, briefly considering the evening thus far. Celia was pretty bossy for a submissive. That wasn't the only inconsistency I'd noticed. Overall, I was having a hard time making this lively, gregarious group of people, who tipped generously and debated Harry Potter, fit into my preconceptions of slavering, perverted sex animals. It was annoying.

People were chatting and mingling when I pushed my plate away and followed Celia. She introduced me to everyone we saw, as we made our way toward the back of the room. I had forgotten Dale had been sitting next to Eric! *Shit!*

Dale stood politely when Celia and I approached him. It seemed less like deference than just good manners, although I wasn't sure why I felt the difference. Perhaps if Miss Tracy had been with us, I would have been able to pinpoint the distinction. He nodded immediately when Celia told him I was new, and could use a mentor. He pulled a business card from his back pocket, which simply said "dale" (in lower case, of course), and gave several contact options, including email, Facebook, and cell phone.

"It would be an honor to help you in any way I can," Dale said, inclining his head in a manner that almost resembled a bow. "I'm off Monday, if you feel like coming over for brunch."

I thanked him, and we exchanged pleasantries. I felt immediately at ease with Dale; unlike several of the other men in the room, he hadn't given me the subtle once-over or held my hand longer than was comfortable. He was cute, in an almost boyish way. Although at least in his thirties, he had a young, round face, short, curly brown hair, and a sweet smile. Like most of the men in the room, Dom or sub, he was wearing a black t-shirt and jeans. His t-shirt, however, bore a bright yellow smiley-face…with a bullet hole between its eyes and a trickle of blood. I'd seen the shirt before, and I found it amusing. That, his courtesy, and his palpable, almost puppy-like eagerness to help, made me wonder why he wasn't 'collared'" already.

After Celia and I stepped away, I asked her.

"He was Domina Dawn's boy for about two years," she informed me, "and then he was collared to Miss Tracy. I'm not sure what happened, but she released him from collar a few months ago. They're on good terms, still."

Celia definitely seemed to know at least something about everybody. I glanced over to the front of the room, where Eric was holding an animated conversation with Kernan. He had moved away shortly after Celia brought me to Dale, presumably to allow us privacy. I couldn't help myself. I told myself it was my journalistic instincts, but even I knew I was lying. "What about him?" I asked Celia, nodding just enough to indicate Eric.

"Sir Falcon?" she asked, and I nodded in confirmation.

Celia sighed, looking troubled. "He's a terrific Dominant," she told me, "and a completely amazing Top. He can do things with a singletail that make me *drool* just to think about. He was teaching Sir Nightwind, but…"

"But?" I prompted. There was a sadness in Celia's face, and it distracted me from thinking about that singletail comment. Somewhat. Even the word made me shiver!

"Well, he lost his girl, Majyck, about six months ago. It was completely unexpected, and it really threw him. Don't let anyone know I told you, but…there was a robbery at the retail store where Majyck worked, and she got shot."

"Oh, god, that's terrible," I said softly, meaning it.

Celia nodded. "He didn't come to anything at all for about a month, and when he did start showing back up, he was…different. Kind of crazy. Scary, dangerous crazy. Kernan almost told him to stay away from the munches, but…it seems like he's getting his head on. He's gained some of the weight back, and he's calmer, more together now. He hasn't played, or even shown an interest in playing, since Majyck died."

81

"You've known him for a while, then? He's a…regular?"

"Yeah, for about two years, or so. They moved up here from Virginia, something to do with his job."

Well, there went my theory he had invaded my munch group…and two years was about as long as he'd been investigating the missing women, so it made sense. The reporter in me couldn't stop. "What kind of work does he do?"

"I have no idea. I think something with computers."

I bit my lip, thinking about what I'd just learned, and trying to reconcile it with what I knew about Special Agent Grayson. Once again, I had a hard time fitting him into my preconceptions.

"He is a hottie, though, isn't he?" Celia asked, misinterpreting my silence.

I nodded absently.

"Come on, I'll introduce you," she grinned, pulling me by the arm. "Who knows? Maybe you'll be good for him!"

I panicked. I couldn't very well wrench my arm out of her grasp or deck her, not without causing a scene. Celia had momentum and the element of surprise, and she was headed directly for the two men. I followed behind helplessly.

Celia stood patiently while the men finished their conversation, which had something to do with Eric—*Falcon,* I reminded myself—giving Kernan money for a party admission in private. Her demeanor changed instantly when the Dominants shifted their attention to us. I got a flash of an image of two wolves looking speculatively at two deer. I looked down, studying the carpet and Eric's shiny, black motorcycle boots. Harness boots, I think they were called.

"Yes, Iris?" Kernan asked Celia. I blinked, then remembered Celia's online 'scene name.' There it was, though…that *tone of voice* when Kernan spoke. It was the same tone of command Eric had used a few times, the same tone Miss Tracy had used when she'd reprimanded the table and Blade. I couldn't define what it was, but it made my stomach tighten in empathy for Celia. That tone of voice made me feel…exposed. It made me feel like…prey.

There was no hint of playfulness about Celia now. "Sirs," she said respectfully. "I'd like to introduce a guest. This is Chloe. She's exploring the lifestyle, and this is her first munch."

There was silence, and it seemed to stretch. I glanced up, wondering if I were supposed to speak now, and found both men openly examining me. I felt my face heat, and it took everything in my arsenal not to squirm under their scrutiny. Both men were alphas…and I was a doe.

"Welcome, Chloe," Kernan finally said, his voice friendly and warm, but still intimidating.

I nodded, glancing quickly up at Kernan, and then back down at Eric's boots. *What in holy hell was wrong with me?* It was a simple introduction, but I felt as tongue-tied as a first-grader in the principal's office. The thought brought a flush of anger—I was *nobody's* doormat, nobody's submissive! Yet, for the life of me, I was frozen.

I looked up quickly when Eric spoke to me. "So, is this what you expected, girl?" he asked drily, one eyebrow raised.

They were waiting for my answer.

"Not…exactly," I replied, my voice thick, "Sir."

I thought I would choke on the word. My face

burned, a combination of anger, embarrassment, and...*oh, good god! That was* not *arousal!* Eric's face remained neutral, but his eyes were glinting with amusement.

Kernan looked over at Eric, and nodded slightly. "Good eye," he said inexplicably, and then he walked away without another word, moving over to another group of people and joining their conversation.

That seemed rude to me, but I wasn't about to say anything. There had been silent conversations going on between the two men, dialogues happening around me, to which I was not privy.

Eric smiled warmly at Celia. "Thank you, Iris," he said, and even I recognized the dismissal.

"Of course, Sir," Celia said happily. As abruptly as Kernan, Celia turned and left, throwing me completely under the bus, and leaving me alone with Eric! He studied me silently, and I felt my temper flare.

"You...dismissed her!" I accused, keeping my voice quiet.

To my surprise, Eric nodded, unconcerned. "And?"

"That was...rude!" I sputtered.

Eric raised an eyebrow at me again, not denying the charge, merely unaffected by it. I felt my face flush hot again.

"There's a play party tonight at Bubba's after the munch," he told me, the change of topic catching me off-guard. "This group only holds them every three months or so. I've bought your ticket. You're coming as my guest."

I started to tell him where he could shove that ticket, but I stopped myself. I thought about it. Celia hadn't mentioned the party. She either didn't trust me yet, or she didn't have the 'authority' to invite me. I wanted to

84

make inroads into this community, to get to know the people and start steering conversations around to Callie…'fetishgirl,' but gaining their trust was going to take time. Time was a luxury I didn't have. The party was a good opportunity, and Eric wasn't obligated to provide it to me.

"Okay." I nodded my agreement.

"'Yes, Sir,'" Eric corrected me, not joking at all.

Oh, good god—of all the nerve! "Fuck. You. Sir!" I hissed quietly, a meaningful pause between each word. Then I smiled, a sweetly venomous smile.

To my surprise, Eric laughed. It was an unexpected sound, rich and warm, completely uninhibited. I wasn't the only one surprised. Several others glanced our way. Miss Tracy nodded approvingly at me, and Celia beamed, looking for all the world like the proud hen who had just laid her first egg.

"You are getting a piece of my mind when we get out of here," I promised Eric sweetly.

"Oh, I'm counting on that, Chloe."

He was infuriating, and he seemed completely aware of the fact, which only increased my frustration. His eyes sparkled in amusement, and I felt my own tighten with anger. He had really nice eyes—sharp, clear, blue-gray, a nice contrast to his dark hair and tanned skin. He had this way of looking at me, as though he were looking inside me. His examination didn't stop at the leather skirt or the scooped neckline; it went deeper…probing, penetrating, analyzing.

Two could play that game. I looked at Eric, examining him with the cool objectivity of a reporter. He was six, maybe six-foot-one, not a heavyweight bodybuilder, but definitely athletic. The black t-shirt fit him, but it was tight, conforming to the hard muscles of his chest and stomach, and straining slightly at his biceps. There was a thin, silver outline of a jaguar's face and shoulders, with one claw raised threateningly, seeming almost to reach off the shirt to swipe at the person standing in front of him. Beneath that, silver letters, almost illegible from having been washed repeatedly, stated, "Big cats play rough. Norfolk Jags MC." Over the shirt, he wore a leather vest—a bar vest, not a suit vest. There were several pins on the left side of the vest; I would have to examine them more closely another time.

"How would you rate your acting ability?" Eric asked.

I didn't hear that slight tone of mockery in his voice, so I looked up at him. He nodded toward the rest of the room. People had started leaving, and Tommy and Verlaine were busily bussing tables and picking up tips.

"Um. Good, I guess," I replied.

"I know you do deer-in-the-headlights well," Eric said, the tone dry enough to make me flush again, "but what about arousal?"

"Excuse me?"

"We're headed to a party, Chloe, and the stuff you're likely to see at this event is going to be tame compared to some other BDSM venues. If you're going to pursue this, you need to not just act your cover, but become it. You're here because thoughts and fantasies about BDSM excite you, turn you on, *make you wet.*"

I winced at Eric's words, and he nodded his head. "If you look like you want to punch someone every time you see or hear something that makes you uncomfortable, you will not last in this community. More importantly, though, you'll put yourself in danger."

It was the kindness in his voice that got through to

me. If he'd been smug or arrogant, I could have retaliated in kind, but he seemed, at least for now, as if he were genuinely trying to help.

"I can do this," I told him decisively.

He studied me for a long moment, deliberating. I looked back at him levelly, neither staring him down nor retreating from him. He nodded slightly, more to himself than to me. I felt a surge of victory. If I had interpreted it correctly, Eric's slight nod meant he had accepted me...my presence on his turf, at least, if not my actual partnership.

"You know where Bubba's is?" he asked me, as we walked past my former table. He took a couple of bills out of his wallet and put them down next to my place setting, without glancing at them. I glanced. I couldn't help it. He had laid down two twenties, which was almost twice the cost of my meal, which I had *not* asked him to pay for, in any case! That was absolutely ridiculous! No wonder Tommy and Verlaine had been so prompt and attentive—this weekly munch group was the damned mother lode!

"I don't know Nashville that well," I admitted, following him outside the restaurant. The back of his vest was covered with a large 'Norfolk Jags' patch; there were three smaller patches along the bottom of the vest – one of them said 'Louisville Vipers L/L.' *Louisville?* I wasn't aware of any motorcycle club called the 'Vipers.' I'd heard of the Gypsy Raiders, of course—everyone knew about them—but I'd never heard of the Vipers. I didn't cover the crime desk, but still...I would have heard.

The sun had gone down, and there was a slight, warm breeze in the parking lot. It felt wonderful after the frigidity of the excessively air-conditioned restaurant.

87

There was a scent in the air … the fragrance of heat, and grass, and summer. I relished it for a moment, as we stood together.

"Then I'm driving," Eric said, continuing the conversation.

I looked, wondering which vehicle was his. He handed me a black motorcycle helmet. We'd been standing next to a motorcycle while talking, and apparently, it was Eric's method of transportation. I balked.

Eric straddled the bike easily, tipping his head at me and waiting. "Problem?" he asked, that hint of a sardonic smile playing at his lips.

"Not at all," I replied briskly, shaking my hair back so I could put the helmet on.

It was bulkier than I thought it would be, and it felt heavy on my head. I pulled the visor up, not liking the way it dimmed my vision. Eric watched, saying nothing. I adjusted my skirt, well-aware the thigh-high leather bunched up almost to my ass, and climbed onto the motorcycle. He didn't say a word about my death grip on his shoulder, and neither did I.

I wouldn't know one type of motorcycle from another, but the Harley-Davidson logo was familiar enough. The bike didn't look new, but it was well cared for, and clean. The seat was actually very comfortable. I settled myself and then put my hands lightly on each side of Eric's waist. I felt him chuckle, as the machine roared to life beneath us. It was a lot louder than I'd anticipated, and for several seconds, I regretted the bravado of my decision.

Eric twisted the handlebars, and the bike pulled out smoothly. The sudden sense of motion was terrifying, and I tightened my hold, definitely regretting the bravado of my decision. He stopped the bike at the end of the parking lot, his feet on the asphalt. He took my hands and pulled them so they encircled his waist, pulling me close to him.

"Lean into the curves," he told me, his voice carrying easily over the sound of the engine. "Hold onto me tightly. If you don't trust me, you'll get both of us hurt."

I don't know if he felt my nod, but I held on tightly. This time when Eric pulled out, he accelerated. I gasped at the sudden wind in my face and turned my head against it, completely unwilling to move my hands to lower the visor. There was no appropriate place for my head to rest…except against Eric's back. The leather of his vest was supple, and it smelled good, an indescribable, heady, masculine aroma. I could feel the warmth of his body against my cheek. I closed my eyes for a moment, both for respite from the wind and to enjoy the sensation. I could learn to appreciate this!

Being on a motorcycle was a completely new experience for me, something to memorize and categorize for later contemplation. I was starting to get comfortable when Eric turned onto the on-ramp to I-40, accelerating and leaning the bike into the curve. I suddenly felt like throwing up, and I white-knuckled it until we were upright again.

"Don't fight the bike," Eric called over his shoulder. "Centrifugal force is our friend!"

I couldn't think of anything nice to say, so I kept quiet. When we were on the straightaway (and upright) again, the ride was fun, even exhilarating! I liked the sensation of the wind on my face, and I liked the way I could eliminate the wind by burying my head into the smell of leather and warm, male body. But I definitely did not like leaning into the curves at sixty miles per hour and seeing just how close the asphalt actually was. *Centrifugal force*—not *a fan.*

***

Bubba's had once been a dojo, but that had been years in the past. The beautiful bamboo floor was all that remained. Now, Bubba's was a seedy bar in a seedy part of Nashville…but it was rocking! Not bouncers-blocking-the-door-and-selectively-admitting-just-the-hotties rocking, but still, a-hundred-people-drinking-and-dancing-to-a-live-band rocking. Eric kept a hand on my elbow—either protectively or possessively—as he escorted me in.

The bartender closest to the entrance was an enormous man, who made Lord Boydton look trim. He must have weighed four hundred pounds, and he was tending bar seated, in a backless office chair. The floor had been raised, so he was able to wheel from customer to customer and deftly pour out drafts or cocktails. He was busy and proficient, and he shouted a running conversation with several patrons as he served them.

He looked over at us and grinned.

"Well, Falcon, now you're here, I can officially say it—ladies and gentlemen, the pree-verts are in the house!"

"Yeah, fuck you, too, Bubba," Eric shot back. "What kind of shit band you got in here tonight?"

Bubba shrugged. "Hell if I know, and whadda you care? You ain't sticking around for the music anyway!"

Eric laughed and, apparently, the exchange was over. He guided me around several tables, and we skirted a huge dance floor to emerge into a dimly-lit hallway near the back of the bar. He opened an industrial steel door, and we stepped into a stairwell, the lights seeming

90

uncomfortably bright in comparison to the club. When the door closed behind us, the volume of the music was cut in half. I could hear myself think again, which was a relief.

"You doing okay?" Eric asked me, not even having to shout the question. I nodded, and Eric started toward the stairs, heading up. I reached out to stop him, and he turned back to me questioningly.

"I wanted to say thanks," I said, the words coming out stiffly, nowhere near as nonchalantly as I'd rehearsed.

Eric smiled at me, and my stomach fluttered in reaction. *What the hell was up with* that?

"You're welcome, girl," he said. He took my hand, and we went *up* the stairs to the dungeon. Yeah. Go figure.

Gerard
The Search

It had taken awhile, but Johanssen had finally called out
sick. It might have had something to do with my
'concerned' comments over the past couple days. He
didn't really look pale, but my grandma used to tell me,
'If someone says you look sick, lie down!' I had gambled
the same principle would work with Johanssen, and,
finally, it had.

That…or by the power of suggestion, the poor
schlep really did catch a stomach virus.

It didn't matter to me either way. The important
thing was he was off-duty for the night, and that meant
I was doing my rounds alone. *That* meant I could finally
search Lau's office.

I already knew Jimmy kept nothing damning on his
computer. He ran a cleaning program every night before
leaving the office. He carried a flash drive with him, and

that was it. That was probably where the information leading up Lau's chain of command would be stored, but I had to do a thorough search anyway, just in case there was any other incriminating evidence to be found. Unfortunately, the thumb drive never left Jimmy's person, and I wasn't stupid enough to try to pick it from his pocket. I couldn't testify against the motherfucker if I was dead.

As soon as I'd learned Johannsen had called out, I triggered a little subroutine I'd secreted into the code of Lau's security software. He was a paranoid bastard, and his security sweeps were excellent, so I'd be deactivating it soon. Until I deactivated it, though, cameras ten and eleven would display images of an empty hallway outside Lau's office. I let myself in with the master key and flipped on the lights. As Lau's chief of security, I had legitimate cause – so far – for everything I was doing, presuming the subroutine remained hidden.

I went through Lau's desk first, using the set of lock picks I'd brought with me for that purpose. There was nothing of interest. I moved to the small closet in the corner of the office, one perhaps originally intended for linens. The shelves were neatly stocked with every kind of office supply imaginable, and with exactly three of each item. Three printer cartridges, three reams of paper. Three boxes of staples, three rolls of scotch tape. Either Lau took his dedication to the Triad Society way too seriously, or the fucker had a solid case of OCD.

I re-locked the closet door and went to the solitary filing cabinet in the office. That lock was a bit more challenging, but it gave after a couple minutes of jiggling.

I found a few interesting things in the filing cabinet. Both Chen Sut and David Phan made more money than I did, even though I'd been with Lau longer and had more responsibilities. It was the Asian version of discriminatory pay practices.

I reached for a folder labeled 'exports,' hoping Lau would be stupid enough to list the girls with the legitimate inventory he traded. My hopes were not high.

The office door opened. I barely had time to move my hand from the folder to another section of files, before Jimmy Lau stepped into the room with his bodyguard walking behind him. Today, it was Juan.

Lau blinked at me in surprise, but he was not yet suspicious. "Gerard? What is going on, my friend? What are you doing in my office?"

I thought fast and nodded toward the filing cabinet. "Came by on my rounds, and saw this cabinet drawer open about an inch," I improvised. "I know that's not like you, so I came in to check."

Lau raised an incredulous eyebrow, so I continued, "As long as I was in here, I figured I'd check Johanssen's personnel file. He's missed two days of work in just the past month."

Lau's eyes cleared, and his body relaxed, but still he frowned at me. "You are not cleared to be in here, Gerard. You know this already."

I shrugged, unconcerned. "So write me up," I said amiably. "I go a lot of places I'm not cleared to be." It was the right approach to take.

Lau chuckled, and held the door open for me to precede him. I stepped out of the office and into the hallway, while he moved over to a small urn sitting on the desk, then reached inside and pulled out the thumb drive he'd forgotten.

Fuck! I'd been that close, and hadn't even realized it. I knew, despite Lau's ready acceptance of my explanation, he would never hide the thumb drive in that urn again. Odds were high he would also begin digging deeper into my pre-war background.

That didn't worry me. The CIA had set my cover up, and it went all the way back to the fictitious Little League I had never belonged to. Lau wouldn't find anything on me the Company didn't want him to find.

On the other hand, I'd spent four years of my life getting close to the viper, gathering evidence to ensure a solid RICO case against him. If he decided I wasn't trustworthy, that was four years of intensive investigation work down the shitter.

Eric
The Dungeon

Hope and I stepped into the dungeon, and, thank god, the door immediately cut the noise. That techno crap from downstairs could barely be heard, and instead, the sultry, erotic strains of one of the tracks from Enigma's *Cross of Changes* filled the air. The additional sounds of adults at play came from behind the curtains blocking off the play space from the social/dressing area. I watched Hope's reaction from the corner of my eye while I handed the party passes I'd gotten from Kernan to Nymphette, the current door monitor.

"I'm glad you came, Sir," she told me respectfully. "It's been too long since we've seen you at a party."

I smiled, acknowledging her expression of sympathy. She had been sitting at Hope's table during the munch, so she would be a familiar face to the inquisitive reporter. As I expected, Hope smiled at Nymphette and seemed to relax marginally. I guided Hope into the social space and found us a table near the snack and soda spread. She kept glancing at the curtains, the curiosity eating her alive. I would have laughed, if only to piss her off, but I had a role to play, too.

"Sit," I ordered, when we'd reached the table I'd selected. I was surprised when she obeyed, but I didn't let it show.

With the music and other noises providing a sound barrier, Hope and I would be able to talk semi-privately, as long as we kept it low. I still had serious reservations about what I was planning to do, but Hope had made it clear she wasn't going to sit home and tend to her knitting. So, I had made my decision at the munch, when I'd watched her stand and introduce herself. She'd been the consummate actress…the perfect new submissive, shy, uncomfortable, but determined to pursue her kink. If I could give her six months' experience and the depth of a slave before introducing her to Lau as an 'acquisition,' he would never stand a chance. She would be utterly irresistible to him. Perfect bait, just as Majyck had been.

I could also convince myself it was safer for both of us if I kept Hope close to me, and, in all honesty, it was. If she stumbled into Lau's nest of vipers on her own, I could do nothing for her. If I brought her in, I could protect her, at least to a point. I would pull the plug if the risk got too high. It was a viable plan. Of course, if ASAC Zewicke found out I was using an unauthorized civilian in a Bureau investigation, convincing *him* of that would be another issue entirely.

In fact, it would be impossible. Involving Hope without getting her Bureau-sanctioned consultant status would mean my badge, flat out. There were no acceptable excuses, no reasonable appeals. If we brought Lau down, though, it would be worth it. Even if they took my badge, they could (and would) use my testimony to put the son-of-a-bitch away.

I'd been toying with the idea of leaving the Bureau for months, anyway. Since their screw-up, and my stupidity, had gotten my partner killed, I'd been operating on autopilot. It was only this case that kept me working at all. If I could use Hope—her safety being paramount—to bring down Lau, then I could weather whatever fallout came from the Feds. I had a solid enough reputation and enough support from my colleagues that, as long as I could avoid indictment, I could find work. I also knew my ASAC. Zewicke could be a prick, but overall, he was a decent cop. If I brought Lau down, he would write me a glowing reference letter with one hand, even as he stripped me of my gun and badge with the other. He'd been a field agent long before becoming an ASAC, and he hadn't yet forgotten the realities of the game. As long as Hope survived, and we brought in enough evidence against Lau to convince a grand jury, I could come out of this relatively unscathed.

I could totally screw the pooch just as easily.

I sat next to Hope, studying her for a long moment, as I considered the possibilities. She broke eye contact first, her cheeks reddening slightly. I wondered what thoughts were making her blush, but I didn't ask.

"What am I going to do with you?" I voiced the thought aloud.

"What options are you considering?" Hope asked, her brown eyes twinkling mischievously. "Perhaps I can help you decide."

I didn't smile. "You're getting in way over your head, girl," I threatened softly. "You don't know what you're doing."

She was perceptive. She picked up on the tone and the danger in my words. Her pupils dilated slightly in reaction, and her chin lifted marginally. "That's my choice to make, Er—Falcon." She noticed the mistake, and I immediately jumped on it.

"That's what I'm talking about," I snapped at her. "You're going to get me killed."

I had guessed correctly and zeroed in on her weak point. She blanched, as my words penetrated, and she closed her mouth abruptly. She had been prepared to argue her case, but I'd knocked her feet from under her before she could even get started. She could play fast and loose with her own life, but I'd just reminded her she was holding mine in her hands as well.

She shook her head miserably. "I have to find her," she said, her eyes shining with tears she wouldn't shed.

Fuck me. She had found my weak point, as well. Months after going undercover, I'd realized I couldn't resist a genuine plea from a strong submissive woman. Majyck had known that. She had played me, and she had died for it. Hope wasn't playing me, which made it all the worse.

I went with my decision.

"All right," I said. "We work together. But we do it *my* way, by *my* rules. Are you good with that?"

She nodded quickly, as I'd known she would, and then, she surprised me. "Yes, Sir," she said steadily. There was no hesitation or mockery in her tone; it would have passed.

"That's a start," I muttered, wondering already how long I would live to regret this. It wasn't the first time I'd put my job, and my life, in the hands of a complete stranger. With Jimmy Lau on the playing field, though, it could well be my last.

"I'm at the Extended Stay on Brandsford," I told her. "I have documentation you'll need to become familiar with. A *lot* of documentation. There's a play party—the real deal, not like this—next Saturday. You will need to be up to speed by then. If you slip up, there are no second chances. You ready to take that on?"

"Yes," she said immediately.

I shook my head, annoyed at her quick response. "Chloe, you don't even know what you're agreeing to. The men involved in this organization are dangerous. They won't hesitate to kill you, if they believe you're a threat to them."

She reached across the table and took my hands in both of hers, looking at me levelly. "It doesn't matter, Falcon," she told me, her voice quiet but purposeful. "If it means bringing Callie home, I'll do anything needed. Anything. I'm not just saying that, I promise you."

Okay. It was time to test her proclamation.

"Do not move." I made it an order. She nodded her head in perfect acquiescence, and I left the table and went to speak to Nymphette. Of course Hope had said she would do anything now—she had no idea what 'anything' could encompass. The Nashville play parties were a lot of fun, but they were tame. Eighty percent of the players were middle-aged, overweight, stay-at-home moms, or balding CPA dads. They drove minivans with car seats and 'Baby on Board' caution stickers. They got naked in public, they tapped into the energy exchange of sex play, and, for a while, they pretended they were dangerous. Then, they went back to their real lives, no harm, no foul, feeling good about themselves and their chosen partners. It was good, clean fun for everyone involved.

100

Lau's parties, on the other hand, took the game up several notches. His clientele didn't have to pretend to be dangerous; they were. There was a world of difference between one of his parties and this. Still, I might as well put Hope through her paces on a dry run.

I came back to the table with the objects I'd borrowed from Nymphette. I don't generally use other peoples' tools or toys, but I hadn't intended to play tonight, so I hadn't come prepared. Additionally, tonight would be Hope's coming out cotillion; we would be making an impression that would reverberate through the Nashville BDSM community. That meant it was remotely possible Jimmy Lau would hear a whisper, or two, about a hot new submissive on the scene, which would pique his interest. It was time to test Hope's resolve.

Hope was sitting where I'd left her. She was watching Sir J. and Kitten, who had come out of the play area and were sitting at another table. J. was holding Kitten on his lap, and he had her covered in a warm blanket. He was speaking to her…quiet, comforting words of aftercare…and she was purring, totally spaced out on that endorphin high some masochists get from a well-controlled scene. It was where her scene name came from. I had made her purr a few times myself. Good fun.

I held the play collar up in front of Hope and allowed myself the satisfaction of smirking when her eyes widened. I stepped around behind her and moved her long brown hair out of the way, enjoying the silkiness of it in my hand. I put the collar around her neck and the small padlock through the locking clasp. I made sure the lock closed with a decisive *snick!* so I could fully enjoy Hope's reaction when she realized she had a leather dog collar *locked* around her neck. I wasn't at all disappointed.

101

I moved back in front of her and held the leash in my hand, but didn't attach it yet. I held her chair politely, gesturing for her to stand. She did so, her eyes hoot-owl wide, watching me with a combination of panic, trust, and ... yes, that one ingredient of perfection Lau would certainly notice...arousal. I felt an answering tightness in my jeans, and ignored it.

"Strip. Everything but panties."

I wouldn't have thought it possible for her eyes to get bigger, but she proved me wrong. Her face was expressionless, her control tight. Only her eyes and the thin line of whiteness around her lips betrayed her emotions. Her hands trembled when she removed the off-white blouse, pulling it over her head. Her arms immediately pebbled into gooseflesh, and it wasn't that coolness of the social area. I know she expected me to look away for the sake of her modesty; I didn't. I skimmed my eyes over her body, trying to minimize my appreciation for her soft curves. She was property I was inspecting for defects, nothing more.

Her hands shook so badly when she tried to un-knot the laces on the right side of her skirt, it became an issue. I considered letting her struggle through it and then decided to push her harder instead. I'd noticed the cords earlier—several times, actually, since the view was no hardship—and they were only corset laces. Easily obtained, easily fixed—but I was willing to bet Hope didn't know that.

I pulled my six-inch Tac-Force switch out of the front pocket of my jeans and clicked it open. Before she could protest, I grabbed the knot at the cord of the skirt and sliced it open. Hope gasped, startled because I had just 'ruined' her expensive leather skirt. It took a second, but she pressed her lips together and didn't protest, which was the one factor that kept her still in the game. Cutting the cord—literally and figuratively—had been a power play, a test of her reactions. If she had protested, it would have been game over.

"Continue," I ordered firmly.

Hope's face flushed in that deliciously erotic combination of mortification and compliance. I reminded myself she was a civilian who was consulting with me on a case, not a submissive. I was a federal agent. I really had no business enjoying the show as much as I was. It was completely unprofessional, and, on a personal basis, utterly dishonorable. I enjoyed the hell out of it, anyway. Hope had very long, tan legs, enough belly fat so her pelvic bones didn't jut out like a skeleton covered with skin, and beautiful, rounded hips hinting at a very nice ass. She had stopped glancing at me to see if I was still maintaining eye contact during my visual appraisal of her body. That was a shame. It would have increased her embarrassment, and it would have been nice to see that lovely combination of anger and pride, fear and defiance, in her expressive brown eyes.

She'd untied enough of the cord on the other side of her skirt that she was able to step out of it. She struggled momentarily for balance, and I waited it out, resisting the impulse to reach out a steadying hand. She was wearing low heels, for Christ's sake—if she couldn't manage in those, she'd never be able to manage the spikes she'd be wearing next Saturday.

Hope finally stooped down to pick up the skirt. She folded it over the back of her chair, adding it to the blouse. She stood then in her lacy black thong and plain white cotton bra. She had not intended to get naked, that much was obvious!

I kept my amusement controlled while Hope stood

there trembling. I said nothing, watching her face as she struggled with herself. She remembered the bra, but she was self-conscious about exposing her breasts, apparently even more than the situation warranted. There were nude or semi-nude people all over the social area. I wondered why Hope was so hesitant. She was young enough, and well-proportioned. There shouldn't be a significant loss of muscle tone, none of the 'sag' many of the other women—submissive and Dominant alike—complained about. *Perhaps she had scars, or an unattractive birthmark?*

If it felt like a long moment to me, I'm sure it was an eternity for her. Awkward silence is sometimes a Dominant's best friend. She finally reached behind her back and unhooked her bra, letting it slip off her shoulders and adding it to the rest of her clothing. There was absolutely nothing wrong with her breasts, nothing she needed to be ashamed of. She was beautiful…uncomfortably so, for me. I enjoyed her discomfiture, her reddened face and neck, her quickened breathing. However, these manifestations, pleasing as they were to my sadistic side, were a dead giveaway that Hope didn't routinely get naked in public. We would have to work on her presentation.

I matter-of-factly attached the leash to the O-ring on the front of her collar, giving it a slight tug just to get her attention. She was a good actress, but she was going to have to be better. Her face was neutral enough for the consensual BDSM munch-group crowd, but Lau was a shark. He would smell her fear like blood in the water. I would have to work her hard this week to get her ready. If she couldn't pass, I wouldn't take her in, period. I'd already decided that. I didn't know what would happen to Callahan if we had to wait another month, but that simply couldn't be my priority.

I led Hope into the dungeon, holding the curtain aside for her to step in before me. I watched closely for her reaction; to her credit, all I noticed was a slight stiffening of her back and shoulders.

The Nashville dungeon was typical of many smaller community BDSM play spaces. It was a fairly large, open space, dimly lit, with small spotlights placed appropriately near each play station. There were two St. Andrew's crosses set up, two waxing or massage tables, four spanking benches, a heavy A-frame ladder with attachment points on both sides, a bootblack stand, and about half a dozen heavy steel eyebolts set into the bare wall as attachment points.

The far side of the room, near the fire exit, was designed for blood and medical play; the lighting was better, and the floor was covered with a heavy-duty tarp, duct-taped onto the carpet. A medical curtain closed off part of the area, and several people stood clustered outside the play space, watching the scene within. There were safety and cleanup stations just inside the dungeon entrance, and another set near the medical play area. A volunteer dungeon monitor, wearing a neon-orange safety vest with the words 'Obey Me' stenciled on the back, walked conscientiously from station to station. Like the play equipment, the vest belonged to the munch group; it was passed off from one DM to another as they took their shifts.

I scanned the area for an overall impression and then tried to see it through Hope's eyes. It's been a few years, but I still remember the first time I ever stepped into a dungeon, so I tried to view everything from that perspective. The first scene to attract Hope's attention would be the flogging being done by Boyd on one of his

105

girls. I couldn't remember which one she was; Boydton tended to cycle through 'kajirae' pretty quickly.

The girl was medium height, somewhat pear-shaped, with a heavier bottom than top. She was nude and bound to the St. Andrew's cross with thick leather wrist restraints attached to eye bolts with the same quick-release 'panic snaps' I use. Boyd was a jackass, but he wasn't an irresponsible player; his toys were laid out on a clean towel, his girl was well-secured, and, judging from the whimpers and moans of pleasure she made, she was having a good time. Her back and ass were fire-engine red, with a bit of bruising and several nice welts.

She yelped as a misstrike wrapped around her right hip, and I glanced at Boydton to see if it had been deliberate. He was concentrating on her completely, and he was in full control—it had been intentional. The girl would be proudly showing that bruise off to the other submissives in an hour or so, gushing to one bottom or another about how 'intense' it had been.

I gave a gentle tug on the leash and moved Hope over to the next station, an elevated spanking bench. Dale was positioned with his ass in the air and his balls, sensibly, tucked close to the bench. Tracy and Stephen were alternating strikes with matching wooden paddles, and Blade was rubbing and squeezing Dale's nipples between each stroke. Dale's ass was already deeply bruised, and his reactions were muted, his moans of pleasure sluggish; he was totally cooked, and they'd be taking him down in a few minutes.

"How can that possibly be fun?" Hope whispered to me.

I just looked at her. You don't explain the sunrise to someone who's been blind since birth. You *can't*.

We moved into the medical play area. A female Top

106

I didn't know had made two neat rows of capped needles going from her female bottom's shoulder blades to her waist. Hope stiffened slightly at the sight. While we watched, the Top took off her gloves, and then started lacing the needles with a bright red string, crisscrossing them in a pretty corset-like pattern. I didn't like that she'd removed the latex, but it wasn't my scene to interfere with. I didn't know if the couple was blood-bonded; presumably, they'd cleared the edgeplay with a DM beforehand. I moved over to the next scene in the medical play area, and this was where Hope lost her shit.

It was an intricate cutting scene. The bottom was young; if I'd been the one on the door, I would have carded her, which I was sure Nymphette had done. If there had been a less responsible submissive on the door, I would have considered asking the DM for verification the girl was eighteen.

She was another bottom I didn't know. Jim, the Top, rarely attended munches, demos, educational events, or fundraisers, but he somehow managed to make it to almost every play party. The bottom was a very small, very slim blonde girl who looked to be about fourteen. She was straddling a recline bench, her back facing us. Jim was sitting on a metal folding chair behind her, and Velvet was beside him, holding a stainless steel medical tray with an assortment of scalpels, sharps, and a large supply of gauze. Another girl I didn't know was standing next to the bottom, wiping blood whenever Jim indicated. Several people were gathered around watching the scene; there was an occasional murmur from one of the onlookers, but they were, for the most part, appropriately silent.

The girl had a large, partially keloidal sunflower-shaped scar on the middle of her back, the petals stretching past her shoulder blades and up her neck. Jim was using a scalpel to meticulously fillet along the outline of the flower, drawing the edge repeatedly along parts of the design that had not scarred prominently enough. The girl was whimpering and crying softly, and her knuckles were white from her tight grip on the support bar of the recline bench.

Hope glared at me accusingly, her face horrified. I met her gaze levelly, raising a challenging eyebrow at her. She turned her face away from the scene, unwilling to look anymore.

I struck instinctively, my hand shooting out before I'd even considered the action. Until this moment, I hadn't actually touched Hope in any way that could be construed as assault, but when she looked away, I had no choice. I grabbed a handful of her hair at the base of her neck and jerked her head back sharply, forcing her to face what she had turned from. She stifled a gasp, and a few of the onlookers glanced over at us. I didn't care. If Hope wanted to play at Dominance and submission, she would damned well learn to submit!

I kept my hand tight in her hair, forcing her to watch the scene for several more seconds. When the bottom cried out, and Jim changed to a sharper blade, I released Hope's hair. I continued to glare at her, though, staring her down. She looked away first, but she was shaking visibly, and she had tears of anger in her eyes. Her expression was a combination of rage and empathy; I wasn't on the receiving end of the empathy.

I watched the scene for another minute or so to make my point, and then I looked at Hope and cut my eyes over to the social area. She started walking that way immediately, and I hid a smile of satisfaction. Without even realizing it, Hope was beginning to react like a submissive. I hadn't had to direct her verbally or tug on the leash; she'd read my intention. Granted, 'out' was where she wanted to go anyway, but that wasn't relevant. If we could get past her reaction to tonight, we stood a decent chance of getting her ready for the real party next Saturday.

Hope
Background

I didn't kill him right there in front of everybody. *That had to count for something, right?*

I couldn't get out of that 'play room' fast enough. I honestly thought I was going to puke before we made it to the social area. I've never been all that great with blood anyway, and there was no way in *hell* Eric was going to convince me that young girl had been having fun, or was on an 'endorphin high' or some other such shit!

I briefly considered dumping Eric, getting a cab, and going after Callie myself, but I discarded the thought. It simply wasn't practical. As much as I suddenly hated Eric, and everything to do with BDSM, I needed him. He knew something about Callie's predicament I didn't, and he already had a way into some 'real deal' play party which might lead me to Callie. I didn't know if I could handle anything more 'real' than this, but I simply had to.

What I had finally realized, though, is that Eric needed me, too. He was a logical and focused man—maybe even cold. He was a federal agent, for Christ's sake! He wasn't tutoring me in BDSM because of my cute ass, or the goodness of his heart.

When I finally stepped outside the curtain, I felt like I could breathe again. I hadn't thought much past that point. I hesitated, glancing back at Eric. His face was expressionless … which I suppose was an improvement over the disapproving glare he'd worn a few moments ago. The anger in his eyes had scared me, and I was still trying to decipher my own feelings. I wasn't scared *of* Eric; I knew he wouldn't hurt me, even though he could.

I had been scared of…disappointing him! *What the hell?!*

I walked back to the table where my clothes were and then turned to face Eric, ready to have at it. Almost imperceptibly, he shook his head…a warning. I bit my tongue and waited for him to speak first.

When he did speak, it wasn't to talk about what we'd just seen. His voice was quiet but firm. "I'm going to remove the play collar now," he said.

I stared at him, puzzled. I wasn't sure why he announced it—normally, Eric just did whatever the hell he wanted to do. I got my answer a second later.

"Kneel."

I know my mouth gaped. I understood why he'd given me the warning, now. If he'd just ordered me to kneel out of the blue, I probably would have punched him. Instead, I glanced over to the door where Nymphette was chatting with a man in…*surprise!*…black leather, pretending she wasn't watching Eric and me. My

111

face was flaming, but I tried to handle it as gracefully as I could. I knelt and looked up at Eric.

I watched the expression on his face change. The coldness melted, replaced by something gentler, something almost warm and even a little…vulnerable. I was still furious with him, and I was still going to kill him the second we were alone, but…it affected me.

I could admit it. He was an attractive and very compelling man. The knuckle-dragging caveman routine worked for some women. Obviously, it had worked for Callie. I wasn't impressed by it…but every once in a while, there seemed to be something more, something deeper, that I was missing. Whatever it was, it pulled at my core, tapping into something so far back in my lizard brain I didn't even recognize it.

At Eric's nod, I bent my head so he could get to the lock behind my neck. He could have just taken the damned thing off the same way he'd put in on, but nooo. I studied his boots while he unlocked the collar. They were hot. Too bad he was a dick.

Eric held his hand out to me when he had the collar off. I didn't want to take it, but I wanted even less to fall on my ass in a graceless heap trying to get up by myself.

"Get dressed. We'll discuss this later."

I didn't reply, just turned away to get my clothes on while he went to return the leash and collar to Nymphette. I adjusted Callie's skirt as best I could with the cut lacing, knowing I'd have to get on the motorcycle anyway.

I couldn't get the sound of that girl's sobs out of my brain. *God, she was so young!* She looked all of fifteen, and I was going to have a hard time getting to sleep tonight. That could have been Callie ten years ago.

I smiled politely to Nymphette when we left and

nodded to the guy she'd been talking to. We retraced our path down the stairs and into the nightclub, where the music thrummed through me with a frantic techno beat. It was close to midnight, and the earlier crowd had just been warm-up. There were so many bodies on the dance floor now, people were unintentionally gyrating against the wrong partners. Eric took my hand, but I jerked it away and glared at him. We were not in front of the BDSM crowd now, and I didn't have to play the role. *Fuck him, and the Harley he rode in on!*

Eric raised that annoying eyebrow at me again and nodded toward the front entrance. I wended my way through the tables, and the people standing between the tables, and the people dancing between the people standing. I stepped outside as soon as I reached the door, not waiting while Eric exchanged goodbye pleasantries with the bartender.

I turned on Eric as soon as he stepped outside, but he cut me off sharply.

"Not here," he ordered.

I didn't know why 'here' wasn't as good a place as any, but I gave him the benefit of the doubt. I silently took the helmet when he offered it, slung my purse over my shoulder, and climbed awkwardly onto the motorcycle behind him. I put my arms around his waist, as I had done before. I was pissed, not stupid.

I still enjoyed the ride, and I still disliked the curves. I'd calmed down significantly, but I kept my head up—I would not lean against Eric's back. I would still work with him on the case—there was no choice really, for either of us—but it would be on *my* terms now, not his. He obviously needed me—or any 'submissive,' I reminded myself—as badly as I needed him. At least, I'd gained the moral high ground and upper hand…that was satisfying to me, on a much-too-personal level.

I was deliberating how best to present my position, when I realized Eric had missed our exit. I didn't say anything, figuring he would bypass the interstate and take Jefferson Avenue instead, but a few minutes later, he passed that turnoff as well.

"You missed your exit!" I told him, raising my voice over the sound of the motorcycle.

He either didn't hear me, or he ignored me.

I tapped him on the shoulder. "Eric, you missed the turn to the restaurant."

He turned his head so I could hear him. "We're not going to the restaurant."

I absorbed that. For just an instant, I felt a shock of genuine fear, the fear every woman would feel when a man physically removed her from perceived safety. I dismissed the thought. Eric was a law enforcement officer, and while some cops were rapists and killers, it wasn't the norm. Besides, I had very good instincts about people. As much as I disliked Eric, I still trusted him. Yes, even with my life.

"Where are we going then?" I shouted. He ignored me, so I tapped him on the shoulder again, a bit harder this time.

"Hope, shut up and enjoy the goddamned ride."

I shut up. For now.

***

We arrived at the Extended Stay hotel about fifteen minutes later. Eric pulled the bike into a parking spot near a private unit, set as far from the registration entrance as possible, and killed the engine. His motorcycle and the Crown Victoria he'd driven to Callie's home were the only two vehicles in this part of the parking lot. I gave him the helmet, which he wordlessly secured to the bike. I added this little detour of his to the mental barrage I was preparing. *Safe, sane, and consensual, my ass! I had* not *consented to go to his hotel room!*

I didn't say a word to him, as we walked up a sidewalk with pretty flower beds on either side of it, to a private door in what looked more like a tiny condo than a hotel room. Eric maintained the silence, using his key card to let us into room 914, which was actually a two-room suite.

It was definitely…lived in. There were take-out containers and fast food bags on the counters in the small kitchenette, and an empty pizza box on the desk next to a Dell laptop. Dirty dress shirts and slacks grew in a pile near the sofa. Empty bottles, mostly Dr. Pepper but a few Heinekens, decorated the end tables near the couch and chair. A weight bench and a pile of weights sat in the corner opposite the television in the living room section of the suite.

The living room/kitchenette was separated from the bedroom and bathroom by a set of folding doors. The archway above the open doors had allowed just enough room for Eric to hang a red, ten-speed bicycle from two hooks that had been embedded into the wall to support each tire. Eric, like Callie, clearly made the time and opportunity to exercise. I admired their dedication, and, fleetingly, wished I shared it. In the bedroom, there were at least a dozen paperback novels on the two night stands, with additional bottles of soda and Big Grab bags of corn chips and pretzels. At least, he wasn't a complete health nut! The king-sized bed was unmade, and several pairs of white boxer briefs littered the carpet around it.

For just a second, Eric looked slightly abashed.

115

"Sorry about the mess," he muttered.

"I'm not your mother," I replied stiffly.

He grinned, his eyes twinkling in amusement at some unexpressed thought. He really was cute when he wasn't looking so grim and serious...or angry. I had to remind myself I was still seriously pissed off at him.

"Want something to drink?" he asked, stepping over to the full-sized refrigerator and pulling out a Heineken.

"You have anything diet?"

Eric looked at me as though I had just grown antlers, so I shook my head.

"I'll pass, thanks."

He twisted the top off his beer and took a deep pull. I watched his throat work as he swallowed, and struggled to remember I was angry, not attracted. *Definitely not attracted!*

He set the beer down on the desk and removed his leather vest, carefully hanging it and placing it in the closet near the hotel room door. I stared at him...more specifically, the shoulder holster and handgun. I hadn't realized he'd been carrying his weapon the entire time. It made sense, of course; I just hadn't known...and I'd had my arms wrapped around him! Eric pulled the desk chair out and sat, nodding at the other chair for me. I remained standing, my arms crossed in front of me.

"Okay, let's have it," Eric said calmly. "What's bothering you, Hope?"

"You really don't go by the book, do you?" I asked, keeping my tone civil.

He stiffened slightly, and raised an eyebrow at me again, but he wasn't taken in by my civility. He spoke carefully, his demeanor tense, slightly defensive. "Why would you say that?"

"A couple of things," I replied mildly. "A few things

that happened tonight were *blatantly illegal,* and you didn't step up to the plate." My tone had hardened, and, conversely, he had relaxed. That wasn't how this was supposed to go.

"Such as?" he prompted.

"Well, at the munch, for starters," I said. "Sir Kernan clearly told law enforcement officers to identify themselves, and I heard nary a peep from your corner of the room."

I watched him for his reaction to that one, which was just my initial shot across the bow. I didn't even get an eyebrow, which was slightly annoying. He waited patiently. "But the main thing I have an issue with is you – we both – witnessed a felony tonight! A young girl was assaulted and *maimed,* and you didn't act on it!" I pulled the trump he'd just given me. "For god's sake, Eric, you were armed! That 'play scene' should have been stopped, and you had both cause and means to do so!"

He waited a long moment. "Are you done?" he asked.

I frowned. That was *definitely* not how this was supposed to go. "I'm done. I would like some answers, though."

Eric took another swallow of his beer, and then fixed me with a hard glare. "One," he said, his tone icy and uncompromising. "Do *not* call me Eric. Not ever. If you and I have any shot of working together, Hope, you don't even *think* of me as Eric, not at any time. I am Falcon or Sir, and those are the only names that come out of your mouth in connection with me."

I glared at him, stubbornly refusing to acknowledge his point. *Power freak, much?*

He continued. "Two. What in the name of hell makes you think I would acknowledge I'm a federal agent when I'm working an undercover assignment? That's stupid, at best, suicidal at worst. If the munch group were a drug cartel, instead of a bunch of middle-aged kids playing sex games with each other, identifying myself as a cop would guarantee me a bullet in the back of my head. And in case you're curious, no, there is *nothing* in the law that mandates I identify myself if someone asks me to, and any arrest I make is one hundred percent righteous unless I violate an actual law enforcement procedure."

"Then why—"

"Don't interrupt me, girl," he warned, in that steely, authoritative tone of voice that made me simultaneously want to scratch his eyes out and melt into a puddle in front of him. God, I was learning to hate that tone!

"Three," he softened, but only marginally. "I know what you saw with that girl tonight upset you…"

"It's not that—"

He slammed his hand down against the desk, hard enough to make both me and the bottle of Heineken jump. "I told you not to interrupt."

I bit back my reply. If I hadn't been completely certain my best friend's life was in danger, I would have told him to shove his arrogance up his ass and walked out of the hotel room. As it was, I fumed silently.

"What you aren't considering," Eric continued with steely calm, "is the submissive was in that chair completely by her choice. She wasn't restrained, and she could have stood up and left that scene any time she wanted. In fact, she didn't even need to do that much. If she had simply said one word—the group's safe word is 'red'—Jim would have stopped the cutting immediately. If, for some bizarre reason, he didn't stop, he would have *been* stopped, forcibly, by every person in that room,

118

Dominant or submissive.

"There was absolutely no call for me to interfere in that scene, Hope, and for Christ's sake, there was no reason for me to even *think* about pulling my weapon! This isn't *CSI,* girl. Drawing my weapon when I don't intend to shoot is absolutely inexcusable. As much as I think Jim is an ass, he wasn't being irresponsible, and I wasn't about to shoot him. What the hell were you even thinking?"

I suddenly didn't feel quite so righteous in my anger. I was remembering the girl's hands squeezing the hold bar so tightly her knuckles were white. Eric was right; there hadn't been any restraints on her wrists, as there had been on the girl Boydton had been whipping. My objection sounded weak, even to myself. "He was *hurting* her, Falcon. There is no way she was having a good time or getting off on that."

"You're right, he was hurting her," Eric acknowledged. "Scarification's not about getting off. Have you ever thought about getting a tattoo, Hope?"

My stomach sank with my last reasonable objection. I actually had—briefly—considered a tattoo. When the seventies had come back a few years ago, I'd thought about how cool it would be to have a rainbow-colored peace sign on my ankle. I had decided I didn't want one badly enough to tolerate being poked by needles hundreds of times. I wanted to say, 'But, that's different—a tattoo is body art!' but even I could see the hypocrisy in the argument. It was my own prejudiced thinking. The girl in the dungeon had considered the scarification of her back to be body art, too, and even though it had bothered the hell out of me to watch, I had to admit the tattoo analogy was legitimate.

Dammit! I hated the taste of crow!

119

"I…guess I overreacted," I admitted reluctantly.

"A bit." Eric smiled at me, but it was a gentle, understanding smile, not mocking or smug as I would have expected. He was being a lot nicer about this than I would have been.

"This is all just so…wrong," I tried to explain. I walked the few steps to the sofa and sat, pulling my feet up under me.

"It's different, Hope," Eric chided. "Different isn't necessarily wrong." He pushed back from the desk and brought his beer with him, coming over to the couch and sitting near me. It was a friendly gesture, and it tore down even more of my defenses. This had been so much easier when he was a dick!

"For what it's worth," he continued, "I've been exactly where you are, and I've felt the same things you're feeling now. I was undercover for months before I really started to understand why kinky people do the things they do."

"So, explain it to me, then," I said. "Why *do* kinky people do the things they do?"

He shook his head. "I don't know how to explain it. I don't have the words, and I don't know if anyone else would, either. The best analogy I can come up with is it's kind of like sexual orientation. People are meant to be gay, straight, or bi, and I don't know if that's how they're born, or if something happens along the way. The reason really doesn't even matter, because it doesn't change what is. I believe it's exactly the same for kink."

"I guess that's one way of making sense out of it. I have a gay cousin."

"We all do. Or a sibling, coworker, or friend."

I nodded, hesitating a long moment, and finally bit the bullet. "Thank you for not getting pissed at me."

Eric looked at me for an equally long moment, his expression unreadable, and I tried my best not to squirm. "You're welcome," he said simply. "So, are you ready to get to work?"

"I thought you'd never ask."

Eric killed his beer and went over to the closet near the door. He bent to open the hotel room safe—a large one, I noticed in surprise—and I admired the view while his back was turned. He was such an attractive man, when he wasn't scowling or glaring daggers at me! He had an athletic body, a strong, handsome face, and gorgeous eyes. More importantly, he was intelligent, dedicated, and passionate. I allowed myself the brief, senseless luxury of wondering what he would be like in bed, before shaking it off. This was about Callie, not me. Besides, Mr. Wuzzles was my man.

***

By 2:00 a.m., I had read or skimmed over every document in the three thick folders – the 'bare bones' of the Lau case—Eric had pulled from the safe. I was much more informed than I had been, but I was drained, mentally, physically, and spiritually. I was also scared to death. Satan himself couldn't have had a more impressive dossier than Jimmy Lau. There were dozens of photographs of Lau in the file, showing a 53-year-old, fit, attractive Asian man, with short black hair and a small scar over his left eyebrow, usually wearing expensive, tailored business suits.

Lau was born into the Chinese mafia, or the 'Triad Society.' Both his father and grandfather were '49ers'— hired muscle—for the criminal organization, and Jimmy was impressed at a young age with the wealth and power of the Shenzhen crime lords, and those whom they

121

favored.

Determined to climb higher up the organizational ladder than his familial predecessors, Jimmy made his first mafia-sanctioned kill in 1970 at the age of nine. *Nine!* He was used as a courier or 'runner' after that. The Triad often used young children—'gutter rats'—for transporting drugs or stolen goods, because the children were small, fast, and less likely to arouse suspicion—at least, until their faces became known to the Shenzhen police.

Lau proved to be loyal, clever, and resourceful, and those qualities set him apart from the other gutter rats. He was eager, ambitious, and ruthless, distinguishing himself from the rest of the 49ers in the Triad. He went through several years of 'observation' and 'loyalty assessment' while still a teenager. The terms were obvious euphemisms, but the documents in Eric's file didn't clarify them. As soon as he was old enough to undergo the initiation rites, Lau joined the organization, and his career path was set.

Lau did his work efficiently and well; he rose steadily in rank and responsibility. He made many friends within the organization, and those who were not his friends kept that information to themselves, or died very suddenly.

In the mid-1990s, Lau diversified his power base. In addition to drug-running, he moved into prostitution and human trafficking, shifting the majority of his business interests from China to the United States He concentrated on big-city markets while keeping his operational bases in small, rural, southern communities. He achieved his boyhood dream of surpassing his father and grandfather in the Triad Society; he obtained the prestigious rank of 'Red Pole Enforcer,' and was on the short list for promotion to 'Deputy Mountain Master.' That was a position of greater prestige within the organized crime syndicate than he had even dared dream.

He became a person of interest to the FBI three years ago, when the stepdaughter of a Virginia state cabinet member went missing. Twenty-four-year-old Melissa Ivy Bainbridge was identified with Lau in a grainy, poor resolution security image shot at a liquor store in Nashville, Tennessee, a week before her disappearance was reported to authorities.

Lau was actually detained and questioned by local authorities, but nothing came of it. He claimed he had gone into the liquor store to make a purchase, and had said hello to the pretty blonde woman; however, he had not known the girl, and hadn't seen her before, or since. There was no reason to doubt his story. At the time, Lau had no criminal record in the U.S., and the local authorities had no idea he was affiliated with the Triad Society. It was only a chance hit on the CIA's international facial recognition software which put him back on the FBI's radar several months later. Unfortunately, there wasn't enough evidence to warrant an investigation.

Several other attractive women between the ages of twenty and thirty went missing from the eastern U.S., but there was nothing to connect them to Lau, and the investigation stalled again. Then, almost a year later, a woman named Emily Murphy came forward, battered and bruised, reporting a Chinese business owner had held her against her will for almost a month. She heard herself referred to as 'merchandise' to be 'exported' to China. She had found an opportunity to escape her captivity when a maid mistakenly entered the locked bedroom where Murphy was being held.

Before Murphy even came into the Nashville FBI office, she made her arrangements to leave the state. When pressed, she gave the interviewing officer the name and number of her sister in Denver; however, when the next agent assigned to the case, Eric Grayson, tried to call Murphy for a follow-up interview, the name and number proved to be fabricated. Emily Murphy had quit her job, closed her bank accounts, terminated her lease, and, for all practical purposes, vanished from the face of the earth. There wasn't enough justification to put out an APB, so Grayson had let it go.

I touched the crucifix I was still wearing in a mildly superstitious gesture. I hoped she was living somewhere off the grid and wasn't one of those Jane Does I had learned about from Sgt. Brooks.

If nothing else, though, Emily Murphy gave the FBI their first vital tip; she told them she met Lau at his exclusive, members-only Nashville night club, the Sandmarian Garden. She was invited to a party at the club by a member of the Nashville BDSM scene. That was the information that pulled Special Agents Eric Grayson and Marjorie 'Majyck' McAdams onto the case. Grayson had prior experience infiltrating underground communities; he'd become a member of both an outlaw motorcycle club and a Leather/Levi patch club, both of which incorporated elements of sadomasochism into their activities. McAdams not only fit the criteria for 'bait,' but she had a sterling field record. She'd also been instrumental in breaking up a prostitution ring in Austin, so she had experience in undercover sex work. The investigation had been re-opened.

Eric ordered us a pizza—thank god for all-night delivery—while I continued reading the file. I saw telephone records, electric bills, and blueprints for the Sandmarian Garden, and for Jimmy Lau's opulent home, located a few miles from the club. The address was on Tyne Boulevard, not far from the Warren's Steakhouse where we'd eaten. I saw photographs of Lau's associates and business partners, as well as several of the women he was seen with publicly (none of whom disappeared or showed any signs of abuse). I saw numerous itineraries from Nashville International Airport, showing Lau traveled frequently between China, Scotland, and the U.S. I saw the medical reports from when he had a torn ligament in his right knee (from playing tennis), and when he'd had a urinary tract infection. I saw pages and pages of his most recent financial transactions, and Eric assured me there were additional mountains of both paper and digital evidence in the Knoxville FBI office.

Pizza arrived, and we ate silently, while I looked at photographs of the Sandmarian Garden. Some of the photos were professional publicity shots, but most were clearly taken by non-professional photographers, using average digital cameras. As Eric explained it to me, Lau had chanced upon an interesting business concept with the exclusive club; the front (literally and figuratively) of the club was a contemporary Asian restaurant and meditation center. It attracted every wealthy Buddhist, pagan, vegan, or New Age follower in Nashville. Lau made a completely legitimate profit from the restaurant alone, and that profit was increased by the sale of candles, incense, herbal teas, hemp clothing, and spiritual literature.

Lau invested a veritable fortune into soundproofing the back area of the Sandmarian Garden. Behind the meditation center were a dance club and two dungeon play spaces, one very large and elaborate, the other much smaller—about the size of a large bedroom—and clearly intended for private 'play.' Lau hosted monthly BDSM parties, by invitation only. The clientele who patronized Lau's dungeon were not the bourgeois who attended public munches. They were universally wealthy to ultra-wealthy, and most, though certainly not all, were Asian businessmen. They demanded absolute anonymity in their choice of sexual recreation, and Lau guaranteed that.

Again, though, everything up to this point was a legitimate business venture. Lau did not supply prostitutes on site, and he actually had a solid team of security officers acting as Dungeon Monitors to ensure nothing illegal happened on the property.

The playrooms had been raided by Nashville Vice, several times. Not surprisingly, the cops always entered the building through the restaurant's front entrance, and they spent a good deal of time searching the seating area, kitchen, and Playroom A. In all the raid reports, they never once approached the corridor where the security elevator was, nor did they notice the 'hidden' door to the more private Playroom B. Obviously, someone was on Lau's payroll to guarantee that level of inefficiency.

The Sandmarian Garden had even been raided jointly by ATF and the FBI once, in response to an 'anonymous phone tip' reporting teenage drinking in the club. Although it was nowhere in any official report, that raid had, in actuality, been a fishing expedition set up in cooperation with Eric's undercover team. Both Falcon and Majyck were inside the dungeon at the time of the raid. There had been no underage drinking, of course, and no arrests had been made. In fact, Lau handled the unexpected raid with such quiet efficiency, most of the bottoms, and even a few of the Tops, were unaware the authorities had even done a walk-through.

The floor above the main level contained several private 'guest rooms.' Eric had been invited upstairs only once by Lau, for a private meeting in which he was given an excellent bottle of scotch and condolences on the death of his submissive, Agent McAdams, whom Lau knew only as Majyck. Eric wasn't able to take photos, clearly, but he included a sketch of the upstairs layout, as far as he knew it, including a detailed description of the room he was invited into. It resembled an exquisitely-appointed hotel room, with only the subtle addition of attachment points to indicate it was something other than what it appeared. The most insidious detail Eric had identified was the placement of several not-quite-hidden cameras, and the presumption there were several more hidden cameras he'd been unable to locate. Only his trained eye had found the few he'd spotted. Lau, seemingly, liked to watch the guests he invited to enjoy the lavish accommodations of his hospitality...from every angle.

The floor below the playrooms and restaurant, which Eric presumed to hold at least Lau's security operations room, was the current area of interest to the FBI. From inside the club, the basement appeared to be accessible by elevator only. Blueprints obtained from the city showed several rooms and an egress point up to street level, but Eric wasn't able to confirm that. He had yet to find the opportunity to get down to the basement, without blowing his cover.

That's where I came in.

I finally finished reading and sat back on the sofa, pushing my paper plate away. Eric glanced at my second, half-finished slice of pizza, and I nodded to him, hiding my smile at how quickly he moved in. He'd already eaten four slices of the small pepperoni and green pepper pizza. We should have at least gotten a medium—what were we thinking?

"What goes on in Playroom B?" I asked, tapping the blueprint with my fingertip.

Eric frowned around the pizza in his mouth, chewing and swallowing before answering me. "Selection process, we presume. We've never gotten an operative inside, although my former partner and I had an invitation, not long before she was killed. What we assume is Lau watches a private play scene with a girl he's interested in dispatching to China. If she's responsive enough, stimulating and sexy enough, he adds her to his inventory, and she's shipped to China in a matter of weeks. If she's not … well, no one is quite sure what happens to the washouts, but it's probably not a happily-ever-after."

I winced at the word 'inventory.' It sounded so…pecuniary. "What's the plan going to be?" I asked, rubbing my eyes and trying unsuccessfully to swallow a yawn.

"For tonight, you take the bed, and I'll sleep out here," Eric replied, sidelining my question with an extremely tempting distraction. "In the morning, we'll go to Callahan's church service."

I'd almost forgotten. "It's a ten o'clock service, but I'm not sure of the address. I need to Google Map it.

"I'll take care of it," Eric said, taking the Dr. Pepper bottle from my hand. I hadn't realized my grip had loosened so much the empty plastic bottle was about to fall. "You. Bed," he ordered. It was 2:30 in the morning, and I hadn't slept much the night before. Bossy or not, he didn't have to tell me twice.

I felt a twinge of conscience when he closed the

folding bedroom doors behind me, leaving him without a bathroom or a bed. It wasn't enough of a twinge to stop me from stripping down to my panties, straightening the sheets and blankets a bit, and then crawling under them.

Mmm. They smelled good...just a faint scent of leather and a remnant of whatever woodsy, spicy cologne Eric used. I pulled one of the extra pillows to me and hugged it, realizing then Eric didn't have a pillow or even a blanket. That was so rude of me!

I was asleep before I could remedy the situation, my last thought something to the effect I'd never invited him to go with me to Callie's church.

***

~Somewhere else~

He loved her curly red hair. She smiled, floating dreamily in the happy fog. It was good that he loved her hair. It made him happy, and it was important he was happy. The fog was happy, she was happy, and he was happy, too.

She looked at the girl lying on the mattress next to hers. Libby? Libby smiled at her. Libby was in her own happy place. There was another girl, another mattress. Jasmine, with the mocha skin and coffee-colored eyes. Oooh...she wanted coffee! It had been days since she'd had coffee!

There was something about the other girl, Jasmine...something that bothered her, worried at the edges of her happy fog, like an annoying fly. It kept coming close to her mind, then buzzing off. Buzzzz...yeah, she was buzzing. She giggled, thinking she should tell Libby about the fly. The thought drifted

129

away, and she let it go. It was nice he loved her curly red hair.

She rolled over onto her stomach, feeling so dizzy when she moved. She was forgetting something really important. She frowned, trying to remember, and then that thought drifted away, too. It was okay. She didn't want to remember anything.

The sun was rising. The beams came in through the little window at sunrise. She loved the little window, and she loved the sunbeams.

The sun glinted next to her eyes, and a little rainbow appeared, just for a second. It was pretty! She moved her head, squinted her eyes, and the rainbow came back. She loved the rainbow.

She reached out for the rainbow, her fingers touching the edge of its prism. She gasped at the sudden sharp sting on her fingertip, and then she relaxed again, and smiled as the pretty redness welled up. The blood was soooo beautiful, so rich and red! How could she have never noticed it before? She drew her finger down on the tile next to her face, doodling with her blood-ink. The tile floor was smooth and cool, and the ink was so red.

The ink stopped before she was finished with her doodle…so she reached for the rainbow. It was a small sliver of glass, about the size of a dime. She made more ink.

She loved her doodle. It made her happy. She smiled when she was finished, and then put her finger in her mouth, sucking it thoughtfully. *What if he didn't like her doodle?*

She pulled the blanket up around her, rocking herself gently in an almost fetal position, then she pushed the blanket off to the floor beside her, bunched up on top of her doodle. *There. All better.*

She smiled and drifted back to her happy place in the fog, wondering about Jasmine's still form, the blue tinge around her lips. She frowned, but then the worry drifted away. He loved her curly red hair.

Eric
Preliminaries

I woke, as always, at 7:30 a.m. My neck was stiff, and my feet were cold from hanging over the arm of the couch. This wasn't what I'd had in mind the couple dozen times I'd allowed myself to imagine spending the night with Hope. I sat up on the couch, stretching. I needed to piss, and I was exhausted. Five hours' sleep was normally plenty for me, but they had been a crappy five hours. My *per diem* covered a decent room in Nashville and most of my rent in Knoxville, but both places were confirmed bachelor pads. It was a hella uncomfortable couch.

I stood, dropping the extra hotel blanket onto the floor, and pulled on a pair of briefs from the clean laundry I had dumped into a basket a few days ago. I considered getting dressed, but I was already across the room and opening the bedroom doors before I'd finished the thought. Morning wood had convinced my bladder I would simply have to mutter through an apology if I woke Hope up.

There was apparently little chance of that. I stopped and stared at her for a moment, watching with guilty pleasure as she slept, one breast bared, her nipple pebbled in the cool air. Her thick brown hair was loose, and it was all over the pillow. She slept on less than half of the damned bed, I noticed resentfully, stopping myself before I could follow that thought to its logical conclusion. Her mouth was slightly open, and she was breathing deeply and easily, puffing lightly on each exhalation.

I made myself stop looking and went into the bathroom, politely closing the door before emptying my bladder. I kept with the courtesy theme and lowered the lid after I flushed. I stepped out to the sink and watched her in the mirror while I turned on the water and stuck my hands under it for a few seconds. She didn't even twitch.

We were about forty-five minutes from Callahan's church in Chatham Hills. Assuming an additional forty-five minutes for Hope to shower, dress, and do whatever else she had to do to get ready, she could still sleep another hour.

I went back out into the living room, closing the doors softly behind me.

Clothes. That would be important, at least a skirt or pair of jeans. Hope's blouse from last night would suffice, but even if I could find corset laces to repair the skirt on a Sunday morning—which I couldn't—there was no way I could see her wearing that hot little number to a church service. Not even a Unitarian church service!

I pulled on shorts, a t-shirt, and running shoes. I double-checked to ensure I had my wallet and key card, and then headed at a jog to the hotel lobby. I'd check with Rich at the front desk to get my mail, then I would find Maria or Carletta to see what their stock of lost-and-found women's clothing entailed. If they had something appropriate, we could get moving more quickly. I would order breakfast, and by the time I got back to the room, we'd be able to start the day.

Maria was off; it was Sunday, so she was taking her grandmother to church. Carletta took me to the laundry facility and showed me the box of clothing they had collected over the past few weeks. My lady friend was welcome to anything she needed; nobody ever called about the clothes, she informed me. The guests only wanted to reclaim their jewelry or cell phones.

I found several items in an assortment of sizes that seemed appropriate, thanked Carletta, and promised we'd return what we didn't use. She waved me off with a grin, and a reminder: if I was going to need more towels, I had to put my dirty ones outside the door again. Or, if I wanted to put all my 'top secret work' away and take down the 'Do Not Disturb' sign, she and Annette would be sure to clean my room thoroughly. I told her I'd consider it. I stopped by the hotel restaurant, just opening for the day, and placed two orders to be sent over by room service.

It was almost eight when I re-entered my room. I figured I would find Hope fixing coffee, drinking a Dr. Pepper, or at least showering. Nope. She was still out cold. *Must be nice.*

I dropped the garments on the couch, did some stretches, and started on the bench. I was into my fourth set of reps before I heard sounds of life from the bedroom. I considered cutting my workout short but decided against it; she would be a while, I was sure. It was sexist, but it was also a truism of life: women were *always* 'a while' in the mornings.

It was probably the smell of bacon that finally enticed Hope from the shower. She emerged wearing the thick white hotel robe and a towel turbaned around her hair. I'd already started on my second mug of coffee and had eaten half my breakfast by the time she came out. I was all about gentlemanly behavior and courtesy, but a man had to eat and I didn't like cold eggs. She could deal with it.

She looked at the second entrée, still covered, on the room service cart, and I nodded. She smiled; it was a glorious, happy, sunshiny smile…and then she took the plate and dug in like a trooper. I liked that about her, too. She enjoyed eating. She wasn't emaciated, and she didn't starve herself, and she wasn't constantly bitching about how desperately she needed to lose five pounds. That, in itself, made her unique in my experience of women, Majyck excepted. Hope also had a personality, was smart and attractive, and had—figuratively speaking—balls of steel. She knew what Lau was. I'd watched the color drain from her face when she read the file the night before, but she was still determined to go after her friend. I gave her kudos for not tucking tail and running. She was notably loyal to her friends…at least, to Callahan.

They were all excellent qualities, traits I admired and found attractive. They were traits I planned to exploit ruthlessly.

We didn't speak until Hope had finished her breakfast and was into her second cup of coffee. I indicated the pile of clothes on the sofa.

"There's a selection from stuff people have left in the hotel," I told her. "Everything's been laundered, of course, and it will save us time if you can find something you can wear to church while I take a shower. Otherwise, we'll have to be late in order to give you time to go by Callahan's house to get something. I understand the dress code for a Unitarian church is about as relaxed as you can get, so anything you pick will be fine."

I didn't wait for her response, just drained my coffee and hit the shower. I could tell she didn't like the idea of wearing 'a stranger's' clothing, but assuring her everything was laundered had eased the wrinkle off her forehead. I hid my laugh, adjusting the water temperature and stepping in. She was cute.

Thoughts of how cute she was necessitated me cooling the water temperature a bit, so it was a quick shower. When I came out, Hope was wearing a pair of nicely snug black jeans along with her low-necked blouse and the gold crucifix from the night before. She had occupied the mirror and sink directly outside the bathroom with a small bag of the war paint women always pile on to cover their perfectly acceptable natural appearance. Not that I'm sexist…or would that make me anti-sexist? Whichever. I hated heavy makeup, and I needed my third cup of coffee.

I moved past Hope, holding the edge of the towel around my waist. Her eyes followed me in the mirror. I grinned, and she immediately turned back to her war paint, her cheeks coloring quite nicely on their own. That gave me food for thought while I pulled clean slacks, a short-sleeved shirt, and a casual sport coat out of the closet in the bedroom, and then stepped into the living room to dress. Hope had been peeking. *Awesome!*

I felt a warm sense of pleasure at the realization. Part of it was typical male pride, of course, but another part was something deeper than that, something that warmed even more than my cock. I frowned. That 'something,' whatever it was, needed to be put away and thought about later. I was working, and I had a civilian in tow. My cock, and anything else, could wait until the job was done.

We were pushing it for time, and I was beginning to get edgy when Hope finally emerged from the bedroom. *Goddamn, she was amazingly hot!* I had noticed before, of course, but this morning she was...incredible. She was curvy, in a glorious, healthy way, but it was that face, and those beautiful, expressive eyes.

I studied her, liking what I saw. Far from being troweled on, her war paint was light, only accenting her cheekbones and eyes slightly more than God had already done. She'd done something with her hair—it was twisted up into some kind of loose, soft bun. She looked clean, fresh, and breathtaking. My cock twitched in my pants—it didn't want to wait until the job was done.

Hope held out her arms slightly for my approval. "Good?" she asked, her voice a bit uncertain. A look of frustration immediately crossed her face, as if she hadn't meant to ask for my approval.

I gave it, anyway. "Beautiful," I replied, giving her what I hoped was a professional smile of approval rather than a horny leer. It worked. Her expression eased, and she bent to grab her purse.

"You don't happen to have one of those bandana scarves, do you?" she asked, as we headed to the door.

I laughed. "No, but we'll take the company car today. Your tax dollars will ensure you don't mess up your hair."

She made a face at my comment, but she seemed more pleased than disappointed to forgo the Hog for the Crown Vic. When I unlocked the car doors, she buckled

137

in without complaint. I got behind the wheel and pulled out, heading for Chatham Hills.

"So, what's on the agenda for today, Falcon?"

I liked that she was giving me the lead without a lot of crap. I liked even more that she wasn't calling me Eric. "Interviews at Callie's church, then talk to the staff at the Italian restaurant. I may or may not have to deal with calls from my IT people, who will be helping us kill Lau's security on Saturday—depends how far they've gotten. We also really need to get you up to speed on BDSM, and the dynamics of Dom/sub relationships, enough at least for you to be able to pass in front of Jimmy Lau and his employees. We need to have you acting and looking the part by Saturday."

"Lau's party at the Sandmarian."

I nodded, although it wasn't a question. "You'll need to be able to pass as the real deal. If you can't, we don't go in." I cut off her objection before she could speak. "This is serious, Hope. If Lau even suspects you're looking for a specific girl—much less that you're a reporter, or you're working with the FBI—he will kill you. He will do it slowly and painfully, with no safe words, to serve as an example to others. He will torture you to death, and he won't even blink." I took my eyes off the road long enough to assess her reaction.

She met my eyes steadily, then gave a slow nod. "I've thought about it…a lot. I promise, Falcon, I am taking this *very* seriously. There are only two people in the entire world I would risk this for—Callie, and my dad. Him, theoretically, because I doubt Lau would…you know."

I laughed. We talked easily for the rest of the drive, and not about the case. I don't know if it was deliberate for both of us, but it was the right move. Things were easy between us by the time we hit Chatham Hills. She told me stories about her high school days with Callahan, her adventures in Louisville, and her cat. I heard more about her cat—*what the hell kind of name is 'Mr. Wuzzles,' anyway?*—than I wanted, but it was a pleasure listening to her, so I put up with the subject matter. Her voice held such a tone of light amusement and genuine love, I actually felt jealous of the damned beast.

In exchange, I told her about my disastrous marriage and divorce, and about my three-year-old daughter, Annie, the one good thing to come out of that train wreck. Hope was an excellent reporter; she grilled me relentlessly, and we arrived at the First Unitarian Universalist Church of Chatham Hills before I realized it.

I walked around to her side of the vehicle while she made some kind of makeup adjustment, totally screwing up my rear-view mirror. I frowned at myself as I opened her car door. I was skirting some dangerous territory here, and I knew it. I enjoyed the feeling of opening the door for her, and giving her my hand. I enjoyed—even for a moment—the fantasy of being on a 'church date.' The smile Hope flashed me when she exited the car seemed genuine, too, and it went straight to my gut. We were definitely going to have to establish our professional boundaries before I started training her. I pushed the thought away, because it wasn't as much fun as listening to her chatter while we walked into the church.

Despite my heavy foot on the accelerator, we stepped in mid-opening hymn. An usher handed each of us a program and indicated two seats near the middle of the meeting hall. The seats were cushioned and comfortable—they could have been movie theater seats. We stood dutifully through the song like the rest of the congregants. Hope immediately found her place on the screen displaying the lyrics and started singing along.

I scanned faces in the crowd, typing them by age and appearance of economic background to cull the groups or individuals I thought Callie would be likely to associate with. There were about seventy people at the service, and the majority seemed to be couples in their well-established yuppiehood. I assumed there was a Sunday school or children's service somewhere else in the building, because there were few kids in the room, and most of those were toddlers or younger.

A group of five twenty-somethings to the left of the choir—*band?*—seemed to be our best bet. I caught Hope's eye, and glanced over toward the group. She looked, nodded, and continued singing. Throughout the service, I kept part of my attention on the group I'd targeted, committing faces and mannerisms to memory, while following the somewhat-familiar protocols of worship on automatic pilot. Sit, stand, pray, sing, dig out a dollar, stand, sit. I half-listened to the sermon, while I studied the rest of the people in the church. After eight years in the Bureau, I'd honed my attention to detail, and I was certain I could describe any one of the target group well enough for a sketch artist. By the end of the service, I was also certain I could sight-recognize any of the congregants or clergy by mug shot.

It was only when people started filing out to 'Blessed Assurance,' I noticed Hope smiling crookedly at me.

"What?" I asked.

"Don't stop," she chided. "You have a lovely baritone."

I'm pretty sure my ears went pink. "It's one they haven't politically corrected, yet," I muttered, a bit guardedly. "I still know the words." I took Hope's hand quickly, and led her over to the group of young people we'd pegged earlier.

When Hope showed photographs, four of the five did recognize Callahan; regrettably, not well enough to be of any help. She had been attending the Unitarian church irregularly for about a year, but had not yet joined the youth committee. They were each appropriately alarmed she was missing, sympathetic, willing to pray for her, and willing to call me with anything they might think of, no matter how irrelevant it seemed. None of them recognized the photograph of Daniel Fletcher. I also showed photos of Jimmy Lau and two of his preferred thugs; none of them recognized any of those men, either. I handed out five business cards and led Hope back to the Crown Vic.

We were halfway back to Nashville before she spoke. I had respected her silence, knowing she was disappointed our interviews had been a waste of time. Hope was still learning the lesson new detectives learned quickly – ninety percent of their 'leads' led nowhere.

"I guess it just couldn't have been that easy, huh?" she asked finally.

"Never is."

"She's been missing almost forty hours now."

I didn't respond to that. There was no response that wouldn't sound bleak, patronizing or insincere.

"What now?" she asked.

I hated the dejection in her tone, so I countered with a matter-of-fact confidence I didn't actually feel. "We keep going until we find her," I answered. "We get your car from Warren's, and we swing by Callahan's house to pick up whatever necessities you need for the next several days. Then, we go shopping and get you a fetish outfit for Saturday, including a pair of four-inch spiked heels. You learn how to walk in them, and we get you into character as my submissive. At four, when Stefano's opens for their dinner hours, we conduct more interviews and pass out more business cards."

Hope
Training

"Drive straight to Callahan's house," Eric ordered, as he held my car door open for me in Warren's parking lot. "I'll be right on your tail, so don't lose me at the lights or in the merge lanes. Keep your cell phone in your hand at all times, and do not get out of your car until I'm in the driveway behind you."

"Paranoid, much?" I asked teasingly.

The joke fell flat. "No. Cautious." He frowned, his forehead wrinkling as he carefully phrased his words to me. "Hope, as of last night, you're under law enforcement protection. The details you know about Jimmy Lau make you dangerous to him, and if he ever realizes it, you will be a target. You do understand that, right? I'm your goddamned shadow until Lau is in custody, and even then, you'll need witness protection until he's packed away. You don't go to the bathroom

143

without me knowing about it, and if it takes you more than thirty seconds to pee, I'm coming in after you."

He was absolutely serious. For the first time, I realized Eric was genuinely afraid of Jimmy Lau, and it shook me. I had read graphic details about murder, drug-smuggling, gun-running, prostitution, and human enslavement, but more than anything I'd seen or read last night, *that* scared me. It scared me like nothing I've ever experienced in my life…it was a snake, coiled deep down in my stomach, the kind of fear that made me wish I was a kid again, and Daddy was tucking me into bed at night. It was the kind of fear that made me want to drive home as fast as I could, lock my doors and windows, and hold Mr. Wuzzles in one hand while I held a gun aimed at the door in the other.

My next thought was incredibly, terribly cowardly of me…but it was also true. I knew if Jimmy Lau wanted to get to me, he would have to go through Eric first. Eric was a formidable opponent. While the feminist in me *despised* myself for taking comfort in that, I still felt safer. The simple fact of the matter was Eric was an alpha…no, a *Dominant*…male, and he saw it as his responsibility to protect me. He would do anything, including put his body in front of mine, to keep me safe.

That pissed me off—at Lau, not at Eric. Whenever we found Callie, Jimmy Lau was going to go away for a very long time, and I was going to do everything in my power to make that happen. Eric had pointed out to me not even China would press for extradition, as long as we could prove Lau was involved in human trafficking. We were coming after Callie, and that meant we were coming after Lau, after his livelihood and his freedom. He didn't know it yet, but he had just as much reason to be scared of me as I was of him.

Jimmy Lau had proven, though, he simply killed what he feared.

This wasn't going to be over, even when it was over. Eric had said as much when he mentioned witness protection. Even if—*when,* I reminded myself sharply— we got Callie home safely, she and I would both have to live to testify against Lau…and that wasn't necessarily going to be easy.

Eric studied me, his eyes appearing more blue than gray in this light, as though he had read my every thought. "You'll be fine, girl," he assured me. Something about the confidence… arrogance…of Eric calling me 'girl' hit me low in my stomach and squeezed, surprisingly, in a not-unpleasant way. I didn't know *what* to do with that feeling.

"Yes, Sir," I replied, teasing, but not mocking him. He smiled at me, tapped the roof of my car twice, and walked around to his sedan in the next space. I waited until he was belted in and his engine started, and then I backed out.

What a difference a night could make! Fifteen hours ago, I'd been hanging on for dear life, but secretly loving every minute of the thrill ride, as I sat behind Eric on his Harley. Now, I was checking my rear-view mirror even more frequently than the road in front of me to be sure he was following close. I was genuinely scared, and I didn't like it one bit.

***

Callie's house was exactly as I had left it, save for the stripe of yellow crime scene tape across the front door. I really hadn't expected otherwise, but I found myself adopting some of Eric's sense of hypervigilance. After ducking under the tape, he locked the deadbolt behind us and followed me upstairs to Callie's bedroom. He wandered out into the hallway, while I dug through my suitcase before deciding it would simply be easier to just take it with me. I'd lugged it all over the state of Tennessee and hadn't actually unpacked it yet; why should I start now?

I was looking through Callie's closet, eyeing those corsets again, when Eric called to me. I went into the hall, and then to the bathroom, where he stood in front of the sink.

"One of these yours?" he asked me, nodding toward the two toothbrushes in the cup.

"Yeah, thanks," I said, a bit puzzled. I took my toothbrush and turned to leave, then stopped. Eric pulled a latex glove from his jacket pocket and snapped it onto his right hand. He carefully picked up Callie's toothbrush and placed it into a Ziploc bag, then put the bagged toothbrush back into the pocket of his sport coat.

My curiosity won out. "The hell?"

"Saliva," he replied levelly, "for DNA."

I turned away from him sharply and went back into Callie's bedroom without speaking. I was shaking with anger and fear, but I tried to tamp it down and concentrate on the corsets I was examining. Eric was simply doing his job.

"Hope?"

He had followed me, and perched on the edge of Callie's bed. God *damn* him!

She had a black leather corset, which was probably the most appropriate, but she also had one made from hunter green tapestry fabric, and, my favorite, a cobalt blue satin with what appeared to be delicate silver

146

bamboo fronds embroidered into the fabric. I touched the cloth softly, my eyes blurring.

Eric came up behind me, and turned me into him, holding me tightly. I stood stiffly against him for a long moment, before tentatively leaning into his strength. He held me for a long time before I could trust myself to speak.

"She's alive," I asserted.

Eric tightened his hold on me without replying, and that's when I cried.

I can't say I felt better afterward, but some of the tension I had been carrying in my shoulders was gone, as though he had siphoned it from me. DNA or not, I would not lose my hope. Callie was alive and still savable, waiting for us to rescue her. Eric was the cop; he could be the realist, too.

"Do you think she's alive?" I hated myself the moment the words came out.

To my surprise, Eric met my eyes levelly and nodded at me. "For now, yes," he answered, "and I promise you, Hope, I'm going to do everything I can to keep her that way."

I nodded, and faced the corsets on the shelf in Callie's closet. "I don't know how to put these on, but they might work as fetish clothes for me. Which one do you think?"

He immediately selected the blue corset. I smiled, surprised at his choice, and pleased he hadn't chosen the leather. He stepped out of the closet and gestured to me. I hesitated; we weren't at a party now. Eric waited, watching me, and I pulled my blouse off over my head and laid it down on the bed near my suitcase. I still had trouble with the bra. I felt my face burning slightly as I reached behind myself and unhooked it, and then shrugged out of it and put it next to the blouse. I couldn't look at him, so I stared at the carpet and his black harness boots.

The corset was laced very loosely. Eric put it on over my head and fitted the front busk piece to me, like a breast plate. "Hold it right here," he instructed, placing my hands. He moved around behind me and adjusted the back panels and laces slightly, and then…*oh, my god!*

His hands moved in a quick, alternating rhythm from the middle of my back upward and then downward. Whatever air I had in my lungs vanished, squeezed out by steel boning and heavy fabric. I made a sound of protest, and Eric stopped.

"Too tight?" he asked, concern in his voice.

"Yes!" I gasped.

He pulled the cords sharply, making them significantly tighter! "Good," he replied cheerfully. If I could have moved, I would have punched him. He tied off the laces and tucked them up under the bottom of the corset, flattening them out evenly. I gasped for breath…or tried to. I was getting very little oxygen, but at least I hadn't passed out. Yet.

Eric came in front of me to inspect. He was smirking, amused by my discomfort—*that asshole!*—but then, as he looked at me, something in his eyes changed. I felt it as much as I saw it, a sudden heat coming to my face as his pupils widened, then darkened. Eric looked away from me quickly, taking several seconds to close the closet door, then nodded me over to the mirror to look at myself. I stepped over, surprised I was able to walk, and looked.

Between the corset and the size-too-small jeans, I had the figure I'd always wanted. And—*oh, my god!*—I had breasts! My B-cup ('B for bee stings,' Callie had

148

always teased me) breasts had been pushed upward, as though ready to spill out of cobalt goblets. Callie's crucifix nestled perfectly between them.

"Wow," I said, more to myself than to Eric. The longer I wore the corset, the more I was able to breathe, and although it was by no means comfortable, I could almost see the allure. The results were…

"Exquisite," Eric said quietly. His voice was slightly husky, and his gaze openly appreciative, but he had gotten control of himself. He stood behind me, looking at my reflection in the mirror, and I looked at his. I admitted it to myself then; a moment ago, he had looked at me with absolute lust, his want naked and raw. He had quashed it, but I remembered…and savored…the moment.

"I should wear this Saturday?" I asked, fishing just a bit.

"Oh, hell, yeah. It's perfect."

I smiled, feeling myself flush with pleasure. Finding Callie was absolutely paramount. After that, though…I resolved, I was going to find out just how 'special' Special Agent Grayson was.

I grew accustomed to taking shallow breaths, so the feeling of relief that burst over me when Eric loosened the corset was intense. My lungs loved me again!

Eric averted his eyes when I slipped back into my bra. It was the first time he'd ever looked away to allow me modesty. *Interesting.*

I mulled that over while I dug into my suitcase for a change of clothes. I'd worn the blouse long enough, and the black jeans, while adequate, weren't mine. I found a yellow summer sundress that didn't need pressing and slipped it on, pulling the jeans off and pulling a pair of sandals from my suitcase.

149

"Bring the leather corset," Eric instructed. "It's more durable, and we'll use it this week."

I packed it away, then frowned at my black heels. "Will these work for the party?" I asked Eric. "I don't have any other dress shoes, and Callie's won't fit me."

Eric shook his head. "No, but we'll drop your car outside my room then stop at Stella's on the way to dinner," he said, picking up my suitcase and heading downstairs. I grabbed the jeans and blouse and followed after him, wondering who Stella was.

***

Stella's was a sex shop. My face was crimson from the moment we stepped inside until the moment we left, about forty minutes later. We had several yards of corset lacing and aglets with which to repair the leather skirt Eric had cut, and a pair of amazingly sexy, black stiletto-heeled boots for me!

Seriously, I'm not a prude. I've been to a sex shop before, several times, even. Granted, I always went with Callie. It was different with Eric. He kept picking up some of those...things, and gazing at me speculatively. Occasionally, he would test a paddle or flogger on his forearm, and then put it back on the shelf. I didn't touch anything, not even the swatches of rabbit fur, which looked temptingly soft.

The knee-high boots Eric chose for me, though, were incredible! They were so hot, even though they looked ridiculous under my sundress. The leather was soft and supple, fitting my calves like a goatskin glove. The heels were four inches high, which was going to be a challenge because of the stiletto points, and Eric made me swear I would practice walking in them. They cost over three hundred dollars, which took my breath away!

150

Eric charged it to his business credit card without even blinking. It was nice to see my tax dollars at work. It was even nicer the boots were considered a 'disposable personal item' by the FBI, which meant I got to keep them! I happily tucked them back into their box and carried them out to deposit into Eric's trunk. It was an absolute shopping WIN! I couldn't stop myself from beaming at him.

We arrived at Stefano's Italian Ristorante at around 4:15. It was early for dinner but late for lunch, and I was starving. Surprisingly, we weren't the only diners there, despite the early hour. There were already several other tables and a few booths taken, and the restaurant continued filling steadily. I waited at the table while Eric spoke to the manager. I saw him present his I.D. and one of the photographs of Callie, and I saw the manager nod cooperatively several times. He and Eric shook hands, and Eric returned to the table.

"He remembers Callahan," Eric told me, pulling his chair in. "He'll send the waiter who had their section over in a few minutes."

I nodded, unable to suppress the flare of hope Eric's words engendered. I knew better than to get my expectations up, but I did it anyway. I studied the menu, concentrating on trying to decide what I wanted, while not salivating like one of Pavlov's dogs. The aromas wafting from the kitchen made that a challenge. Embarrassingly, the moment our waitress stepped up to our table and set down glasses of water, my stomach growled loudly enough for Eric's lips to turn up. *Good god…was I going to spend my entire life blushing around that man?*

I looked back at the menu, still undecided, and listened while Eric ordered his meal. "We'll have the bruschetta and *mussels di Napoli* for an appetizer," Eric said. "Then I'll have the classic lasagna, and the lady will have the chicken alfredo."

"Very good, sir," the waitress replied. "And to drink?"

"A Heineken and a Diet Coke with lemon."

I think it was the surprise more than anything else keeping my mouth shut while the waitress took the menu from my hand and left. For a moment, I simply didn't know what to say. I suppressed my immediate impulse, which was to recommend Eric try some anatomically impossible sexual gratification, and thought about it. Callie hadn't told me about this rule, and I hadn't read it on the internet, either.

"So…for clarification, Falcon…the Dom orders the sub's food?"

"Not all Dominants. But I do."

"What if I didn't like alfredo?" I raised a challenging eyebrow, curious how Eric would respond to that.

Eric simply looked at me, amused. "You would go hungry."

I thought about letting it go. Seriously, I had to choose my battles with Eric; how big a deal was it, anyway? But, my curiosity was too strong.

"So, why did you select chicken alfredo, Sir?"

"Because that's what I wanted to watch you eat."

I opened my mouth, and shut it again. I had absolutely no retort to that.

The waitress arrived a few minutes later with our drinks, and cheerily told us Ricky would be by to talk to us in a few minutes. Eric thanked her, while I glared at the wedge of lemon floating in my soda. I hated lemon. I didn't even like it in tea! I squeezed it defiantly into the soda before dropping it back into my glass.

"I need to know a few things before we go into Lau's," Eric said. His voice was serious and professional, so I let the little stuff go, and paid attention to him. "I need to know your limits, Hope. Not just what you're willing to do for Callie, but what you are able to do, period."

I nodded. The same thought had been on my mind off and on throughout the day.

"I don't like the idea of being hit," I admitted, biting my lower lip, "but I know I can endure it, if I have to."

Eric surprised me with a chuckle. "I'm not worried about that," he told me, an inexplicable expression in his eyes. "The physical parts of BDSM are the easiest. I'm more concerned about in here." He tapped his temple. "Power exchange is almost one hundred percent emotional, Hope. You have to willingly surrender all of your personal power and responsibility to me, and before you can do that, you have to trust me. Implicitly."

I nodded. "I'll try."

"Do," he ordered, "or do not. There is no try."

I looked up incredulously, and found Eric smirking at me. "You just quoted Yoda?!"

"Master Yoda," he corrected indignantly, "was absolutely one of the greatest Jedi knights ever. We could both learn a lot from that little guy!"

I burst out laughing, and, after a mock glare, Eric chuckled, too.

"Okay, *Master* Falcon," I teased, lightening the barb with a smile. "How do I learn to trust you implicitly in six days?"

Eric nodded approvingly. "Asking the question is a good place to start. The first step is the motivation to learn."

"Callie gives me the motivation," I said quietly.

153

Eric nodded, his grayish eyes somber with empathy. "Right," he agreed, "but the desire has to come from within you, or you had better be an Academy caliber actress. That's the only way this can work. Right now, everything is safe, and you have the seconds—or milliseconds—you need to think and to evaluate whether you will obey me or resist. Once we go undercover, though, we're in Lau's territory, and everything you do *must* be immediate. Instinctive."

It was daunting. "I don't know how," I admitted to Eric. I hated the smallness in my own voice, hated admitting a weakness, but it was the simple truth. No matter how much I read about BDSM, I only *felt* it sporadically. Because of that, I hesitated, even without meaning to. I knew that was what Eric was referring to. That was what would betray me to Lau, and what could possibly get us both killed. "The other thing…"

Eric waited.

I took a breath and plunged on. "Even if I do 'pass muster,' and Lau thinks I'm a submissive, why will he target me? There are so many other submissive women in Nashville, most of them thinner and prettier—"

Eric held up his hand, cutting me off, and I stopped, flushing again. It had taken a lot for me to admit that.

"First," he said, his voice gentle but uncompromising, "don't ever denigrate yourself around me again, either your appearance or your intelligence. I promise you, you won't like me if I hear it in the future."

I shivered at the tone of his voice, and slowly dipped my head agreement. He wasn't playing.

"Second. I've been undercover on the Lau investigation for more than a year, acting as one of his brokers. I'm very familiar with his preferences. The man has good taste, and you're perfect bait for him, physically and mentally.

"Third. Lau won't actually need to 'target' you, girl. I'm selling you to him."

It was fortuitous the waiter, Ricky, came up to our table at that moment, because my mouth dropped open in shock. I had time to close it while Ricky introduced himself to Eric and me. Ricky was young. He had to have been twenty-one in order to serve alcohol, but he was still in that gawky, all-limbs phase of late adolescence most teenage boys endure. He had a cute face, marked by a mild case of acne, and a charming smile. He kept glancing over to his section where his customers and tips waited, so I tried to move things along quickly.

"This is my friend, Trish Callahan," I told him, showing him the best facial shot of Callie. "And this is Daniel Fletcher, the guy she was supposed to be meeting here Friday night."

Ricky glanced down at both pictures, then back over to his section. "Yeah, I remember the redhead," he said, tapping her photograph lightly. "She was really hot, you know?"

"What was she wearing?" Eric asked for confirmation.

"Um…I'm not sure. This dark green slip kind of a thing, with a shirt over it, but not buttoned. It was that soft, shiny material, touchable, like. She was sitting when I got to their table, so I didn't see her come in. Sorry."

He glanced back at his section, and Eric slapped the table, just loudly enough to make both Ricky and me jump. Eric's bottle of Heineken and my glass of soda were unaffected by the outburst.

"Ricky, I have your manager's permission for you to join us at this table," Eric said, in that quiet tone of voice I'd learned to identify as dangerous. "Please sit down and give us your complete attention, so I can ensure this interview is conducted properly. Your other option is to miss the night of work entirely and come into the police station to answer the same questions I'm going to ask you here." Eric's courtesy did nothing to disguise the command in his voice. I wasn't surprised when Ricky pulled up a chair and sat at our table, no longer glancing back toward his section.

"Yeah, sorry," the kid mumbled. "It's just going to be a busy crowd—you know, Sunday night."

"I understand," Eric said flatly, "but a young woman's life is in danger, and that takes precedence over your tips."

Ricky had the good grace to look embarrassed, and gave Eric his full attention. "Yes, sir, I understand. What happened to her?"

"She's been kidnapped," I said, before Eric could reply. He shot me a warning look, but I'd already started. "We think by this guy."

I pointed to the photograph of Fletcher again, drawing Ricky's eyes to it.

I could tell even before he started shaking his head. "No, that wasn't who she was with," he told us. "I've never seen that guy before."

I felt a sense of panic. "Are you sure?" I pushed. "He might have been older, and I think his hair was different."

Ricky shook his head again, studying the picture closely. "I'm sorry, but yeah, I'm sure. Totally. She wasn't with this guy."

I slumped, nodding a thank you and feeling disappointment bloom inside my chest. Another dead end. *Shit!*

Eric pulled a small notebook and pen from his jacket

pocket. "What was the man wearing?"

Ricky thought about it. "Um…a blue polo shirt. I didn't see the rest of his clothes, I'm sorry."

"Can you describe him? What color eyes, what color hair?"

"Oh, he had black hair and dark eyes. He was Asian."

Gerard
Clean-up

Johanssen's voice held an edge of panic I'd never heard before. "Gerard, we gotta problem down here!"

I depressed the button on the radio and spoke, while shoving another fry into my mouth. "Go ahead."

"No can do," Johanssen's tinny voice replied, and I felt the first flicker of genuine concern. "You gotta get down here, man."

With a sigh, I tossed the remains of my dinner into the trash and stood up, glancing around the small satellite office on the third floor of Lau's club and checking the monitor one last time. I flicked the switches to pull up cameras four and five, looking closely for anything out of place. On the screen, Johanssen stood in the basement room with the latest collection of girls, running his hand through his hair. Everything looked fine. The little redhead was sleeping peacefully, her blanket kicked off to the side of the pallet. The black girl was restless, her legs twitching in her sleep as if she were dreaming of running. She was getting ready to awaken soon—the doc would need to adjust her dosage. The brunette was also sleeping. Johanssen was standing near the little Hispanic girl. Her head was tilted oddly, white foam and vomit around her mouth. Her eyes stared vacantly, looking at nothing.

Oh, fuck!

I slammed the door closed behind me, locking it as quickly as I could, and double-timing it, took the hidden stairs three at a time. No wonder Johanssen was freaked! Jesus Christ, the girl was dead!

There was nothing I could do when I got down there. I took pictures with my cellphone before we moved the body. The little red-head looked up at me, her brow furrowed in concern when Johanssen stripped the linens off Jasmine's mattress.

"Everything's okay, hon," I told her. "Relax."

The smile that lit her face was absolute sunshine and innocence. It made me sick to my stomach. I knew what was waiting for her at the end of the line, and I also knew I couldn't save her from that fate.

Hope
Play Date

Forty minutes later, when Eric and I arrived at his hotel room, I was still mulling over Ricky's description of the man. I carried my Styrofoam takeout container and a bag of groceries with – thank god! – a twelve pack of Diet Coke amongst the goodies. Eric carried my suitcase and the box with my beautiful knee-high boots. We hadn't said much since leaving the grocery store, and my stomach was in knots. I put the food and soda into the fridge while Eric set my items in the bedroom.

"You're going to have to get used to the boots," Eric said, matter-of-factly, "so you need to wear them tonight when we play."

"Play?" I asked, only belatedly tossing in the "Sir?" at the end. He arched a brow, but didn't remark on it.

"Play," he repeated firmly. "As in, now."

I watched as Eric unselfconsciously removed the

sport coat and shirt he'd been wearing. He stepped around me to the closet and pulled out his leather vest, putting it on over his bare skin. He laughed at the expression on my face.

"What, you think Doms wear leather because it looks so tough?" he asked, a hint of teasing in his voice. "Hell, no, Chloe. We wear it because the toys we play with fucking *hurt!*"

I had been 'Hope' all day, and now I was 'Chloe.' *Interesting.*

He nodded to the bedroom. "There's a soft-sided rifle case in the bedroom closet, and inside it is the toy rack, and the toys I use. The rack is basically a tripod with a cross-bar attachment. Set that up, hang the toys on the hooks, then put on your boots. Only the boots."

"Yes, Sir," I replied, moving to obey.

I glanced over my shoulder, a bit enviously, as he toed his own boots off with obvious pleasure. He then walked over to the expensive ten-speed bicycle that was mounted on the archway between the two rooms. He easily brought the bicycle down, wheeling it over beside the weight machine and out of the way. I heard chains— *chains!*—clanking, but I stiffened my back and refused to turn to look.

The toy rack was simple, but clever. Once the tripod was raised, a simple screw clamp held the cross bar in place. The cross bar had about twenty small cup hooks screwed into it, leaving a space for each toy to hang. I looked at the toys, suppressing a shudder. I'd seen *Fifty Shades of Grey* with Callie, of course, so I wasn't overwhelmed...but I was impressed. The quality of the implements of torture was exquisite. The whip was braided beautifully, and each item felt heavier and more durable in my hand than they looked. I hung everything

161

up carefully. Eric hadn't said anything about an assigned order, so I hung them in a way that seemed aesthetically pleasing to me, longer toys to shorter. There were floggers, of course, a whip, paddles, canes and many other devices I didn't recognize. There were softer items, including a swatch of the bunny fur I'd seen at Stella's, which pleased me. Maybe I could survive this after all.

Eric was sitting on the sofa, waiting patiently by the time I approached him, nude except for the boots. Uncertain, I stood looking down at him. That didn't feel right, so I knelt, trying to appear as diffident and submissive as possible. I heard a choked sound, and then Eric chuckled. My face flushed immediately, but I didn't look up at him. I didn't dare. I would have glared daggers directly from my eyes into his brain.

"Safe words," he said, once his amusement was under control. "They're largely universal, and for tonight, I expect you to use them. Do you understand, Chloe? I will push you until you say 'red.'"

"Yes, Sir," I replied demurely.

"Red means stop. You are done. The scene is over for that night. Yellow means you still have more play in you, but something is wrong. The Dom is hitting the same place too often, or putting too much power into a strike, or your nose itches…whatever."

I blinked.

"I can stop if my nose itches?" I asked incredulously.

Eric nodded. "Of course. As much as Tops enjoy playing—and, I assure you, Tops do enjoy playing—the bottom's pleasure generally comes first. How can I expect you to enjoy what *I'm* doing to you, if the only thing on your mind is the blister on your toe, or how bad your nose itches? I want you to be comfortable while I beat your ass."

162

I glanced up at him quickly. Nope, he wasn't joking. Not even a little bit. I nodded my head, feeling the relief ease into my muscles. "Thank you, Sir," I said, not having to feign the gratitude.

Eric stood then, and held out his hand to help me rise. It surprised me a bit—it was such a gentlemanly thing to do when he was preparing to brutalize me!

He took me over to the toy rack. "It's going to be important for you to have bruises, so I will be marking you tonight. This is it, Hope. From the moment we begin playing, my career, and probably my life, are in your hands. If you step foot into Jimmy Lau's club, your life is in mine."

"Yes, Sir," I murmured, shivering slightly at the serious tone of his voice. I understood this was the moment he was crossing the line.

He knew I knew, because he nodded before continuing. "You choose one implement for me to use on you. I will choose three. Other than that, I'll use my hands or soft toys only."

Relief washed over me like a tidal wave, and I gave him a tremulous smile. "Which one is the singletail?" I asked.

To my surprise, Eric's face reddened slightly, his ears turning pink. He actually blushed!

"Who told you about the singletail – Celia, or Lori?"

I smiled sweetly, enjoying his discomfiture. "Celia."

Eric removed the whip from the toy rack, handing it to me handle first. I examined it, admiring the workmanship, then carefully handed it back to him. "A rule of etiquette," Eric instructed, watching me with approval. "Do not ever, *ever* touch a Dominant's toys without their permission. That, of course, includes their human property."

163

I narrowed my eyes at the term, but nodded. I'd learned the 'no touch' rule off the internet already.

The cuff he placed over my right wrist was like Nirvana for carpal tunnel sufferers. The leather was soft, sensual, and there was a padded grip bar to wrap my fingers around. Eric tightened the cuff appropriately, and instead of feeling like my wrist was being restrained, it felt like it was being supported. He put the other cuff on and studied me for a long moment.

"We're in a hotel room," he said, taking some strange looking clasps and affixing them to the rings at my wrists, elevating my arms slightly above my head. He attached the other side of each clasp to the chains hanging from the ceiling halfway to the floor. The heavy-duty hooks Eric had used to 'mount the bicycle' were deeply embedded into the studs in the wall. It wasn't a weight-bearing wall, granted, but it would be more than I could do to free myself. I tested them forcefully, and suddenly realized this wasn't a game anymore. Just like that, I was absolutely in Eric's power. He could easily, effortlessly kill me, and I was unable to protect myself in any way. A cold stab of terror was immediately followed by a hot stab of…*seriously? Fucking* arousal*?!*

Eric saw the expressions on my face, and he guided my right hand to the clasp, showing me how to work it. "These are called panic snaps, or quick release snaps," he explained. A twist of the wrist, and suddenly I was free. I found myself almost dizzy with relief. "The real purpose of bondage is to support you. In the middle of a scene, you may feel like your legs are made of wet spaghetti noodles. The cuffs will keep you from falling on your ass, maybe hurting yourself. If you panic, or otherwise decide you don't want to be restrained, this is how you release yourself."

164

"Thank you, Sir," I murmured, genuinely meaning it. I had learned so much in just the past ten minutes.

Eric smiled and adjusted the cuffs to a more comfortable position, clicking the snap into a link of chain at the height he wanted. The elevation lifted my breasts slightly, and I saw him looking appreciatively. I felt the blush crawl up my neck, and tried my best to ignore it.

"Hotel room. Do I need to gag you?"

"What?" I asked stupidly, a moment of confusion throwing me off my game.

"What, *Sir*," Eric reminded me patiently. "I said we are in a hotel room. Do I need to gag you?"

I considered a moment, before shaking my head. Yes, it was a hotel room, but it was also a Residence Inn, an extended-stay hotel, with private access, thicker walls, and better insulation. Also, I suspected Eric had asked for the most isolated room possible, because I still hadn't seen any other vehicles in the lot near his suite. "I think I'll be okay."

"Good girl," he smiled.

A sudden rush of warmth heated my belly. *What the fuck?!*

I didn't have time to consider my feelings, although my body's responses were definitely being filed away for later review. Eric put a soft, leather (of course!) blindfold over my eyes. It was padded around the eye sockets and, like the cuffs, amazingly comfortable. I'd never realized sadists would be so…considerate.

Eric stepped away from me, and I strained to hear where he was going. A moment later, soft music flooded the room. It wasn't an artist I'd heard before; the instrumentals were soft, but the beat was compelling. I flinched when Eric returned, and turned my body

165

slightly. Without my eyes, the rest of my senses immediately heightened, and I became hypervigilant.

"What are your safe words?" Eric asked me, his voice soft in my ear. He ran fingertips lightly down my neck, trailing his fingers down my back to my ass.

"Umm…" I was unable to help myself. His hand felt warm, and it had been a long time since I had been touched intimately. "Yellow and red, Sir."

"Good girl."

I frowned as heat pooled in my belly again. *Why the hell did I react so strongly to those two words—words intended for a damned dog, not a lover!* I tried to grasp a thought; something about the word 'lover' was off, but I was concentrating on the feel of Eric's hand stroking my body. Then it was gone, only to be immediately replaced by the amazingly soft, sensual warmth of a swatch of rabbit fur rubbing up and down my neck and back. My skin prickled, gooseflesh forming. Okay, so while I wasn't a fan of pain and chains, I think I could definitely incorporate blindfolds and bunny fur into my love life…if I ever got one.

"You're quite beautiful, Chloe," Eric murmured. The rabbit fur was gone, replaced by something scratchy. It wasn't an unpleasant sensation, but the contrast was marked because of my heightened sensitivity. I struggled to figure out which implement he was using and realized it was the small dish scrubbing pad I'd left in the bottom of the rifle bag! I smiled to myself; I never would have considered that a toy, and I'd wondered why it was in the bag.

Eric smacked my ass, and I jumped, gasping. I waited a moment, my body tense, and he smacked the other side. I exhaled slowly, waiting for the pain. There was a bit of sting, but it was completely innocuous. I was puzzled for a moment, but then realized Eric was cupping his hand slightly, taking most of the sting out of the smacks and leaving a dull, thuddy sensation in its stead. He was cheating! He knew a way to get me through Lau's party without actually hurting me.

I almost laughed out loud, but I didn't want to push my luck. I was, after all, restrained. It was never a good idea to piss a guy off when he had you tied up.

I relaxed completely then, my trust in Eric established. Whatever he did might sting a bit, but he wasn't actually going to hurt me.

Eric moved around to the front of my body, and I could sense him standing very close, only an inch or two from me. I could feel the heat of his skin, and I could smell the slight, woodsy scent of the cologne he'd applied that morning.

"Spread your legs," he ordered.

It took a moment for me to comply, and I knew, without him saying a word, that moment would have cost me my life in front of Jimmy Lau. It could have cost Eric his, as well, if Lau suspected Eric of bringing in a plant rather than a 'true submissive.'

"Yes, Sir," I said softly, trying to make up for the lapse.

I spread my legs, tensing in the expectation of exploring fingers. I was surprised—and a bit disappointed—when Eric stepped into my body, not even touching the too-sensitive areas down south. He was fully clothed and inaccessible to me. *Not that I wanted him,* I reprimanded myself sternly. I felt his arms go around my waist, and then, with careful precision, he was spanking me with both cupped hands, alternating a strike on each butt cheek. I soon fell into the rhythm. There was a little bit of pain, an occasional strike that was a bit

167

too hard, but for the most part, it was a delicious sensation of thudding impact. Each smack jarred slightly, and I felt my core pull in response to the vibration.

My ass warmed, and Eric began to flatten his hands. I squirmed a bit. It didn't hurt…not really, but there was a bit of sting, definitely less comfortable than the thud of his cupped hands. I knew my butt was getting red, because I could feel the heat, but it still hadn't become too unpleasant. I smiled, breathing deeply. This was completely do-able, at least with Eric.

He increased the strength of the smacks, and I gasped in surprise. I was definitely sensing pain now, but the rhythm was even more compelling. I didn't want him to stop. I wanted to move in time with the beat of the music, the beat of the smacks. After several minutes, he did stop, though, and he grabbed me in a warm, full-bodied embrace. I felt myself going limp as he held me, and then I felt his lips on mine, soft, warm, inviting. I let my lips part, and he immediately took possession of my mouth, his tongue dancing with mine. I sighed as I felt his fingernails scratching lightly along my back.

Eric stepped away from me, and I almost whimpered in disappointment. I strained to hear him move around behind me. A moment later, I felt the buttery soft falls of a flogger drape over my shoulder, then over my other shoulder, as he pulled them slowly away. "This is deerskin," he said, his voice quiet and seductive.

He struck me.

Once again, I tensed, waiting for pain that didn't come. The falls were soft and warm. I could feel the impact, but it didn't hurt like I was expecting it to. Eric struck me again, and again, and soon, he had a wonderful rhythm going in complete harmony with the music. I

168

found my body swaying, almost dancing in time, and I let the wrist restraints bear more of my weight. I relaxed into it, occasionally gasping, as a strike landed a bit sharply or in a surprising manner. I could feel my back heating, could feel an occasional sense of sting, but overall, I enjoyed the sensations that flooded my body with each impact. This was *so* much more relaxing than a deep tissue massage at La Femme!

At some point, the music intensified, and Eric switched to a heavier flogger. He draped it over each shoulder, as he had done with the deerskin, but he didn't tell me what it was, and I didn't ask. He established the same wonderful rhythm again but the impact was more intense and I grunted with each strike, grateful for the support of the chains and the comfort of the grip bars as I maintained my balance in those damned stiletto heels! Eric stopped for a moment, moving around in front of me again, and he put something—*nipple clamps!*—onto my nipples, adjusting the clamps slightly behind the nipple rather than on the tip. I hadn't realized how pearled they had become—apparently, the air in the room was cooler than I'd thought.

That didn't explain the heat between my legs, but I refused to give that thought too much attention.

Eric moved around behind me again, and I heard him at the toy rack. I braced for another flogger, but instead I felt something...or I *almost* felt something...different.

It was a light, stinging sensation, but it was there and gone before I could process it. It came again, and I felt my hair rustle slightly. Curiosity pulled at me as the sensation found its own rhythm, and I found myself squirming, both to avoid and to seek out the sharp little stings.

169

"What is that, Sir?" I asked, my voice sounding distant to my own ears. A moment later, there was a loud *crack!* right next to my ear, as Eric snapped the whip. I gasped in fear, instinctively pulling away, but the rhythmic stinging sensation returned. I strained my ears, trying to filter out the music, and I heard a gentle, rhythmic 'swishing' sound as Eric flicked the singletail from side-to-side across my back, shoulders, and ass.

"You remember your safe words?" he asked, and I nodded.

The whip cracked again, making me jump. "Yes, Sir!" I gasped out, and then the now-familiar stinging sensations returned. I found myself leaning in and out, swaying on the chains that held me as Eric encircled my entire body with the whip. Dear god, who would have imagined this could feel so good!? It *hurt*. The stinging sensation felt like a dozen small paper cuts all over my body…but I was completely, utterly relaxed, a happiness floating through me as every muscle in my body loosened, enjoying freedom for the first time in my life. I moaned, but it wasn't in pain. I *so* owed Callie an apology! Kink still wasn't my thing, but I definitely understood its allure now.

"You're done," he murmured in my ear. I hummed back at him, acknowledging rather than truly comprehending.

I felt the swatch of rabbit fur on my back again and whimpered in pleasure, and then in surprised disappointment as Eric released the clamps that held my wrists to the chains. He carried me over to the bed and lay me upon it, then gently removed the clamps from my nipples. I hissed as blood flowed into them, causing the first sensations of intense pain I'd felt that night. Oooh, I did *not* like nipple clamps!

170

For some bizarre reason, that thought hit me as incredibly funny, and I giggled. I felt Eric's weight, as he lay down beside me and pulled a heavy blanket up over both of us. He was a furnace next to me, and I realized with a start that I was *cold*. Teeth-chattering, frozen-toes-and-fingers cold! I clung to Eric, and he wrapped himself around me like an additional blanket while I shivered. I giggled again, lost in a euphoria of sensation threatening to overwhelm me. God, I wanted...I wanted to come. I badly wanted an orgasm, to have Eric's fingers and mouth on me, to feel him deep inside me. I could feel an impressive erection through his slacks, so I knew he wanted me, too, but the words simply...stuck in my throat. No way could I ask him to fuck me. *Nuh-uh, wasn't happening.*

After several minutes of snuggling, the blanket and body heat warmed me sufficiently so my teeth stopped chattering, at least. Eric helped me sit, and I felt him press a glass into my hand, guiding it to my mouth. I took a sip of the Diet Coke, and then I drank greedily. Eric pulled the glass away before I was finished. "Slowly," he warned, permitting me to drink again after a moment. Okay, so this time I didn't guzzle. I had seen *My Fair Lady;* I could do 'well-mannered.'

"That was...wow." I said eloquently, and then I giggled again as Eric took the glass from me and set it on the nightstand. "Yeah, that was wow."

I could hear the chuckle in his dry voice. "I'm glad you enjoyed yourself, Chloe...Hope."

I nodded my head and reached for the blindfold, stopping myself before removing it. "May I take it off, Sir?" I asked. The word still stuck in my brain, but it sounded more natural coming out of my mouth.

"You may," he replied, his voice evidencing he was

171

pleased with me.

I took the blindfold off, blinking dazedly. Eric had turned most of the hotel room lights down, but I still felt like I was in centerfield at Yankee stadium. I looked at Eric, taking in his sweat-soaked hair and body. He looked like he'd been through the wringer.

I glanced over at the digital clock sitting on the night stand, and looked back at Eric in shock. "Three hours?!" I exclaimed.

Eric
Aftercare

I chuckled at Hope's expression of incredulity as I unclicked the panic snap and removed her first cuff. *Greedy masochists were all alike!*

"Yes, three hours," I replied, gesturing for her to give me her other wrist. She complied, still looking dazed, so I decided to rub it in. "I won't need to bother with my work out tomorrow morning. I'm good."

I almost laughed as I saw her finally take in my sweaty face and chest. I had worked my ass off to session her, and she'd taken everything I'd given. I didn't push her too hard, of course, but I had seriously expected her to safe word well over an hour ago. She was, as the subs liked to say, 'cooked.' The good thing was she would have some excellent bruises. They would blossom over the next several days, and would begin fading by Saturday.

"You—wow. Three hours," Hope repeated.

I went over to the cupboard in the kitchenette where I kept the non-perishables and came back with a Hershey bar, which Hope almost caught when I tossed it to her. The candy bar was halfway gone before I blinked. I set the box of antiseptic Band-Aids I carried in the other hand onto the bed while I unzipped Hope's boots, pulling them carefully off her feet. She hissed. As I suspected, she had a nasty blister already forming on her right heel and a spot of redness where one would form on her left. Perhaps she would be a bit less ecstatic about owning the sexy boots now, but somehow, I doubted it. Just like any masochist was the same when it came to the enjoyment of properly-administered pain, any woman was the same when it came to free shoes.

"I'm going to need to take care of your feet," I told her, as I watched her lick the chocolate from her fingertips. My cock throbbed in response to the visual, but luckily, she didn't notice. "Do you want to shower tonight or in the morning?"

"Mmm. Morning," she mumbled, already half asleep.

I wondered if her answer would have been different if I'd told her I wouldn't let her shower alone, not as stoned as she was on the endorphins. It didn't matter. By the time I was finished with her feet, she was sleeping soundly, the empty candy wrapper on the bed beside her and a smudge of chocolate at the corner of her lips.

I looked out at the couch, and then back to the bed where Hope lay, taking up significantly less than half the space. *Fuck it. I was a growing boy. I needed my sleep, too.*

***

I was awake at 7:30 as usual, but this morning, I was well rested and relaxed. I was also on the very edge of my side

174

of the bed, and completely wrapped up in Hope. I had slept in boxer briefs out of deference to her, but they didn't help. Her slim leg was curled up over both of mine, her knee mere inches from my morning erection, and her arm was wrapped around my chest, her head snuggled close. And, of course, I had to piss like crazy. *Son of a motherless goat!*

I kept my tone normal and spoke quietly, "Hope, you need to move over. I have to get up."

Nothing.

A bit more firmly this time. "Hope, you need to move, hon."

That got an "Mmpf," and a slight shake of the head that brought the aroma of her lightly-scented hair closer to my nose. Okay, morning wood wins every time. I extricated myself from her leg and arm, and wiggled my way out of the bed before I completely embarrassed myself all over her.

When I got out of the shower twenty minutes later, Hope was, surprisingly, awake. She smiled happily at me. "I feel amazing," she said. Her voice was normal, but there was still a bit of that dreamy quality to it, letting me know she was still adrift on endorphins. I adjusted my towel and came over to the bed, sitting beside her.

"I'm glad I was able to make it enjoyable for you," I said with a warm smile that still, I hoped, conveyed professional distance. "Something you need to know about, though, is sub-drop."

Hope nodded. "I read about it online," she told me, eyeing the place where my towel draped open slightly. I bit back a smile, and did not adjust a thing. If she got an eyeful, it served her right for looking.

"Okay, good deal," I told her. "So, breakfast is going to be heavy on proteins, and you'll be drinking a lot of water today."

"Yes, Sir," she nodded.

I stood, and Hope got her curiosity at least partially satisfied. "I'll order breakfast while you shower. I need to meet with my team today to work out some of the logistics of our intervention with Lau's internet this week. What have you got going on?"

Hope rose, too, surprisingly unselfconscious about her nudity, especially considering how reserved she had initially been about showing her breasts. "I think I'll call Dale to see if he can meet this morning, Sir," she said, "and this afternoon, I'll keep that appointment with Callie's shrink, Dr. Rouchard."

"We'll keep that appointment together," I corrected her.

Hope nodded, seeming pleased, which surprised me again. She went into the bathroom and closed the door behind her. Apparently, the immodesty went only so far. I could live with that.

***

We took the bike to Dale's apartment. I'd known the boy for roughly two years, but I'd never really talked to him much. He was extremely respectful of my status as a Dominant, but our interests didn't complement each other. While I was flexible in my choice of play partners, Dale was painfully straight, and submitted only to women. I wasn't sure if he were slightly homophobic, or if he simply preferred the Domme/boy dynamic.

"What do you mean, 'flexible'?" Hope asked when we stopped at a traffic light. "Are you bisexual?"

I considered the question. "Maybe. In a way, I suppose so, as much as BDSM is—in itself—a sexual activity," I replied. "I enjoy beating men, because God designed their bodies to take a hard pounding. I enjoy fucking women for the same reason."

Dale met us at the door, straightening when he saw me. Apparently, Hope had neglected to mention a Dom would be bringing her to his place.

"Sir Falcon, Chloe," Dale said politely. "Welcome to my home. Please come in."

I guided Hope in, waiting in silence until I watched her step into the living room and glance around the neat, almost Spartan area. I remained on the doorstep. "I have some paperwork to catch up on, Dale, but thank you, anyway," I said, pretending not to notice the expression of relief crossing his face. I lowered my voice, fixing him with an expression that made most female submissives quail. "I'll be back for Chloe in about two hours. She's…interesting to me. Please take care of her."

If possible, Dale straightened even more. He clearly recognized I was placing Chloe in his care, and he was both intimidated and honored by the charge. "Yes, Sir, I understand."

I winked and nodded. "Good man," I said, watching the flush of pleasure cross his face. Straight or not, he still wasn't immune to a male Dominant's praise. I'd added a twist of respect by calling him a man instead of a boy. It never hurt to befriend a submissive. Male or female, a sub understood 'loyalty' like no one else. I had no doubt at all Dale would protect Chloe, with his life, if necessary. I also knew it wouldn't be necessary at this point—Chloe was still an unknown to Lau—so I was comfortable enough with the arrangement.

***

It was a twenty-minute drive to the Holiday Inn outside of Nashville. My eyes studied my surroundings as I

177

parked the bike and removed my helmet, but I was still only able to identify one of the Feds stationed outside the hotel room. Damn! Either they were getting better, or I was losing my edge.

I used a key card to get into Room 112, a ground-floor, corner unit. As I expected, the moment I stepped inside the room, two federal agents drew their weapons, re-holstering as soon as they saw it was me.

"Christ, Grayson," Jabroski grumbled, as he did every time we met. "One of these days, I'mma end up shooting you." He said that every time, too.

I chuckled, and nodded a greeting to both men. Peter Jabroski and Todd Vogel were my surveillance and tech team, and they were magicians. They had been a thorn in Jimmy Lau's side for weeks now, intentionally interfering with his internet and electrical services at random intervals. Lau was starting to expect the occasional brownout or loss of power, and that complacency, miniscule as it was, would be vital when it came time for Hope and me to do our thing at his party.

"Don't touch that!" Vogel snapped, as I started to move a pile of paperwork off the last available seat in the hotel room. The room was cluttered with the detritus of surveillance equipment, computer gear, takeout containers, etc. It was disorganized and chaotic, the complete opposite of the unmarked black van parked a few doors down. The van was immaculate, with every single item inside placed precisely to maximize efficiency.

"I'm not standing around holding my dick, Vogel," I growled. "Either move this shit yourself, or I'll be swiping it to the floor in 5…4…"

He moved the stack of paperwork, which also contained some digital components, a hard drive, and some device with wires attached to it. *Okay, so maybe I could have done some damage by sitting down.*

"Give me the latest, guys," I said, glancing at my watch.

They did.

It was a solid plan…as solid as we were going to get with Jimmy Lau and the Triad Society. I was to be given an earbud, smaller even than a hearing aid. Once it was inserted into my ear canal, it would require a hemostat to remove it. I would be able to activate it by pushing a button attached to a money clip I would carry in my pocket. Flipped in one direction, the button would block any nearby transmissions, coming or going. In the other, it would allow me to speak to the team, and call for backup. I was strictly limited on use; not only did the receiver have a one-hour battery life, but Lau's security would be able to detect the signal, and possibly even triangulate on it, when they had electricity and internet.

There would be backup units on standby and Jabby and Vogel were going to be in the van, about a mile from the Sandmarian Gardens, when I took Hope to the party this Saturday. Of course, all the IT team knew is I was taking a local submissive as 'arm candy' for cover. I'd done so several times before. As far as they were concerned, Saturday night would be one more night of gathering a morsel of evidence here, an iota there; the same damned thing we'd been doing for years.

But…I had a serious *frisson* going on, and it told me this was the weekend Jimmy Lau and his entire damned operation was coming *down*.

Between 10:30 and 11:00 Saturday night, there would be a brief flicker of lights followed by a 10-second brownout. That would be my signal to get to the elevator and down into the basement level. Exactly three minutes later, the power would go out. If we were lucky, the intelligence we'd been given from the spooks would be accurate. The bulletproof doors to Jimmy Lau's security center would lock automatically, on full shutdown until the power came up, and, more importantly, until the clear code was given by the Red Pole Enforcer himself. It was the biggest flaw in Lau's entire operation, and we planned to take full advantage of it.

"What's your feel on the intel?" I asked Jabby, helping myself to a piece of pizza even though I wasn't hungry. It would have been rude not to steal their food; it was expected.

"I hate this interagency bullshit, you know that, Grayson," Jabroski grumbled. "The CIA has a guy on the inside, and they say their guy has access to Lau's security. Hell, he could even be tight with Lau himself, they're not sayin'. They're being dicks about sharing most of their intelligence, but I don't think they'd deliberately screw with us, not knowing we were sending a man inside."

I nodded, but I wasn't happy about it. The Bureau wasn't just sending 'a man' inside. Hope would be there, too.

"So, how long will I have until power comes back up?" I asked Vogel. He turned back to the keyboard, his long fingers flying over the keys like a concert pianist on crack.

"About twenty-five minutes – call it twenty to be safe," Vogel replied. He was as melancholy as Jabby was jovial. I'd never gotten to know him well, but his information was as rock-solid as it came.

"I have twenty minutes—we'll call it nineteen—to get down to the basement with the infrared and photograph everything I can. Excluding the security

180

room itself, which will be on lockdown, I'm looking at about 4,000 square feet. It's doable."

"Important thing is you have less than two minutes after the power comes back on to get back up to the main floor and be otherwise engaged. Once they have juice, it'll take about that long for Lau's team to get their system back online, and then they'll be able to spot you on their security cameras in living color from ten different angles."

That would be the highest danger point in the entire evening. If Lau's security personnel were monitoring those cameras and I wasn't upstairs, I was a dead man.

I nodded to Jabroski. I knew. It was part of the job. I needed to be waiting at the elevator the instant power came back up, and take it from the basement to the first floor immediately. If not, I would be another statistic. It didn't need saying, so neither of us said it.

"You're set up to make the call," Vogel said, his monotone even more bland than normal. "Who are you planning to use as bait?"

I shrugged. "No idea," I lied. "I'll pick someone from the munch group, and call her on Saturday. Lau won't hit on her because she won't have what he's looking for, but I'll make sure whoever I pick will be hot enough."

"Make sure she has big tits," Vogel grunted, turning back to his keyboard. At his nod, I picked up my cell phone and hit the speed dial.

"Jimmy," I said a moment later, infusing my voice with warmth I didn't feel. To my own ears, I sounded like a used car salesman. "My man! How are you, *lǎoshī*? Oh, yeah, sure, I hear you on that. Listen, though, I might have some merchandise you'll be interested in… Yeah? No, I was thinking something more appropriate for your personal collection, but it's a beautiful piece, so

181

I'm not entirely sure I'm willing to sell... Oh, well, of course, I'm always willing to negotiate with you, Jimmy, you know that... Yeah, I'll be there Saturday. Wouldn't miss it. See you then."

I hung up with a satisfied nod to Jabroski and Vogel. The trap was baited.

***

Hope was smiling happily when I came to Dale's door, and I felt an instant, hard stab of jealousy. Dale invited me in, and I entered, jealousy dissipating as I saw what they'd been doing together. Cookies, chips, and soda bottles littered Dale's coffee table along with about ten bottles of nail polish and related paraphernalia. *Son of a motherless goat!*

"Dale gives *the* best mani-pedis, Sir!" Hope gushed happily, showing off her bright red toes and fingernails. They did look very professionally done, so I smiled politely and nodded. Dale shrugged at me, but I could see he was pleased with himself.

"He does man hands, too. Would you like him to do you, Sir Falcon?"

I'm not sure who was more alarmed at the prospect—me, or Dale.

Eric
Hope's Place

Hope and I sat in the waiting room at the Chatham Hills Behavioral Health Center for over an hour. We had arrived ten minutes before the scheduled appointment time and had given my name to the receptionist, but we were told Dr. Rouchard was seeing a patient. When Dr. Dana Rouchard, a trim, neat African-American woman in her late forties, finally called my name, she seemed puzzled. The expression deepened when she saw the two of us approach.

"How can I help you?" she asked, not stepping away from the entrance between the waiting room and the offices in the back.

I pulled my I.D. and showed it to her. "We're keeping an appointment for Patricia Callahan," I said, with a courteous, professional smile. "We need to ask you some questions, please."

"Please, come into my office," Dr. Rouchard said

183

stiffly, barely glancing at my creds.

We followed her down a short hallway into a plush, elegant office. Classical music played softly on hidden speakers, and some kind of candle was burning, filling the room with a cloying, flowery scent.

"What can I do to assist the FBI?" Dr. Rouchard asked, smiling warmly at me and a bit more coolly at Hope. Her demeanor spoke of a busy professional woman, who was humoring us only because of the badge in my suitcoat pocket. As if to reinforce my impression, she glanced not-so-subtly at a diamond watch on her left wrist.

"Doctor, we understand Patricia Callahan is a patient of yours?" I asked.

Dr. Rouchard frowned. "Since you're here, Mr. Grayson, I won't att—"

"Agent," I interrupted, with another pleasant smile. "Agent Grayson, Doctor." I didn't usually stand on formality, unless it was for a submissive to address me as 'Sir,' but something about this woman set my teeth on edge and rang all of my radar's bells and whistles. I wasn't going to give her the upper hand, not for a second. By the expression on Hope's face, I realized she had taken the same instant dislike to Dr. Rouchard.

Rouchard flushed slightly, her lips thinning into a smile, and nodded her head. "Of course, please forgive me. Since you're here, Agent Grayson, I won't attempt to deny my doctor-patient relationship with Ms. Callahan. However, I'm afraid that is the only thing I can tell you without a court order, much as I would prefer otherwise. I have a duty to maintain patient confidentiality."

"But, this woman was —"

"We understand," I interrupted Hope. She shut up,

but I could tell she wasn't happy about it. I stood and pulled a business card from my wallet, handing it to the doctor. "How did you know Miss Callahan wouldn't be keeping her appointment today, Dr. Rouchard?" I asked pleasantly, keeping my voice mildly curious. She hadn't told me she'd known Callahan wouldn't keep the appointment, but she had clearly rescheduled the time slot with another patient.

Rouchard smiled thinly. "She left voicemail to reschedule her appointment, but I'm afraid she hasn't done so yet, Agent," she said, accepting the business card I gave her. "Now, I do apologize, but I must dictate some patient notes, before I forget any pertinent information." We thanked each other politely, and Hope and I left the doctor's office, moving back out to the waiting area.

I reached into my pocket, drawing my cell phone out as if stopping there to make a call. When Dr. Rouchard closed the door to the waiting room, I put it back into my pocket and moved over to the reception area, smiling my most endearing smile at the young woman behind the desk.

"May I help you, sir?" she asked, blinking at me.

"Yes…Amanda," I said, with another charming smile. "Could you please tell me the date Patricia Callahan cancelled her appointment with Dr. Rouchard?"

"Certainly," Amanda said, with a flirty smile of her own, turning to her computer and typing briefly.

"Um, apparently, she was a no-show," Amanda said, with an apologetic shrug. "She didn't call to cancel, sir."

That was exactly what I'd thought. I thanked the girl, and we left the behavioral health center. Hope turned to me, fire in her eyes, the moment we were out the door.

"That doctor is a lying bitch!" she exploded. "I don't trust her!"

I nodded as I handed her the helmet. "I don't either. She looks familiar to me, but I can't place her. I'm going to run her through NCIC to see if she has any priors."

***

Hope and I spent the night in the Marriot Courtyard of Chatham Hills, an expense I'd be paying for personally since my *per diem* was already accounted for. We stocked the refrigerator with a few snacks and soft drinks and ordered room service for dinner. I tightened the corset as much as Hope could bear, and had her practice walking, bending, and sitting in both the corset and the boots for about two hours. Overall, it was a quiet, uneventful night, and we both went to bed early, in separate, queen-sized beds.

Tuesday morning, I read over the NCIC report on Dr. Rouchard and made several follow-up phone inquiries. Rouchard had a sealed juvie record, which was of no use at all, but she also had several priors for bad checks, some of which had been passed as recently as this year. That was unusual for a well-paid psychologist, and I wondered where her money was going. I was beginning to suspect the good doctor was somehow involved in either Lau's drug op, white slavery operation, or both, but I wasn't sure how she fit in. In any case, I was unable to prove anything based on what I had. I shot a quick email to Jeannie LeCler, an intern in my D.C. office, asking her to investigate any possible links between our missing women and Dana Rouchard. I didn't expect anything to come of it, but it was another lead to follow.

After breakfast, Hope and I reported Callahan's

disappearance to her employer and interviewed her coworkers at Chatham Hills Regional Hospital. It helped that Callahan had told Hope so much about everyone at her job. She was able to identify most of Callie's coworkers, and she was able to tell me which were sincere in their concern for the girl, and which were not. By the time we sat down to lunch, I knew none of Callie's coworkers had any idea what had happened to her. It was discouraging, but over the years, I'd grown accustomed to setbacks. Hope, on the other hand, looked like someone had kicked her puppy.

With nothing on the agenda for the afternoon, we returned to the hotel room. I hadn't brought toys with me, but they weren't necessary. Hands work as well as either a paddle or a swatch of rabbit fur. Hope was already wearing the stiletto boots, as I'd instructed that morning, so I had her strip down to them and laced her into the leather corset, a bit tighter than I had the night before. She was doing well with the hasty corset training; well enough, at least, to be able to pass.

"You'll need to be more comfortable getting naked in front of people," I told her bluntly. "You still carry tension in your shoulders and on your face when I tell you to strip."

"Yes, Sir," Hope said. Her voice was despondent, fear and worry still plaguing her from the morning's hospital visit. I wasn't sure how to snap her out of it, and the only thing I could think of was to work her—hard—in preparation for Lau's party. If she were lucky, the training would distract her from her dejection; if not, it would still be beneficial. She stood awkwardly while I headed toward the small hotel refrigerator for a Dr. Pepper.

I changed my mind, sitting on the chair near the air

187

conditioning unit. "Bring me a Dr. Pepper, please," I said. Despite the 'please,' it was an instruction, not a request. I saw Hope's eyes register the difference, her spine stiffening infinitesimally. She turned, walked to the refrigerator, and pulled out a bottle of soda, bringing it to where I sat and handing it to me.

"No," I said. "Again."

"What?"

"Did I stutter? Take it back, and bring it to me again. Only this time, *serve* me."

Hope was definitely not in the mood. I could see that plainly on her face, and it made me all the more determined to proceed.

Hope turned smartly, walking back to the hallway where the refrigerator was recessed into the wall. She placed the bottle of soda into the refrigerator then stood. She glanced back at me, but I simply watched her, giving no encouragement.

She bent, took the same bottle from the refrigerator, and brought it back to me, this time handing it to me with a strained smile on her face.

I gave it back to her. "No."

"What am I doing wrong?" she asked, not *quite* sullenly.

"At this point, it would be easier to tell you what you're doing right," I snapped. "Think about it, Chloe. Think about what you observed at the munch. The things Dale talked to you about, if he covered service-oriented submission while he was painting your toenails, and if not, the way he acted. Scenes you've seen on television, when there are butlers and maids and such, or what you've read online about submissives." I struggled to come up with a better example, then nodded. "Think about what you know of Japanese geishas."

188

I watched her mind work. She took the soda back and started again. This time, she took a plastic glass from the countertop and added a few cubes of ice from the bucket, pouring the drink over them. Her face was a pleasant-looking mask when she brought the drink to me.

"Better," I said, "but not there yet. Again."

Hope visibly swallowed her frustration and served me again, and again. And again. Each time she changed something, I commented on the change, indicating whether it was an improvement. I watched her frustration grow, even as her performance improved.

"Can you at least give me a suggestion?" she finally asked, exasperated.

I thought about it, mentally comparing her service to Majyck's, and to the ridiculous 'serves' of the Gorean kajirae. "It's…about beauty, as much as about service," I said finally. "Think like a geisha. What do you know about them?"

Hope frowned, considering. "They were—are, I suppose—Japanese courtesans, well-trained to act as hostesses and entertainers. They're talented—in music or dance, usually, but also in the art of conversation. They wear distinctive white makeup, red lipstick, and—"

"Never mind what they look like," I interrupted. "Keep on with the description of what they do, or how they act."

"They're…graceful," Hope struggled.

"What else?"

"I…I don't know."

"What was their main purpose, other than to entertain or provide sex?"

"To bring pleasure to the men they entertained, to

189

enable them to feel good about themselves."

"That's a big part, yes. But it goes further than to make the man feel 'good.' Their purpose was to make the man they entertained feel pampered, indulged. Everything they did was to make things beautiful and uncomplicated for their guest. From the way they served tea to the way they slid open a bamboo door, it was all designed to be pleasurable to all of the senses. They needed to agree with whatever he said, but to do so in an ingratiating, yet not obsequious manner, so he would believe he really was the smartest guy in the universe. They needed to make him feel…worshipped."

She nodded understanding, and we started again. Her acting ability cranked up several notches, despite her increasing anger. I was impressed. I wouldn't have known how irritable she was becoming if I didn't know her fairly well by now. I didn't blame her. I knew the boots had to be uncomfortable by now—we'd been at it for more than three hours, and I hadn't allowed her off her feet for more than a few seconds at a time.

"Again."

Hope rose gracefully from her kneeling position, swaying her hips invitingly as she walked back to the refrigerator. She knelt, the pose utterly feminine, to replace the Dr. Pepper, and again to remove it. She carried the glass back to me, her eyes lowered demurely, and sank to her knees at my feet, glancing up at me with a quick, shy smile, before lowering her eyes again. The glass of soda rested on her flattened palm, held surreptitiously by her thumb, and she raised it to a comfortable level, not allowing the glass to wobble. I was able to take the drink from her hand, without having to fumble with her fingers covering the glass.

"Thank you," I said, my voice peremptory as I took

the drink and had a sip.

Hope's eyes shot up in surprise, and her mouth dropped slightly. "That's it?" she asked.

I nodded, and Hope's eyes lit up with victory and relief. I held the glass out to her, and she accepted it on her open palm, shifting it slightly to get a more natural grip.

"Now, again, Chloe," I ordered. "This time, bring a snack as well."

I don't even think Hope realized she was going to do it. I certainly didn't. Her hand flew forward before either of us could blink, and I felt ice cubes and cold soft drink splashing my face and shirt. The anger in her eyes was primeval. "Even when you say 'thank you,' there's an air of entitlement in your voice!" she snapped. "I hate that arrogant smugness! It's so fucking...Republican!"

I clenched my teeth hard to keep the bellows of laughter from exploding, and forced my facial expression into an angry scowl. I'm also a good actor, and six years of assorted undercover work had perfected my ability. It worked. Hope's eyes grew, as she realized what she'd just done, and the implications of her actions. I watched her own teeth clench as her chin lifted slightly, telling me she wasn't about to apologize, or—more appropriately—prostrate herself and beg forgiveness. My scowl deepened, as I fought harder with the laughter. The righteous fury and indignation on her face squeezed something inside my chest, and, for just an instant, Hope was there, where Majyck had left a hollow. I wasn't ready for the sharp pain of that, and I turned away from her quickly, before she could see my eyes.

"You've had your one tantrum," I said, my voice steely. "Now, get a towel and clean me up. Then, we'll see to your punishment."

I said the last automatically. I realized as soon as the words were spoken, though, they were the only appropriate ones I could have said. I had no choice but to follow through. It's the course I would have taken with Majyck...with any submissive, honestly...but something in my gut told me it was the wrong action to take with Hope.

I reached out to her, taking her chin in my hand to make her look at me, and my voice was gentle when I spoke again. "This will also be a test," I said, doing my best to mitigate the damage. "Before I take you into Lau's territory, I need to know how well you can handle pain – real pain. I won't be able to let you sub-drop on Saturday, so today will be a first run for that. There won't be any warm-up, but I expect you to safe word when it gets to be too much."

Hope nodded stiffly. A slight change in her expression told me she'd rather eat a bug than safe word, and that somehow eased the tension in me. She had accepted this as a test of her endurance, in addition to punishment for her transgression. We were on solid ground again.

I watched while she moved into the bathroom, wetting a towel under warm water and bringing it over, wiping my face, neck, and arms. "Would you like a clean shirt, Sir?" she asked. Her voice was tight, but only just. I nodded, studying her while she went into the suitcase I hadn't bothered to unpack, and got me another t-shirt.

Every person has a pain threshold, myself included. Two years ago, I'd subjected myself to every instrument of torture I could imagine using on Majyck, both to understand what she would be enduring and to find my own threshold. It had been very...unpleasant. As time went on, though, Majyck's initial pain tolerance increased, seemingly exponentially, until she became a true masochist. Her ability to handle, process, and actually enjoy pain had so far surpassed mine, there was no comparison.

I shrugged into my t-shirt, then gestured for Hope to turn around so I could unlace the corset. "Boots off," I told her, as I folded the corset and placed it on the unused bed. She complied, barely stifling a sigh of relief, then held my shoulder with one hand to keep her balance while I lifted each foot in turn to inspect them. The corn pads and Band-Aids we'd used to protect the blisters were working, and her feet were doing well, all things considered.

"You ready for this?" I asked. Hope hesitated for just an instant, then nodded.

Hope
Stripes

Was I ready? For punishment? *Was he out of his* fucking *mind?!*

I didn't trust myself to speak, so I lied my ass off by way of a nod.

Eric studied me for a long moment, and when he spoke, his voice was impersonal, with a slight edge that made me want to curl in on myself. "Do I need to explain why I'm punishing you?"

I shook my head, surprised at the sudden flush of shame—*What the fuck!?*—I felt coloring my cheeks. "No, Sir," I said, fighting the urge to grind my teeth. "I understand what I did wrong."

Eric nodded, his voice gentle again. "I know you do."

He stepped around me and moved over to the bed while I stood waiting, my eyes on the carpet. My parents hadn't believed in corporal punishment. This would be

194

the first time in my life someone used pain as a means to chastise me. The thought was…unsettling. I watched from my peripheral vision as Eric pulled three of the pillows from the head of the bed to the middle, making a raised surface. He left the fourth pillow up at the top of the bed.

"Use that pillow to dampen any sounds you make," he instructed, his voice curt and businesslike. "Now, get into position."

My stomach clenched, and for a moment, I was frozen. I snapped out of it, before he would have to repeat himself. I risked a quick glance up at his face, hoping, perhaps, for a glimpse of mercy. I was disappointed. There was no anger in his eyes, but no quarter given, either. I took in a deep breath and stepped over to the bed, risking my first glance at his hands. I regretted it instantly. Some things, you just don't want to see coming. I hadn't noticed it over the past few days, but Eric's hands were huge! They were going to hit like cast iron.

Eric held out a hand as I approached the bed, and courteously helped me crawl into position on the firm mattress. The irony wasn't lost on me, but I was too absorbed in how easily his large hand had enveloped mine to appreciate the finer intricacies of the moment.

"Stripes," he said, when I adjusted myself on top of the three pillows and let out a quivering breath. "You'll count."

I turned my head to him, startled. I hadn't expected that. My stomach knotted, and for just a moment, I was afraid I was going to puke. I fiercely reminded myself of Callie. She needed my—our—help, and I wasn't going to let a few minutes of discomfort stop us now. Also, Eric was right; we had to know if I could handle it, or if

I'd fall apart in front of Lau on Saturday. *I could handle it,* I reassured myself. *I would handle it.*

I watched Eric unbuckle his belt and slide it from the loops around his waist, my head scrambling to adjust my expectations from the solid impact of his hand to the stinging bite of leather.

"C-count," I acknowledged, steeling myself. "Yes, Sir." I was an adult woman, and this was a choice I had made. I gripped the pillow tightly, the smell of freshly-bleached hotel linens assaulting my senses. For a quick moment, I wondered what the young Vietnamese housekeeper I'd seen earlier in the day would think if she could see me now. I put the thought out of my mind, preparing myself for the whipping.

The first lash caught me by surprise, the snap of leather burning hot and deep across my ass, the pain so much more intense than I was expecting. I screamed, thankfully into the pillow, shocked at how hard the strike had been, how deeply it burned. I was suddenly very uncertain I could handle any of this!

"Count," he reminded me, the mildness of his voice incongruous against the shrieking pain.

"One, Sir," I gasped out, just as the second lash burned a trail cruelly close to its predecessor. "Two, Sir!" The third lash landed flat across the "sweet spot," the place where the ass and legs meet together in a bundle of nerve endings. "Three, Sir!" Tears spilled from my eyes, unsettling me, but I gritted my teeth hard, denying the 'red' from being voiced. The fourth lash burned across my ass with a vengeance and I gasped, squirming off the pillow for a moment and turning my backside away from Eric, my hand reaching behind me to feel the hot, raised welts. Tears ran down my face, but I refused to say the word. I wanted it to stop—more than

196

anything—but I refused to ask.

"Resume position, girl," Eric commanded, his voice still the same quiet, deadly calm.

I had to fight myself. The safe word was right there, right at the edge of my lips, waiting to be released into the air. I could say it, and the pain would stop now. Or…I could resume the position. I knew he wouldn't go easy on me…he'd proven that. It was nothing…nothing but sheer, stupid pride that made me resume the position.

Eric saw it the instant I made the decision, and his eyes lit with respect. That *almost* made it worthwhile. I resumed position, my sweat-covered body holding the pillow lifeline close.

I was right. He didn't go easy. The next two lashes were unbearable, and finally, pain won out over pride. "Red!" I gasped, as the sixth lash landed on my ass and upper thigh.

It was over. It took a moment, but when I was able, I looked over at him. He stood straight and tall next to the bed, the belt still in his hand. There was no expression of pleasure on his face, none of that strange, soft arousal I had noticed when he'd removed the wrist restraints the other day. This had been punishment for both of us.

He pulled me into his arms and held me. My makeup smeared against his new t-shirt, but neither of us cared. For just that moment, his embrace was emotional balm, and I needed it badly.

"I'm proud of you, Hope," he said, his voice warm with praise and a tinge of surprise. He placed the belt on the nightstand beside the bed and continued to hold me, rubbing my back in a comforting circular motion. "You handled that well. No one could have done better."

I let the words soothe my wounded pride as I reached a hand back, feeling the six hot welts that crossed my ass. Well … at least, there would be no worries about me having enough bruises to look like a submissive. My ass was going to be deep purple and blue by the time Saturday arrived.

Eric
Hope's Place

We were eating an early dinner in the restaurant of the hotel, Hope sitting gingerly in her chair. "I know you're discouraged," I told her, killing off the last of my Heineken as I spoke. "I've been there, Hope. I understand how hard this is, but you need to keep the faith. It's important for you, but it's even more important for Callahan."

She nodded, giving me a shaky smile. "I do have faith, Sir...I'm just not sure where it is right now."

"What would make you feel better?" I asked. "Other than having your friend next to you right now, what one thing could we do that would make you feel better?"

She blinked, as if surprised at the question. "Other than Callie...I just wish I could go home," she said quietly. "I want to...I don't know. I want to play with my cat, and read a book, and sleep in my own bed, just

199

for tonight."

I nodded thoughtfully. I knew it wasn't just the lack of progress today that had Hope down; she was also sub-dropping, hard. I'd only had the one Heineken, and that was with a full meal, so the drive wouldn't be an issue. "We can do that," I told her. "We'll grab our bags and check out, then we'll head to Louisville. We can be there by ten."

Hope's smile was like sunshine emerging from behind clouds, and I felt a pulling sensation in my stomach I hadn't felt in eight months…not since Majyck and I stopped being lovers, two months before her death. Damn.

Our breakup had been amicable, but I wondered then, and I still wondered, how much it had contributed to her sense of recklessness, the same recklessness that had gotten her killed. I think it was a question I would never have an answer for.

The four-hour road trip with Hope was probably a huge mistake. Telling her at the outset of the trip we were 'taking the night off' was *definitely* a huge mistake. The barriers broke, and her vivacious personality came out like a torrent of gushing water. We needed to work on her ability to submit with ease, but I also knew she was crashing from her first endorphin high and her second, less enjoyable, beating. Hope needed the relaxation of 'vanilla' conversation and laughter as badly as I needed to know she wouldn't make any fatal mistakes on Saturday.

On the other hand, we had four more days to put her through her paces, so she could afford one night of recovery. Knowing she didn't have to perform in any way, except to continue addressing me as 'Sir,' took the weight of the universe off both of us, and we talked, laughed, and teased each other mercilessly.

I was genuinely disappointed to pull up to her apartment complex shortly after ten. It had been one of the more enjoyable drives I could remember.

But Hope was beginning to drag, and, truth be told, so was I. I was looking forward to sleep, and I was hoping for a guest bedroom rather than a living room sofa. We brought our bags up, yawning rather than chatting. Before Hope even unlocked her door, there was an eager, incessant 'meowing' from the other side, as Mr. Wuzzles paced back and forth in clear consternation. Hope opened the door and a small, but pudgy, orange tabby cat *climbed her* until it reached her left shoulder, where it settled in comfortably, purring loudly. I watched, stunned, as Hope dropped everything, kicked the door closed after I'd stepped in, and sat down right in the entranceway, all of her loving attention devoted to the cat. She repeatedly reassured him she was home for the night and confessed she was a bad mommy for leaving him. How could she have done such a thing?

"No, you aren't wasting away, Mr. Wuzzles. I've only been gone since Friday, and I know Debi fed you, you precious widdle boy! But I know, it's been hard, honey. I have the special treats right here to make it up to you!"

I thought I was going to gag. Hope pulled a bag of cat treats from a shelf in the entryway closet and gave a small handful to the cat. I watched in bemusement as Mr. Wuzzles made it through four treats without so much as acknowledging my presence. Pity I couldn't maintain that luck.

Once his need for love and domination of his human had been met, followed by his need for special treats to ward off pending emaciation, Mr. Wuzzles decided to check me out. He hissed, making it clear he was not

201

impressed. Being honest, he didn't do much for me, either. Only exhaustion and courtesy as Hope's guest stopped me from hissing back.

"He's a little territorial," Hope apologized, finally gathering her purse and overnight bag and moving us into the living room.

Her place was small, but it wasn't overcrowded. It was tidy, and tastefully decorated. More than anything, it exuded warmth and comfort, two qualities I hadn't been able to bring to either my temporary work residences or my own home in D.C. I couldn't care less about my work housing, but I wanted Annie to love my house in D.C. when she was old enough to appreciate such things. Perhaps, when the Lau trial was over and Hope came out of Witness Protection, I could ask her for some decorating tips, maybe even spend some time with her and get to know her on a more … personal level. It would be good for Annie to have a sane mother figure in her life. I pulled myself up sharply. *Where the hell had* that *come from?* Damn, I knew I was tired now.

I shook the daydreams out of my head and followed Hope as she showed me to the bathroom so I could shower first. When I was finished, I waited in the living room while she took her own shower. I spent about three seconds trying to befriend the glaring demon-cat before giving up and turning on the television.

Hope emerged about half an hour later, her hair slightly damp. She wore a pink bathrobe, and I could smell the fresh floral scent of her body wash from where I stood. I could also see the fatigue in her eyes. I'd resisted the urge to snoop around while she was in the shower, so I still didn't know the layout of her apartment.

"Would you like me on the couch?"

Hope bit her lower lip in a moment of indecision, then shook her head. "It's not comfortable, Sir," she said. "We've slept togeth…in the same bed before."

Her bed was only a double, so my feet would hang off the edge, but it had a good, firm mattress. I stripped down to briefs, then watched while she turned her back to me, taking off her robe and revealing an overly-large nightshirt beneath. I bit back a chuckle when she turned around. Darth Vader graced the front of her shirt, and beneath him it read: *Come to the Dark Side. We have cookies.*

We both knew the night would be entirely platonic, of course, but we didn't realize we would have such a conscientious chaperone. Mr. Wuzzles enforced the verdict by the protective way he clung to Hope, climbing right up onto her chest the moment she lay down, and turning toward me with an angry glare. Hope petted him, her eyes closed. I watched, the illumination from the street light outside Hope's bedroom window more than adequate. The cat did that 'biscuit-making' thing cats always do, then began licking Hope's face, thoroughly cleaning her cheeks and nose.

"He loves me," she murmured.

"He's taste-testing you," I corrected. "One night, he's going to eat you in your sleep."

Luckily, Hope was asleep by then. The cat turned to look at me again, his eyes narrowing. I could almost read its devious little feline mind. *MY human. Back off!*

I shrugged, pulling up the blanket and shifting into a comfortable position. Some women had mace; Hope had Mr. Wuzzles.

Hope
Biding Time

The next morning, we woke early and headed back to Nashville. It almost killed me when Mr. Wuzzles cried, as I headed toward the door. "Soon," I promised him, holding him close for a few seconds. "This will all be over soon, baby-boy, and Mama will be home then."

I pretended not to notice the glare my cat shot Eric, just as I had pretended not to hear Eric's snarky remark the night before. Mr. Wuzzles was jealous of anyone who 'stole' the time and attention that was his rightful due. I wasn't sure what Eric's issue was.

Our 'off-duty' time ended as soon as we pulled up to Eric's room at the Residence Inn. My car and Eric's Harley were the only vehicles in our part of the lot, but there were two new cars parked three units away. Eric carried our bags inside while I retrieved Callie's computer and thumb drives from the trunk of my car.

"Work?" Eric asked, when I began to set it up on the desk.

"It's Callie's," I said. "I…borrowed it."

His eyes narrowed at my blatant violation of the law, but he didn't challenge me. I sat at the desk, opening the laptop and my spiral notebook. I had thought to number Callie's flash drives from one to eighteen, and I picked up where I'd left off—thumb drive number three.

Eric read over my shoulder for a few minutes, and then he pulled out his own laptop, grabbing thumb drives ten through eighteen and settling down on the sofa. We resolved ourselves to a long, tedious afternoon of research.

Periodically, one of us would come across something which might prove relevant, and we would read that section aloud to the other, analyzing its significance.

I found contact information for Rory, Callie's brother, just as I finished the last of my room-service dinner. His name had a work number with an NYC area code listed, with 'Glory Hole Dance Club' beside it. *Glory Hole?* I frowned, considering what I knew about the term. Pieces of my past tumbled together as I remembered Callie's flashy, flamboyant brother: the delight he took in teaching Callie and me every form of dance I could imagine; the almost-constant ridicule he endured from other boys at school; the stiff way his father spoke to him when I visited; and, most of all, the handful of gay porn magazines that had spilled from Tom Quinn's gym bag the week after he'd called me 'Dopey Hopey.'

It didn't matter to me, of course. I was perfectly fine with Rory being gay; but…was that the reason he had left home so early? *Was that why he had seemingly cut Callie completely out of his life? Would she want me to contact him, or leave well enough alone?*

I looked at the time display in the corner of my laptop. It was 8:10 p.m. A dance club would be open, but hopefully not at the busiest time of the night. I dialed the number before I could change my mind.

"Glory Hole, this is Wendy."

I hadn't been expecting a woman to answer, so I was slightly taken aback. "Um, yes. Is Rory Callahan working tonight, please?"

"He's finishing up a set. Hold on."

I held, listening to the thumping bass of a popular dance song and the sounds of chatter and laughter coming from, I presumed, a bar area.

About three minutes later, the music paused. I heard Wendy call, "Yo! Ro! You got a phone call!"

I came this close to hanging up.

"This is Rory, the answer to alllll your wet dreams. How can I help you, honey?"

I hesitated, as a new song began thumping in the background, then said, "Hey, Rory. It's Hope Pendleton. Long time no see."

There was a long moment of silence from the other end of the phone, and I wondered if he had hung up.

"Wow," he said finally. "Talk about a blast from the past! How've you been?"

"I'm okay," I said, meeting Eric's eyes as my own filled with tears. "I need to tell you about Callie…"

***

Rory and I talked for about fifteen minutes until he had to go back to work. He said he would ask the club manager for time off, and would fly in to Chatham Hills as soon as he could. I gave him my cell phone number, wiped my eyes, and rang off, a bowling ball of dread settling in the pit of my stomach. I was glad I had reached Rory; he needed to know what was happening with his sister. *But why did it feel like I had notified Callie's next of kin of her death?*

We knocked off the research shortly after my phone call. Between us, we'd examined all but four of the thumb drives. We had found very little, and I didn't hold much hope for the rest of our efforts. Eric instructed me to get into the leather corset and boots and, with a groan, I obeyed. I spent the next three hours struggling to breathe and practicing how to walk until he finally called it a night and I dropped, exhausted, into the bed.

***

The next three days passed in much the same manner. Mornings and afternoons, we poured over Callie's computer files, reading everything we had originally passed over based on the title of the document, and in the evenings, we trained in service elegance, corsetry, and spike-heeled boots. We talked *ad nauseam* about possible scenarios that could play out on Saturday night. Eric drilled me on the blueprint specs of Sandmarian Gardens, even taking me out to the parking lot to run through the layout, counting steps from the entrance of the restaurant to the hallway, to the elevator, and back to the exit.

Friday afternoon, Eric opened an email from the FBI intern he worked with in Washington. I watched him read it, the furrow on his brow suggesting it wasn't good news, and I braced myself.

"Well, son of a motherless goat," Eric muttered, when he had finished reading.

I bit down on my impatience and waited.

"Seems like Dr. Rouchard is as dirty as we thought

she was, but everything's circumstantial," he said, turning the laptop to face me. "I'd hate to be as fucked as she is."

I read the report, stunned at the personal information it contained. Dr. Rouchard had a substantial, six-figure income from her counseling practice, but she was indebted up to her eyeballs. Her home, valued at more than four million dollars, carried three mortgages, two of which were in default. There were several liens against the property, she had outstanding Warrants in Debt, and her credit score was abysmal. She had also been convicted of passing cold checks, which we had already learned from the initial NCIC report.

Jeannie LeCler, Eric's intern, had also included unofficial information; apparently, the reason for Dana Rouchard's financial afflictions was one Dennis Alvin Rouchard, age twenty-nine. Dennis, Rouchard's son, had been in and out of various drug rehabilitation programs with clockwork regularity since the age of fifteen. A chronic recidivist, Dennis had been denied re-entry into several programs for failure to comply and consistently dirty urine tests. Rouchard had spent hundreds of thousands of dollars to alternatively support her son's heroin addiction and attempt to clean him up. LeCler had found recurrent payments to Three Star Recovery, Inc., a pharmaceutical manufacturer which she believed to be a shell corporation for Lau Enterprises. She was continuing the investigation, hoping to be able to link the corporations definitively.

"Son of a motherless goat," I murmured.

***

Friday evening, we went to a NAMTA 'demo,' where I

208

learned about erotic wax play and got to dip my hands into liquid paraffin. I recognized several people from the munch, Dale among them. It was good to chat with him for a while; he was just so incredibly *nice!* I think, perhaps more than any other submissive I'd met, Dale genuinely lived his lifestyle choices. He was always polite and helpful, and he seemed to be genuinely interested in the well-being of others in the group.

I both dreaded and anticipated Saturday evening's party.

Hope
Party

"You look stunning. It's perfect. With the demure act you've perfected, and those gorgeous, expressive eyes, Lau will be on you like white on rice. No racism intended."

My eyes shot up to Eric's face. I looked to see if he were teasing…apparently, he was not. He thought my eyes were gorgeous! My face heated, as the blush crawled up my neck, but I didn't look away. He had taught me to take a compliment, if nothing else. "Thank you, Sir," I murmured, with a heady mix of sultriness and diffidence in my voice. I barely recognized myself in these clothes and with this…enhanced…self-perspective.

I was wearing Callie's blue corset with the silver bamboo trimming and the repaired laced-up leather skirt I had worn to the munch. Of course, I was also wearing the boots Eric had bought me from Stella's. I was as prepared as I would ever be. Every day this week, Eric had discussed the ins and outs of the submissive mindset, and every evening, in addition to wearing the come-fuck-me boots, I had been laced into that damned leather corset and had practiced different types of service, from food presentation to foot rubs. Eric had tightened the hateful corset once every hour I wore it, until I actually felt dizzy-headed from the lack of oxygen. It had been a relief for bedtime to arrive each night, simply because I knew he would take the iron beast off of me!

Tonight, by comparison, the other corset felt loose and roomy, although it still gave me the figure of my dreams and held the girls up on a cobalt serving platter. I understood now why he had made the garment so tight the rest of the week; by comparison, I felt comfortable, and therefore, I looked as if I had been wearing a corset for years. I actually *was* comfortable, whereas a week ago, I would have been completely miserable, even with the laces pulled to the same tautness.

Eric was dressed in mouth-watering black leather pants, a tight black t-shirt, his vest, and a Master's cap. He exuded sex appeal, and by the confidence in his bearing, he knew it.

"For inside your right boot," he said, handing me a thin, beautifully made stiletto.

I looked up at him in surprise. "Sir?" I asked uncertainly.

"Lau has a strict no-weapons policy in the Sandmarian Gardens," Eric said, as if that clarified, rather than muddied the instruction. At my puzzled expression, he added, "Ninety percent of the patrons violate that policy. I don't actually expect you to stab anyone."

211

I smiled in relief. "Thank you, Sir," I said softly. I had noticed the strange flaps of leather inside each boot, but I hadn't considered they were actual *sheaths*.

Eric smiled, and handed me another item, a tube of lipstick. I already had my makeup impeccably applied, but I didn't object. "Thank you again, Sir," I said, in that quiet, reticent voice I had perfected over the past four days.

"It's also a knife," he told me, taking the lipstick back and removing the cap. He twisted the base of the tube, and a small blade arose. "This is wicked sharp, so be careful with it. It's razor-edged. It's meant for slicing, not stabbing."

"Very nice, Sir," I said with a smile. "Is that an FBI super-spy gadget?"

Eric laughed. "No, it's a novelty item from a BDSM convention. Basically, it's meant to be cute, but some masochists really are so addicted to adrenaline and endorphins, they use them as portable 'quick fixes.' Boss stressing you out at work? Pop into the bathroom, whip this puppy out, do a quick cutting, and back to it."

I considered his words. A week ago, I couldn't even have imagined it.

"Keep it on you," he continued. "Again, you're not actually going to use it."

I accepted the tube and tucked it into my décolletage with a modest smile. Eric gave me his arm and escorted me from the hotel room to the Crown Victoria.

***

An hour later, my stomach dropped. Eric and I were sitting at a table in the Sandmarian Garden, having just finished a light meal of salads and breadsticks. It was never a good idea to play hungry; it was an even worse idea to play after a heavy meal. The Asian man, whose face I would recognize in the middle of Times Square, walked up to our table, flanked by security guards on either side of him. I looked down quickly, hoping my face had betrayed nothing as Eric greeted his 'friend' and made introductions.

"Jimmy, this is my girl, Chloe Anderson," Eric said, smiling warmly as he stood. "Chloe, this is Mr. Lau, the owner of this fine establishment."

I smiled demurely, then quickly glanced down as I got to my feet and proffered my hand. "A pleasure, Sir," I said softly, my pulse frightened-rabbit rapid in my throat.

"Enchanté, cher," Jimmy Lau said, pressing his lips to my hand as though we were enacting a scene from an old movie

If I had been drinking, I would have snorted liquid through my nose at his heavy Cajun accent. As it was, I arched an inquisitive, and flirtatious, eyebrow at the man I knew in my gut had kidnapped Callie. "You have a beautiful place, Mr. Lau," I said, flicking my eyes up to meet his before lowering them again.

"You add to its beauty tenfold, little one," he said, and then he nodded to Eric. "Enjoy the party, Falcon."

Eric smiled back, the men shook hands again, and we resumed our seats. "I always do, Jimmy."

When Lau was a good distance from the table, I opened my mouth to speak but Eric shook his head slightly. He took his cash from an inside pocket of his vest, and set it onto the table, messing with the money clip for a few seconds. "We can talk now, for about two minutes," he told me with a tight smile.

I blinked at the device. "Another novelty item?" I asked.

Eric shook his head. "FBI super-spy gadget. What was your initial impression of Lau?"

"He's a player," I said immediately. "He thinks he's charming above and beyond anyone else. He knows he's in a position of power."

Eric nodded, pleased with my analysis, then a frown of worry wrinkled his forehead. "He hasn't invited us into the private playroom, and that concerns me. We'll have to go through the evening, and see how it flows. If we don't get in today, next month we can try…"

"Callie will be gone by next month," I interrupted flatly.

Eric nodded, his face expressionless but his eyes somber. "In all likelihood, yes."

"Then why—" Eric shook his head infinitesimally, and I shut up as one of Lau's thugs approached our table, carrying—of all things!—a dessert tray.

"With Mr. Lau's compliments," the thug intoned. "He recommends the key lime pie."

"Then, the lady will have the key lime pie," Eric said, "and I'll have the chocolate cheese cake."

We danced after dinner. It was actually enjoyable, and for a few moments here and there, I had to remind myself I was not on a real date with Eric. There were several waltzes, a few formless dances where people just held each other and swayed, and then, surprisingly, a tango. Eric looked at me with question in his eyes, and I nodded. Of course, I could tango! Callie's brother had taught us both ballroom dancing in high school, and, though it had been years since I had performed the dance, the steps were familiar. I knew already Eric was an excellent lead, so I followed in his steps, laughing softly as we moved with the music.

"I think we have Jimmy's attention," Eric whispered

in my ear, just before rolling me out into the final turn. I could have stayed on the dance floor another hour, happily, but at the sound of a quiet gong, people began moving toward the back hall. Toy bags and fetish wear had been moved into the playroom by the wait staff as people had dined. I saw the blue and yellow card with the number seventeen placed on our table and presumed I would find its match in the playroom.

We were next in line to enter Playroom B, when one of Lau's goons stepped toward us, speaking quietly to Eric. I had to strain to hear the words. "...Lau...you and your lady...more comfortable...private room."

I bit the inside of my cheek to keep my features calm and smooth. *We were in!* I didn't know if I was more elated or terrified, but we were one step closer to Callie. I was certain she, too, had played in Lau's private space.

Eric stepped out of the line and guided me with a hand at the small of my back. We followed Lau's security officer down the hall, past an elevator, and into a small, unobtrusive room. The lights inside were dim, but each wall was mirrored so the lighting was reflected. As a result, the room felt cozy and intimate. Classical music—Tchaikovsky, I think—played from hidden speakers. The room was a small theater, of sorts. Three rows of comfortable seating surrounded a round, raised dais, upon which stood a gleaming, polished oaken St. Andrew's cross. Beside the cross stood Eric's toy rack, everything already neatly displayed and ready for use. Jimmy Lau sat in one of the theater-style seats, a cocktail on the tray beside him.

I balked, looking up at Eric in feigned, wide-eyed panic. "Sir, what—" I began, and Eric shushed me.

"Be still, Chloe," he ordered quietly. "I'm the only one who will touch you tonight. I promised you,

215

remember?"

I nodded tremulously, smiling nervously at Lau and doing my best to appear doe-like and timid. It required more acting than I thought it would. This close to the man, I felt wolf-like and vicious; I was enraged this son-of-a-bitch was still drawing oxygen into his lungs while my friend—and other women, also, I allowed—were suffering because of him. I pretended to cower before him, noting the self-satisfied expression on his face, and promising myself that he would *eat it*. Jimmy Lau would have his day in court, and I vowed Callie and I would be there to watch every sordid moment of it.

Eric handed a CD to one of Lau's men. There were about four thugs in the small room, making the theater seem claustrophobically small. Three of the men left, leaving only Lau and a bodyguard. A few moments later, the now-familiar strains of Enigma filled the small room. Eric and I had played several times, and my body had some impressive bruises and even a few blood welts. Other than the marks from the belt, I'd been surprised to see the physical evidence of the damage Eric had inflicted; he was so skilled at warm up I rarely felt pain during a play session, and when I did, it was fleeting. Tonight, as he had warned me, would be different.

"I'll need you absolutely alert," he'd said earlier, as we had gotten ready for the party. "I can't have you dropping into that happy masochist space, not tonight. So you'll see—and feel the difference. It will be similar to punishment, but not quite that harsh. Every time you get close to dropping, I will strike harder, or out of rhythm, or in the wrong place. I promise, you won't daze out on me."

I stepped out of my skirt easily and untied my boots, turning to place them neatly beside the play station. I made certain Lau got an eyeful of my black-lace thonged ass, as I bent with perfect feminine poise to fold the skirt and lay it beside the boots. I stood then and gracefully turned my back to Eric, facing Lau. He smiled as I held the corset in place by the breastplate while Eric expertly unlaced the garment. I removed it without hesitation, giving Lau another eyeful. This time, I returned his smile with a charming nod of my own as I again bent to place the corset gently on top of the skirt.

Eric kept his promise. I never even came close to the happy space I had felt earlier that week. Also, I learned it was a hell of a lot harder to fake sub drop than it was to fake an orgasm! I couldn't *think* gooseflesh onto my body, nor could I make my teeth chatter, or my lips go slightly blue.

Luckily, Lau kept his seat, respecting Eric's 'ownership' of me. About forty-five minutes after we began playing, Eric took me down from the cross, holding me gently and covering me with a blanket. I huddled in his arms, as if seeking warmth, when the fact was I was sweaty, hot, and sore as hell! *Who would have thought a technique as simple as cupping a hand would make so much difference in the way a spanking felt! Who would have thought there was so much skill involved in the practice of BDSM?* I had always perceived BDSM to be extremely painful; tonight, it had been. The tears on my face were genuine, and I could see the pain in Eric's eyes while he murmured words of aftercare to me.

This is for Callie. Suck it up, buttercup! I told myself fiercely. So yeah, it hurt. No big deal. Now I knew the difference between a skilled Dominant and a wannabe, and the next time I played, after Callie was home safely, I could immediately stop the scene if the guy didn't know what he was doing.

Next time?!

Lau approached us before my mind could lock onto that thought. He shook Eric's hand amicably and smiled at me. "You are a lovely lady, Chloe, and I am a true aficionado of submissive beauty. You are welcome in my club any time you wish."

I murmured a quiet thank you and snuggled into Eric, pretending to zone out as the two men talked. Lau told Eric he was definitely interested in that export item he had for sale, and promised they would meet during the week to discuss the matter. Eric's voice was warm as he thanked Lau for his hospitality and the privilege of the private audience. As soon as Lau and his entourage left, Eric handed me my clothes, quickly helping me into the boots and corset.

"I want us at the bar right away," he whispered in my ear. "There's going to be a brownout and then a power loss. I need to be down in the basement right before the power outage."

We were sitting together at the sushi/saké bar. I had been nursing my Midori Sour for almost fifteen minutes before the power flickered once, causing everyone in the room to gasp slightly. A moment later, the lights dimmed, and Eric stood, held my seat, and escorted me in the dark to the ladies' room in the hallway between the kitchen and playroom.

"You stay in here," he told me. "If it goes as planned, I'll be back in twenty minutes."

I nodded at Eric, seeing the whites of his eyes and the light sheen of sweat on his forehead. They were the only indications I had, but I knew exactly what they meant. Something my father had told me, years ago, whispered in my mind: 'Honey, a hero ain't nothin' but a scared man who doesn't walk away.' Impulsively, I grabbed Eric and kissed him on the mouth, hard.

Eric
Reconnaissance

I left Hope, immediately putting her out of my mind as I strode toward the elevator. It had been two minutes, by my count; in another, the power would go out, making the elevator useless. I approached the hallway and flipped the button on the disguised jammer to temporarily block any signal Lau's security team should receive, then I hit the button calling the elevator to me. Luck was, so far, not my lady tonight. Instead of opening immediately, the elevator hummed, clearly coming down from the floor above at nursing-home speed. I slid into it, feeling the sweat begin to pool in the small of my back and on my palms. This was the first part of tonight's plan where we found out how good Jimmy Lau's security team was. If they had eyes on the elevator at all times, I was likely to have a welcome party when I hit the basement.

I flipped the switch on the money clip, turning off the jammer, and drew my weapon. The elevator stopped, and the doors just began to open when the power went out. My count was off by ten seconds, or the crew was antsy, and had jumped the gun. "Cutting it close," I muttered.

Luckily, I was able to pry the doors open far enough to squeeze through. Even luckier, there was no security crew standing in the pitch darkness, weapons leveled at me. I quickly pulled out the night vision goggles and low-light camera and began snapping shots, sweat dripping down my neck and back as each minute ticked by. I was quick, but careful, photographing the general layout first, then getting into more specific details with offices and conference rooms. I was running out of time when I hit the last room, and I almost bypassed it.

There were four filthy mattresses on the floor inside the room. Rumpled bedclothes and coarse blankets topped the beds and the smell of urine, feces, and vomit filled the room. I stepped inside, quickly snapping as many shots as possible. One mattress had the blanket pulled over onto the floor and it was only chance that made me look down. There were designs of some kind on the tile floor…what appeared to be letters. I didn't have time. I snapped the pictures as quickly as I could, and pulled my switchblade to take a scraping of the paint, wrapping it in my handkerchief. My hands were shaking now. It had been at least eighteen minutes. I covered the squiggles up, then headed back the way I had come at a brisk jog.

I was less than halfway to the elevator, when the lights flickered, then came on. I broke into a flat-out run and slammed my hand against the elevator button, sliding inside it just as the red light over the security

221

camera turned on. I hit the button for the first floor. If Lau's security team was up there, I was dead.

Hope scared the shit out of me, meeting me right outside the elevator door. "An alarm went off," she told me, as I left the car and dragged her to the other side of the hall. "It was silenced almost immediately."

The elevator began moving again, heading up.

We were in trouble.

"You need to go," I told her, my voice quiet but brooking no argument. "Get out of here, now. Here are the keys to the Vic—take them, and meet me back at the hotel."

The elevator stopped a floor above us, and then started down again. We both looked at it, watching the digital display change from two to one.

"Go!" I hissed.

"No time, Agent!" Hope replied. She pushed me against the wall so I faced the elevator. She dropped to her knees in front of me. To my utter astonishment, she yanked open the snaps of my leather pants and pulled my cock out, wrapping her hand and mouth expertly around it, as though she had been sucking on me for the past twenty minutes.

She swirled her tongue under the head of my penis, and I'll be damned if I didn't rise to the occasion! I was scared out of my mind, absolutely convinced Lau and his security team had me busted, but I was also quickly sporting a raging hard-on. I leaned back against the wall, wrapping my hands in her hair and tilting my head back, my eyes half closed.

That was how Jimmy Lau found us, when he and four of his goons stepped out of the elevator, guns drawn and aimed directly at us. I opened my eyes and straightened slightly, but otherwise gave no indication of concern. Lau looked at me for a long moment.

"What are you doing here, my friend?" he asked me, his voice soft and dangerous.

I tightened my hold in Hope's hair and tugged slightly. She released me and glanced around, her mouth gaping slightly as if she were just now noticing Lau and his goons. I took my time tucking myself back into my pants, making sure Lau and his team got the impression Chloe had been at her task for a while.

"I could ask you the same thing, Jimmy," I said. I helped Hope stand, and she stumbled convincingly, as if her foot had gone to sleep. One of Lau's goons stepped forward to help her, and I tightened my grip on her upper arm in an attempted warning. Hope gasped anyway, recognizing Dale.

"G-guns!" she covered quickly. "Sir Falcon!" Her voice held an edge of panic, perhaps a bit overdone, but it directed attention away from Dale, who was either Jimmy Lau's chief of security or, as I sincerely hoped, our spook.

"You're scaring her!" I snapped at Lau. He hesitated a bare moment, then nodded to his men. They lowered their weapons, and Dale returned to his position behind Lau, once Hope was upright beside me.

"What the hell's going on, Jimmy?" I asked, my voice irritated and snappish. "I wasn't expecting to have thirty minutes to cool my heels in the dark!"

Jimmy raised a hand in a conciliatory gesture, the apology not reaching his eyes. "Of course, of course, my friend," he said, with a cool smile. "It is just this is a restricted area unless you are accompanied by one of my security personnel, Falcon. I am having some…in-house problems."

The admission surprised me, and it let me know the

combination of our power outages and internet interrupts with whatever sabotage Dale—if he was our spook—was pulling off, was definitely working on Lau's nerves. He and his entourage were armed for bear…inside his own castle.

"Sir, I'd like to go home, please?" Hope's pleading words were almost whispered, and I had no difficulty at all seeing her as a terrified woman, one just a few words away from a loud, disruptive, hysterical meltdown. Lau sensed it, too, as he glanced over to Dale with a barely perceptible nod.

"Miss Anderson, I'm sure we can arrange something to make you feel more comfortable," Dale said, his voice soothing and his smile charming. "You need to let Mr. Lau apologize for scaring you, sweetheart. It's a matter of personal honor for him to compensate you in some manner. We have some beautiful private rooms upstairs, with large, built-in Jacuzzis and heated towels. I'll have Reynaldo send up some champagne and some of the sweetest chocolate covered strawberries you've ever tasted."

Hope frowned stubbornly, as if she were about to refuse the offer, and I shook my head slightly at her. She bit her lower lip indecisively, then gave a tremulous smile, and nodded at Dale. "That would be lovely, Sir," she said, her voice still betraying uncertainty. God, Hope was a consummate actress! Majyck couldn't have played this better! I watched Lau's men relax infinitesimally.

"Falcon, I will need your weapons," Lau said, his voice nonchalant. He knew I was carrying, and I knew he knew.

"Of course," I replied, and handed over the Glock from my shoulder holster with no qualms. I then pulled my pant leg up, removed the .22 from its holster and the

Tac Force switch from its hilt, handing them to Dale as well.

Lau glanced at Hope, who seemed oblivious for a moment. "Oh!" she exclaimed, then pulled the stiletto from her boot and held it toward Dale, blade first. I immediately grabbed her wrist, drawing a surprised gasp from her, and carefully removed the stiletto from her fingers, handing it to Dale in the appropriate manner. She didn't say anything, but her face turned bright red. I couldn't believe she had genuinely made the stupid error so I was burning with curiosity at what she was thinking of to make her blush that deeply. In any case, it was perfect. Dale took the blade, and Lau's crew relaxed the rest of the way. I was unarmed, and they were now completely certain the stupid white submissive girl would cut off her own fingers before being able to handle a blade. I smiled to myself; I knew they were seriously underestimating Hope.

She did not proffer the small razor lipstick tube from inside her corset, and they didn't search her.

Hope made stiff, polite small talk with Dale while we rode up in the elevator. Lau and the rest of his men continued searching the premises below for indications someone had infiltrated their security. I suspected either Jabroski or Vogel would be making a fast food run to hold them over for a night that was going to be longer than they'd expected.

As Dale showed us to our room, I watched for some kind of signal from him, some nuance or gesture that would let me know he had ID'd me as FBI, the same way I'd ID'd him as CIA. I was disappointed; Dale was strictly professional. For a moment, I wondered if I had miscalculated. If Dale were not the CIA mole I thought he was, Hope and I could be in deep trouble.

Hope
Deep Under

The moment Eric and I were alone, my fear vanished, and I began to enjoy myself, hamming it up in a way that would make my junior year Drama teacher proud. I was playing to the cameras now, not to twitchy Asian men with loaded guns in their hands.

I turned to Eric, throwing myself at him with a sob. Real tears rolled down my face. "Sir, they had *guns!*" I wailed, my voice quaking with terror. "Why did they point guns at us?!"

"Hush, Chloe," Eric replied, attempting to disengage me. I decided my clingy submissive character would cling, so I clung to Eric's neck as though my Oscar depended on it.

"Please, S-Sir, I want to go home," I hiccuped. "I don't w-want champagne and strawberries. Please, Sir, red, Sir, take me home, r-red, red!"

That got a reaction out of Eric. He held me close then, and half-carried me over to the bed, sitting me on his lap and soothing me with words and sweet caresses.

"It was only a misunderstanding, girl," he said, performing as much as I was. If this had been a dress rehearsal instead of the real deal, I would have burst out laughing. "I want you to get a grip, Chloe. Take some deep breaths and calm down. You're perfectly safe here, hon."

I took a few shuddering breaths, and slowly 'got a grip' on myself.

"I thought you said Mr. Lau wouldn't mind if I gave you a blowjob?" I asked, batting my eyes innocently. I noticed Eric's eyes narrow slightly, and decided I'd better cool it a bit.

"I told you, hon, it was a misunderstanding. Apparently, Mr. Lau is having some problems of his own right now. You can understand that, right? Sometimes you can't trust people, even when you think they're your friends? Like your girlfriend, Bitsy?"

Ohhh…so two could ad-lib. I nodded tearfully. "Bitsy's a bitch," I said, with a scowl.

"Right," Eric agreed. "It seems Mr. Lau is having some problems inside his circle right now, but that doesn't really impact us."

"I still want to go home, Sir." I pouted slightly.

Eric sighed. "Chloe, Mr. Lau is a very important business partner of mine, and I really don't want to be rude to him. We're close to making a deal for some important merchandise that is going to get me a lot of money, and is also going to improve my business relations with him. I want you to like Mr. Lau, and I want you to be able to come back here, and have a good time. He invited you, remember? He doesn't invite just anyone."

I deliberated, as if unconvinced, and Eric continued, "I'll take you home if you insist, girl, but I would really appreciate it if you would stay. For me."

I knew hell would freeze over before he said 'please,' so, tempting as it was to yank his chain, I nodded my acquiescence. "Yes, Sir," I said, "of course. For you."

"Good girl." Eric smiled at me and kissed me on the forehead. "Now, go check out that Jacuzzi tub and get it ready for us. I'll be right in."

I smiled, a doe-like expression of docility on my face that almost made Eric laugh out loud. I was quite pleased with myself; I couldn't imagine a single submissive in the Nashville munch group who could have pulled that off as well as I did.

I knew the moment I left the room, Eric would begin a quick, and obvious, search for hidden cameras. He would be sure to miss most of them, but would find at least one and somehow cover it, probably with an expression of smug satisfaction at beating Jimmy Lau at his own game. That, in turn, would give Lau and his security team the satisfaction of getting one over on their guests. We each believed we had the other where we wanted him.

I stepped out of the bathroom a moment later, practically glowing with pleasure. "Oh, Sir Falcon, this place is gorgeous," I gushed breathily. "Jimmy must be loaded!"

"Mr. Lau," Eric corrected me sternly. "Be respectful, girl. Mr. Lau is very wealthy, yes. And since you've been good tonight, we'll see about that Jacuzzi. Come take off my boots."

The champagne, heavy hors d'oeuvres, and chocolate-covered strawberries arrived a couple minutes later. I was actually hungry, which surprised me, so I dug in, nattering happily while we ate, apparently having forgotten all about the guns that had scared me enough to safe word earlier.

I could tell Eric was on edge when we went into the bathroom and stripped down for the whirlpool tub. He'd seen me naked several times, of course, but this was my first glimpse of the full monty. I was not disappointed! I know people say size doesn't matter, but to me, it mattered some. Not as much as sweetness, tenderness, and skill, but an extra-medium or larger cock, combined with someone who knew how to use it, made Hope a happy camper!

With no signs of arousal at all, Eric was showing at least four inches. That made me curious as hell. *How much would that cock grow when it was engorged with lust?* I felt an answering pull in my own body and a wetness between my legs; apparently, I wanted to find out!

Eric climbed down into the whirlpool tub first, offering his hand to steady me. The Jacuzzi could comfortably seat four, and I'd turned the temperature up slightly on my earlier foray, so it felt delicious. Eric hit the button to turn the bubbles up to maximum, then pulled me back against him, wrapping his arms around me, and putting his mouth close to my ear.

"We have a problem, Hope," he said. He was using my given name, so I knew he was counting on the noise of the whirlpool to mask any sound. He also moved his head slightly, so cameras would hopefully pick up nuzzling rather than talking. Accordingly, I leaned back into his embrace, half closing my eyes as if in pleasure.

"Mm, what's that?" I asked, barely moving my lips.

Eric turned his mouth directly to my ear, as though he were kissing my neck. "Lau is going to be watching on security cams. He's going to expect us to have sex, and he'll expect it to be rough. This isn't something I anticipated, and it's not something you signed up for."

I giggled, as though he'd just said something flirtatious, then moved around in the water so I was straddling Eric's lap, facing him this time. I was conscious of our skin-on-skin beneath the water, and I could tell Eric was becoming conscious of it, as well. It was my turn to nuzzle his neck. "I realized that earlier," I murmured, seriously. "I know how deadly this is, Eric. I'm not a virgin, and I trust you." I grinned, kissing him and grabbing his lower lip playfully between my teeth before moving back close to his ear. "Besides…I've always fantasized about being a porn star, haven't you? Kinda hot!" I teased. I burst out laughing, both to perform for the cameras, and so he knew I was jerking his chain. His eyes darkened in a promise of vengeance I thought I might enjoy.

A few minutes later, Eric hit the button of the Jacuzzi. The echoing silence in the bathroom was deafening, confirming it would have been next to impossible for Lau and his goons to have heard anything above the noise of the tub in full jetstream mode.

I stepped out of the tub first, appreciating the heated floors, and moved over to the warming rack for the towels. *I wouldn't object to a few million dollars to allow me such luxuries in my own bathroom,* I thought. I brought the huge bath towels over, wrapping one around myself for modesty sake *(hah!)* and submissively drying Eric with the other. He accepted the service as though he were a god, and I, a mere supplicant; there would be payback later.

***

In the bedroom, I spent the next hour and a half forgetting about Callie and all the rest of my worries. Eric made use of the hidden attachment points on the bed to tie me down, and then he proceeded to 'play' with me and awaken each of my senses, one-by-one. He spent a bit of time with every toy on his rack, and my body reveled in the contrast of sensation as he alternated sting, thud, scratchy, bunny soft, and needle sharp. He allowed me to drop, hard, and I was a quivering mass of gelatin when he finally released my wrists from the restraints. This time, though, he didn't cuddle me, as I had come to expect. He pulled me up to my knees, positioning my legs slightly apart. He made sure the pillows were situated comfortably beneath me, and then he got onto the bed behind me. I heard the sound of foil tearing, then Eric was slowly guiding himself into my wetness. My body spasmed around him almost immediately, and I exploded, seeing white stars behind my eyes from the power of that first orgasm. Once he stretched me, Eric withdrew almost all the way and then slammed back in! I screamed, as my vagina protested in delicious, delighted torment. It had been months since I'd had sex at all, but I hadn't had a man as large as Eric in...well, ever.

He set up a punishing rhythm, and I matched him thrust for thrust, mewling, and gasping, and crying out with every orgasm I had. My clitoris was a throbbing bundle of nerves, and with only an occasional flick of his forefinger and thumb, Eric was able to pull a climax both from my clit and deep, deep inside me. I sobbed with the ecstasy of the best orgasms I had ever had in my life...and it wasn't for the cameras.

I don't know how many times I came—I lost count at four—before Eric's breathing quickened, and he shuddered his release above me. I adjusted my legs, and he rolled over to lie beside me, his cock still buried inside, while the tears dried off my face.

"Thank you, Sir," I murmured, kissing his lips gently. I was drifting to sleep before the words were completely out of my mouth.

***

At 7:30 in the morning, Eric woke, and we went at it again, this time without the kinky foreplay. It was still delicious, powerfully orgasmic sex, and a feeling of languid satiety filled me, even as my fear for Callie ratcheted upward. At 8:00, there was a soft knock on the door. Eric got up, which surprised me, and came back with a tray of breakfast foods, including Bloody Marys and eggs hollandaise with spinach. Eric picked at his, but I devoured mine with enthusiasm.

"Mr. Lau is a very nice man!" I exclaimed, conscious of the cameras once again. "Thank you for talking me into staying, Sir. I'm sorry I was so upset last night. This place is beautiful—so swanky!"

I could have bitten my own tongue, but Eric didn't seem to notice the word I had used, so hopefully, Lau wouldn't either. Callie had been half drugged or drunk…she had called the room 'schwanky.' Sometimes, there were disadvantages to being so close; we thought alike, and that wasn't always a good thing.

We finished breakfast, and were ready to leave before nine. Jimmy Lau met us at the door, and, impulsively, I leaned over and kissed him on the cheek. I'm not sure if Eric or Lau was more surprised.

Eric
Closing In

Curiosity got the better of me, so I asked when we got into the Vic, "So? Kissing Lau?"

Hope looked at me levelly. "I kissed him like Judas kissed Christ," she said, "and now, I'm going to crucify him."

I whistled through my teeth as I took the Donovan Street exit. "Remind me not to piss you off."

***

We sat on the couch in my hotel room in Nashville, the laptop propped open between us. We had been looking at the same digital photos for twenty minutes or more. There were four single mattresses on the floor of the small room. The mattress furthest from the door had a blanket crumpled near it, and on the floor, apparently written in blood, were some letters and numbers.

"It's not a phone number," Hope muttered, yet

again.

"No, not one that makes any sense, anyway."

I had done a reverse lookup on the number and had found an insurance company in Las Vegas, a title company in Jersey, and a restaurant in Washington, D.C. Nothing tied into Lau, directly or indirectly

"It has to mean something! Callie wouldn't have written it if it didn't mean something!"

"Hope," I cautioned, "we don't know if it's Callie's blood. I'll overnight the sample as soon as the post office opens, but the lab won't have DNA results for at least two weeks, and that's for a high priority rush. Don't get your hopes up, hon."

She glared at me stubbornly. "Doesn't matter. It's her handwriting. I *know* Callie's handwriting."

The image had been cut off on the left-hand corner, and it was a bit grainy due to the low resolution, but what we could see was clear enough:

opeless

729*0100

We had already determined—to Hope's satisfaction, at least—that the partial word 'Hopeless' was a direct reference to her, but the numbers had been baffling us for a while. "If it's not a telephone number, what else could it be?" I thought aloud. I stared at the numbers, wracking my brain, frustration welling inside me. We were so close! I was missing something, something simple. I looked at Hope, trying to recall everything in Callahan's file in an attempt to make sense of the numbers. "Was Callie's dad in the military?" I asked.

"Air Force," she said. "Why?"

We both looked at the numbers again, and finally it

clicked into place. 729 could be 7/29 – July 29. If so, then 0100 was 1:00 a.m.

"That could be it," I said, "but what does it *mean?"*

"Helicopter!" Hope snapped abruptly, pointing to the asterisk. "Whirly-bird, chopper blades. It's what she would draw to symbolize a helicopter, Sir! I know she would!"

I considered it, nodding slowly. "The 29th is Tuesday," I said. "That gives us today and tomorrow to figure out where the helipad is, and how to access it. I'll bet a week's pay it's right on Lau's fucking rooftop!"

"The club has a helipad?" she asked.

"No, but Lau's residence does, according to the city inspector's blueprints. I'm calling this in, Hope. Even if the blood isn't Callahan's, as long as it's human, we've got probable cause. It'll be enough to get us warrants for Lau's residence and the Sandmarian. We may actually nail this son-of-a-bitch!"

It was Sunday morning, but I called ASAC Zewicke at his Knoxville home without a qualm of conscience. I explained what we had discovered, emailed copies of the photos to him, and sat on my thumbs waiting for the green light.

Forty minutes later, Zewicke called back. He had authorized the arrest, with the caveat I was to be nowhere near the site. Just in case the whole thing went south, Zewicke explained, he wanted my cover kept intact. I didn't like it, but his reasoning was righteous, so I agreed to sit it out. As though I had a choice in the matter.

Zewicke told me he had already called Judge Hoyt for the warrants, and he would assemble teams to go in for the bust in just a few hours. It was all going down this afternoon.

Hope and I sat around the hotel room, waiting. She made a few phone calls—to her supervisor, to request another few days off from work, and to Rory, although I requested she not give him any specific updates yet. After that, she read a novel on her Kindle, while I worked on paperwork from some of my other cases. And we waited.

The minutes crept by. We ordered lunch, then dinner. Still there was nothing. I called my daughter, as I did every Sunday evening, and Hope checked in with her neighbor to ensure Mr. Wuzzles' continued existence.

Finally, the call came in, at just after 7:30 that evening. Jabby sounded exhausted.

"Hey, Grayson. It was a bust."

My stomach sank. "What do you mean, a bust?" I demanded. "You got the warrants, right? You had teams at Lau's home and at the club?"

"Yeah, man, but he came up clean. There was no evidence of trafficking, or any kind of violation at all—hell, we couldn't even find marijuana on any of his employees!"

"How did it go down?" I asked, my voice bitter with disappointment. "Did the teams go in concurrently, or hit his residence first?"

I heard the shuffling of papers, then Jabby came back on the line. "No, it looks like Metro went into the club first. Our guys hit Lau's front door about twenty minutes later."

I swore viciously. Someone, either in Metro or in the Bureau itself, was dirty as hell. Twenty minutes would have been plenty of time to relocate four young women, and it was nineteen and a half minutes of unacceptable fuck up! Hanging unsaid was the fact that, other than my ASAC and the crews he assembled, Vogel and Jabroski would have been the only team knowing when the bust was scheduled to go down.

"You know this wasn't us, right?" Jabby asked, a bit defensively. "We're good, right, man?"

"Yeah, we're good," I said heavily. "Zewicke will have questions, I'm sure."

"We'll try to have answers," Jabroski said, and rung off.

I stared at my phone for a long moment while Hope hovered nearby, her face reflecting my own discouragement. I couldn't imagine either of the tech heads signaling Metro prematurely, so it had to have been someone on Zewicke's team. *But, who? And how the fuck were we going to flush the rat in time to save Callahan and, presumably, the three other women targeted for export to China?*

"God fucking dammit!" I swore. Hope came up behind me and began rubbing the tension from my shoulders. I should have stopped her, but her hands felt good, easing muscles that had been on high alert all day long.

"What now?" she asked despondently.

I shook my head. "I honestly don't—" I began.

My cell phone rang.

I glanced at the caller ID and my heart jumped. I held my hand up in warning to Hope. She immediately backed away from my shoulders, which was a shame, and sat as still as possible.

"Jimmy!" I greeted, with heartiness I didn't feel. "What's up, *lǎoshī?*"

"Falcon, I can't speak long. I'm having security issues, and I am not certain this line is safe," Lau said, his Cajun accent notably absent under the stress in his tone. "I wanted to enquire about our arrangement."

I was genuinely puzzled. "Our arrangement?"

"Yes. That exquisite piece of merchandise you showed me yesterday. I presume you still wish to sell it?"

I hesitated a moment, my mind working feverishly. Zewicke didn't know anything about my involvement with Hope over the past week, and I wasn't authorized to negotiate anything with the perp. *Still…I never really had been, had I?* "Uh, yeah, about that," I said, feigning reluctance. "That item turned out to be more valuable than I thought, Jimmy. I'm not sure I want to sell it after all."

Jimmy's voice cooled. "I understand, Falcon. I do have a shipment of exports leaving the country, however, so I will need to know your decision very soon."

"Sure. I'll give it serious consideration."

"It is a great deal of money, my friend."

"Yes, it is." I paused a long moment, as if considering carefully. "I also know selling you that piece for your collection will win me some good faith with you. That's very important to me, as well."

After a moment of silence, Lau said, "Perhaps you can show me the piece again, and I can inspect it more closely? I could…potentially…increase my offering price."

That was the opening I needed. I could set up an inspection and potential buy with Lau, but I would still have time to bring Zewicke up to speed and get backup teams in place…presuming we could ferret out the rat in our nest or keep our operation completely dark until the moment of Lau's arrest.

"Sure, Jimmy. It would be my pleasure. How about I bring it by your club Wednesday night?" I smiled inwardly at the silence on the other end of the line. This is where we got confirmation to show if we had been correct in our interpretation of Callie's cipher. Apparently, we had.

"I am afraid I'm leaving town for a business trip late Tuesday night, my friend," Lau said to me. "Perhaps we could meet at the club before my flight departs—say, ten o'clock?"

I grinned and gave Hope a thumb's up. "That sounds fine, Jimmy. Ten o'clock Tuesday night. I'll see you then."

I hung up, accepting Hope's delighted squeal and warm hug with pleasure. I considered whether to call ASAC Zewicke and decided against it, figuring this meeting would require suit, tie, and a face-to-face ass-kissing. *Son of a motherless goat!* We were back in business.

Hope
The Call

The meeting in Knoxville with Eric's supervisor didn't go as badly as I'd anticipated. Of course, I spent forty-five minutes cooling my heels in a waiting room with Anne Bishop's novel to keep me company while Eric, presumably, got chewed a new asshole by a very unhappy Assistant Special Agent in Charge. When I was ushered in to meet said Assistant Special Agent, everything was cool, calm, and professional. He wasted a good twenty minutes of my time trying to talk me out of my involvement in Callie's case, finally giving up on that account and producing indemnification documents for me to sign, as well as a subcontractor's contract. I think he was surprised at both my stubbornness and my knowledge of the very thin line of my own legal rights. Eric looked smug a few times during our 'discussion,' and the ASAC shot him a glare or two when he thought

I wasn't paying attention. I was certain Eric had minimized my ability to be a prodigious pain in the ass.

One thing the ASAC was absolutely unbending about was that I would not be permitted anywhere near the Sandmarian Gardens on the Tuesday night of Lau's arrest. An officer from Nashville Metro P.D. would be assigned for my protection, and if I attempted to leave our hotel room, I was to be detained for my own safety and for obstruction of justice. I liked ASAC Zewicke *much* less than I liked Special Agent Grayson, but, having little choice, I agreed to his draconian terms.

We got back to Nashville and went out to dinner, which I could barely touch. If all went well, Callie would be home safely in only two days! I spent a lot of my time praying and worrying. By the time Eric and I arrived at his hotel room, I was spazzing out. I seriously considered taking a sleeping pill just to knock myself out.

"Come here, girl," Eric said to me. I came to him automatically, and he reached out, taking my hand. "You're on pins and needles tonight. Do you want to play, to take the edge off?"

I blinked in surprise. His offer was unexpected…but, surprisingly, not unwelcome. The rush of endorphins *would* take the edge off, I realized with a start. It would be as calming as any sedative I could think of. But…it was no longer necessary for the case. If I played with Eric now, it would be because…I wanted to.

I nodded slowly. "Yes, Sir. Please," I almost whispered.

Eric smiled, and we made the preparations. He brought the ten-speed bicycle down and dimmed the lights while I set up the toy rack and turned on the CD player. In less than a week, it had become a routine … a

241

comfortable routine.

Several hours later, Eric was hot and sweaty, content in whatever 'Topspace' made it worthwhile for a Dom to work so hard to bring a submissive pleasure. I was flying high. He had outdone himself, and I was absolutely stoned on the epinephrine, serotonin, and opioid peptides floating through my bloodstream. I wasn't quite ready for aftercare, yet, though. Eric pulled the blanket over us, and I scooted under it, finding the zipper of his slacks.

"It isn't necessary, Hope," he said, and then, he didn't say anything for several minutes. Before he could come in my mouth, he pulled away from me and flipped me onto my back, eliciting a yelp of pain, which he ignored. He ripped open the condom and put it on, pushing into me less gently than he had at Lau's club. I rose to meet him with every thrust. *Yes! This is what I wanted!* I had orgasm after orgasm, and the pleasure washed over me as the endorphins flowed through me. By the time Eric reached his climax, I was completely spent, and sleep claimed me where I lay. Eric removed my restraints and his clothes, and we slept entwined in each other's arms, each of us seeking and giving comfort.

***

The following day—D-Day—alternately dragged and flew by.

My babysitter, Officer Reanne Michaels, arrived promptly at 8:00 p.m. Eric didn't know her, but she seemed pleasant enough, and she had even brought a deck of cards, inviting me to the distraction of gin rummy. I played, losing more hands than I should have because I was a bundle of nerves. Eric left shortly after 9:00, needing extra time to swing by the communications van to pick up his wire. That was when the call came in.

I jumped, gasping for air, my heart pounding in my throat as the strands of the *Pink Panther* melody sounded in the hotel room. That was Callie's ring tone—it was ONLY Callie's ring tone!

I knocked the chair back from the table in my haste to get to my phone, eliciting an expression of concern from Officer Michaels. I ignored her and pushed the talk button.

"Callie?" I asked eagerly. My heart sank, as a crisp, professional, male voice responded.

"With whom am I speaking, please?"

"Who are *you,* and how do you have this cell phone?" I snapped back, gesturing wildly for Officer Michaels to come listen. She moved over immediately, and I tilted the phone so she could hear as well.

"This is Sgt. Joshua Brooks with the Chatham Hills Police Department. Again, who am I speaking with, please?"

No wonder his voice had sounded familiar. "It's Hope Pendleton, Sergeant," I said, feeling despair sink into my stomach. "Why do you have Callie's cell phone?"

There was a long, anxious moment of silence.

Brooks finally cleared his throat. "Miss Pendleton. Officer Michaels from Nashville Metro is there with you now, isn't she?"

"Yes," I snapped. "Please tell me how you found Callie's cell phone!"

"I'm sorry to inform you, Miss Pendleton…this telephone was among the personal effects found on a young woman's body. She was brought in to Nashville Metro tonight. Since I'm the lead investigator on this case, I was called in. I'm here at Metro now. Your number was the last number dialed on this cell phone."

243

I sank to my knees on the carpet, ignoring Officer Michaels' expression of concern. "No," I whispered. "Is it…was the body…?"

"The victim appears to resemble your friend," Detective Brooks said, his voice extremely gentle. "We don't know for certain, since she had no identification on her. Could you please have Officer Michaels bring you to the station? I am sorry to ask, ma'am, but … I need you to identify the body."

My stomach lurched and bile came up my throat. I swallowed convulsively, ignoring both the burn of acid in my throat and the burn of tears behind my eyes. I stared at the carpet for a long moment, numbed by shock. I couldn't—wouldn't—believe this. It had to be a mistake.

"Miss Pendleton?" Brooks asked again.

"Yes. I-I'll be there as quickly as I can," I replied, and rang off. I sat there for another moment, while Officer Michaels looked at me sympathetically. Then I scrolled through my contacts until I found Eric's number. I saw Michaels glance at her watch as the call went to voicemail.

"It's Hope," I said, my voice breaking a little. "Sgt. Brooks just called. They think they've found Callie, Eric. I need to go down to Nashville Metro to…to identify her. Please…get that bastard!"

It was a good thing Officer Michaels was there to drive—I remembered absolutely nothing about the twenty-minute trip from the hotel to the precinct house. I followed Officer Michaels through the metal detector and signed my name on the visitor registration, all on automatic pilot.

Sgt. Brooks met us outside an office, his dark eyes bright with sympathy.

This is not happening.

We boarded the elevator, and Brooks pressed the 'down' button while that thought ran through my head like a scratched record. We stepped out into the hallway.

This is not happening.

This is not happening.

This is not happening.

I mouthed the words silently, my lips barely moving, one word for each step I took, one for each breath. The hallway was institutional, harshly lit and silent, except for the slight squeak of my sneakers and the solid, measured steps of the man beside me. He was wearing boots. Not cowboy boots…motorcycle boots, with harness straps. They were black, slightly creased, but shiny and clean. His gray dress slacks covered most of them, but I'd been looking down, staring at my own feet and his as we walked down the long hallway.

This is not happening.

We were in the basement of the building, just like they show on television. The silence echoed around me, pressing in on me, threatening to take the air from my lungs. I glanced up once, to see how much further the hallway went on, and the fluorescent light fixture above me spun dizzily in my peripheral vision. I breathed in and I breathed out, and then again, concentrating on the simple act as if my life depended on it.

This is not happening.

We stopped in the middle of the hallway, in front of a long window, and he tapped lightly on the glass. I paid attention to my breathing, and I stared at my shoes, noticing the scuff of reddish mud on my left sneaker. I heard a noise on the other side of the glass, and my eyes shot up of their own accord. My heartbeat accelerated and my breathing quickened, the fluorescents hazy in my eyes from the sudden tears blurring my vision.

I was relieved we weren't going inside the room...ashamed of my sense of relief, but relieved anyway. There was a gurney on the other side of the window, close enough I could have reached through the glass and touched the motionless form of the woman under the green hospital sheet. I felt myself shaking violently, and the bile in my stomach soured, threatening to rise. I felt the man waiting for me, and I didn't know why. Finally, I nodded once, sharply, lying to tell him I was ready.

Inside the room, the morgue attendant in surgical scrubs carefully folded the sheet down off the woman's face, uncovering her to below her neck. His movements were precise but respectful, and he smoothed the sheet neatly before stepping away from her. She was beautiful...or she had been. She had short, curly red hair, smooth features, full, bloodless blue lips...and she was so very pale.

I didn't realize I was holding my breath. I heard the man's voice from far away, gentle, but insistent. "Miss Pendleton? Is this your friend?"

The tears spilled over, and the window swam in front of me. I shook my head, almost sick with relief. "No. It isn't her," I said.

I gasped, the sudden sharp prick of a needle in my arm surprising me out of my stupor.

"What the hell?!" I asked Brooks, then looked stupidly at the needle in Officer Michaels' hand. She looked back at me, then quickly lowered her eyes, her face flushing with shame. My knees turned to gelatin, and the man with the gray suit and the motorcycle boots caught me, as the institutional tile floor suddenly came up to meet my face.

246

Eric
The Basement

We went in fast and hard. I knew in my gut the girls had been moved into that little basement room beneath the Sandmarian Gardens, where they were now awaiting transport by vehicle to Lau's mansion home, to be airlifted from his helipad to god-only-knew where. It would be the first leg of a very long flight to China.

For once, my gut was wrong. The room that had housed the four women was just as empty as it had been the first night I'd found it. In fact, it was identical in every way...save two; someone had stripped the mattresses completely of linens, and someone had scrubbed the floor where the message had been written in blood. The smell of bleach was strong in the air, guaranteeing no more DNA evidence would be collected from this site.

I walked back into the main area of the basement, where about seven of Lau's security guards sat zip-tied under Jim Hunter's watch. I looked for Dale, not seeing him among the group. Cops and Feds were crawling all over the security center, and I knew Jabby and Vogel would be in geek nirvana soon enough. I glanced at my cell for a time check, noticed the call from Hope, and punched up voicemail while half listening to a conversation between my ASAC and another agent.

"It's Hope," she said, her voice sounding small and broken. I immediately went on full alert as she continued. "Sgt. Brooks just called. They think they've found Callie, Eric. I need to go down to Nashville Metro to…to identify her. Please…get that bastard!"

I hung up, my brow furrowing in puzzlement. *Why was Brooks calling her from Metro, when he should be in Chatham Hills?* I listened to the message again—yes, Hope had definitely said Metro, not the Chatham Hills PD. I shrugged mentally, resolving to get back to the question later.

From the other side of the basement, Officer Morrow shouted, "Over here!"

I ran, with half a dozen cops ahead of me.

"Good work, man," I told the patrolman, who pointed out the barely-visible door concealed in the wall to the north side of the basement. At a nod from ASAC Zewicke, two SWAT officers used the battering ram and, after two solid *thwumps!* the door was smashed open.

It opened into a long corridor. It was a fucking underground tunnel with concrete floors and fluorescent lighting. *Son of a motherless goat!*

I started to step into the tunnel, then froze, holding my hand up to stop the uniform next to me. The woman's foot was an inch away from…

I bent down and picked up the small gold crucifix. All of the blood rushed to my brain, my pulse pounding

248

in my ears, as I put two and two together. I knew that necklace!

"Sgt. Brooks with Chatham Hills P.D. is the mole!" I snapped to ASAC Zewicke. He looked at me in surprise, and I held up the necklace. "This belongs—"

Far down the tunnel, a woman screamed...and, an instant later, there was a gunshot. *Fuck procedure!*

Gerard
Exit

I was getting desperate. Lau had told me that afternoon he was leaving the country with the shipment of girls for an extended visit to China. Won Lei, his second, would be in charge of operations for the months he would be gone, and I would receive my instructions directly from him, as if from Lau himself.

I sat in the security booth, tapping my fingers anxiously on the top of the desk, only occasionally glancing up at the monitors. *What the hell was I going to do?* I was no closer to getting the incriminating thumb drive than I had been four years ago! All the time we had spent, all the funds and training the CIA had wrapped up in this, all my personal time and effort would be for nothing, if I didn't get that drive. Lau himself was secondary at this point; it would be nice to bust him, nicer to put him down, but getting the hierarchy of his entire operation took precedence.

The problem was, I didn't have the opportunity to do either. I was desperate enough to attempt the pickpocket, if I could only get the son-of-a-bitch alone.

I glanced up at the monitors, then looked more closely at number eleven. A female cop in uniform and a male cop in a suit were approaching Lau's office. Between them, they supported a semi-conscious woman, who was stumbling as much as walking. I watched closely. I'd seen any number of women in the same state after being given a dose of Meier's cocktail, so I knew this was the replacement for the little Hispanic girl who had died.

They stopped outside Lau's office, and the girl lifted her head slightly, giving me my first clear view of her face. *Oh, shit!* It was Chloe.

Lau's thug came to the office door at the cop's knock, and a moment later, Lau himself stepped out into the corridor. There was conversation I couldn't hear, and evident pleasure on Lau's face. Lau nodded, and the two cops walked away, leaving Chloe with the Red Pole Enforcer and his guard. I swore bitterly.

Chloe was the new FBI agent my superiors had told me would be entering the field. I was certain of it now. Her fieldwork was adequate, but sloppy. She had penetrated the munch group, a good first step, but then she had moved much too quickly, securing Falcon as a Dom and gaining entrance to Lau's inner circle in the first pass. Now, she was likely to die for it.

It killed me, not just because Chloe was a fellow law enforcement officer, but because I genuinely liked the girl. She was funny and sweet, with a charming blend of world-weariness and naiveté, and she had projected the role of 'newbie submissive' well. I knew the mission

251

came first, above all else…but I resolved to help her, if I could.

I watched as Lau and his thug brought the girl down the corridor toward the elevator. I switched to camera four and watched them disembark, then enter the hallway outside the security booth. I stood, opening the door for them as they arrived.

"Ah, good, you're here," Lau said, by way of greeting.

"Yes, sir. How can I help?"

"This one needs to go with the others, out to the helipad. I will accompany you." Lau turned to his guard, issuing rapid-fire instructions in Chinese. The guard responded, then left, presumably to follow whatever orders Lau had given.

At that moment, Chloe collapsed against Lau, who stepped back with an expression of annoyance.

"They gave her too much, the incompetent fools!" Lau hissed. "Carry her."

"Yes, sir," I replied, and easily picked the girl up. My heart rose, excitement building in my chest. He had dismissed his bodyguard, and I was to carry Chloe to the chopper. That meant I had three-quarters of a mile in an isolated tunnel with Lau, unescorted. It was the perfect opportunity to make my move—it would be the *only* opportunity.

We went to the hidden doorway on the far side of the basement, and Lau tapped the buried access panel in the appropriate places. The door swung open, and we stepped inside the tunnel, which led from the basement of Lau's club to the rooftop of a small warehouse he owned, less than a mile away. The tunnel rose at a steady incline, making it realistic I would be exerting myself carrying Chloe. I breathed heavily, playing it up. It wasn't enough to make him suspicious, but it would be enough to give verisimilitude to my plan.

I watched Lau carefully as we walked. His shoulders were tight, his gait stiff. He was on guard. *I would give him a minute or two*, I decided, walking slightly behind him as he continued up the incline. As I'd hoped, once we were well on our way, Lau began to relax. He chatted with me about operations, giving additional instructions. I kept my answers brief, as though conserving my breath. In truth, Chloe was barely heavy enough for me to notice, as pumped up as I was on adrenaline. Lau didn't know that, though.

About three hundred feet from the exit, I made my move. I groaned, as if in pain, and stopped walking. I set Chloe on her feet, holding her to keep the semi-conscious woman from falling. I hoped she was just playing her part well.

"Sir...I need just a minute, please. She's heavier than she looks."

Lau scowled. "We have no time for this," he told me briskly. "I will carry her the rest of the way."

Shit! That wasn't what I had planned.

Improvising, I agreed, but then mis-stepped directly in front of Lau, colliding with him as he reached to scoop the girl up. Chloe slid to the ground, and Lau glared at me, his eyes cold. In that instant, seeing the cruelty in his eyes, I changed my mind. The girl was just as important as the operation itself. I had just lifted the thumb drive, but I wanted Chloe, too.

I attacked.

I was a trained martial artist, but Lao was, too. Within the narrow hallway, though, neither of us could gain position, and the fight quickly devolved into a fistfight, both of us on the ground punching at each other, each trying to gain the advantage. A few things

253

happened very quickly. There was a thunderous explosion in the hallway. Chloe's eyes widened in a moment of clarity and terror, and she screamed. I felt my throat being ripped out, and I lost my hold on Lau, bringing my hand up to my neck, surprised to find warm, red blood suddenly pumping between my fingers.

Lau, breathing heavily from exertion, stood above me, straightening his jacket and replacing his gun into his shoulder holster. "*Die*, traitorous pig!" he spat. I realized I was going to do just that, and I felt a moment of despair when he picked the girl up and hurried away.

***

Jimmy Lau carried Chloe out to the rooftop where the helicopter waited. Four members of his security team stood in position, and one of them came to help him maneuver the woman into the back of the helicopter, placing her on the seat next to the pale white girl with red hair. As an afterthought, Lau gave an order, and the security man handcuffed the two girls together.

Smiling in satisfaction, Lau settled into the co-pilot's seat and nodded approval. As he buckled up, the pilot began flicking switches, and the slow *thwap-thwap-thwap!* of the rotors began picking up speed.

Lau patted his own suit jacket, as if to reassure himself. An expression of panic, then fury, crossed his face, and he shouted in Chinese to his pilot. The man immediately stopped takeoff preparations, and Lau unbuckled, jumping from the helicopter and storming back to the door from which he'd just emerged. Seeing the anger on his face, one of his security team quickly stepped away.

The Asian businessman jogged through the tunnel, knowing the corpse of the filthy American traitor was only a few hundred feet in.

***

I heard him coming, which surprised me, since my own pulse was pounding so loud in my ears. He had missed the thumb drive, after all. My vision was blurring, and cold was beginning to seep through my body. I was keeping direct pressure on the wound, but it was taking every ounce of my willpower to hold it there and still hold the pistol steady. Cold was spreading through my body faster, and I knew, with aching certainty, that all I needed to do was let go...that's all, just let go. The cold would vanish. It would be replaced by warmth and love so strong, I would never feel pain again. I wanted that. I ached for it. I was so, so tired! But...I still had something to finish.

I saw him then, and my finger gently squeezed the trigger. The gun jerked in my hand as the shot echoed, and Jimmy Lau staggered, hit in the abdomen. I had only grazed him, the bullet barely shifting his jacket to the side. I shot again, and this time he spun around hard, taking the shot in the shoulder-joint. He didn't fall, though, and I didn't have it in me to try again. It was too hard to hold the gun from where I was lying.

In the distance, I heard the continued sound of helicopter blades, but then, from a completely opposite direction, I heard several loud 'thumps.' They came from the other end of the tunnel, far, far back. Lau heard them, too, and indecision showed on his face. He looked at me with utter hatred, as he assessed his odds. I smiled calmly at him, as I felt the coldness cover more of my body. I knew the cavalry was coming. I also knew they wouldn't be there soon enough.

With a snarled curse, Lau turned, and staggered

away. I let the gun fall from my fingertips and moved my hand slowly, each moment agony, reaching for the thumb drive in my pocket.

Eric
Red Door

I pulled my weapon and tore down the tunnel. Other cops ran on my heels, some of them with guns drawn. There were only a few side doors, and I bypassed them, leaving the others to investigate as I ran full-out toward the sound of that scream. It had sounded like Hope. Panic pressed in on me from all sides, feelings swirling in my mind so rapidly I couldn't distinguish one from another. This was Majyck, all over again; I was going to be too late. Pain and grief threatened to overwhelm me, and I forced the thoughts away. I didn't have time. I had never had time. Still running, my feet pounding the concrete, I felt a new fear pressing in on me…fear for myself. For who I would become, if I lost Hope.

Hargrave and Johnson veered off into another of the side rooms, their pistols out. I was now the officer in the lead, and I was well ahead of the others in the pack.

257

Sweat poured from my body, and I pushed myself to go faster, running hard toward the end of the tunnel. I couldn't even hear the footsteps of my backup behind me.

It had finally clicked inside my brain. Joshua Brooks was our mole, the rat who was feeding information to Lau. Dana Rouchard was the one who supplied him with potential girls, after learning from her therapy sessions the girls were relatively alone in the world. I was certain of it now, just as I was certain that scream hadn't been Callahan or one of the others. It had been Hope.

I rounded a corner, barely slowing down. I slipped in blood and stumbled over a body, cursing as I lost my footing and fell. The blood was still warm…and it was still pumping from the wound in Dale's neck. His hand held direct pressure on the wound, but his eyes were already becoming glassy.

"Dale, stay with me," I said, torn. "Come on, man, there's help on the way! People are right behind me, buddy; you're gonna be fine!"

Dale shook his head with a weak smile, wincing at the movement. He knew I was lying. "No time," he rasped, then tried again. "CIA. Tell Transnational…Red Door failed. Agent Gerard down. Give…" He stopped, his eyes filling with pain as I took the bloody thumb drive he held out to me. A coughing fit hit him, and blood pulsed through his fingers. He only had seconds.

"Hang on, Dale," I whispered, and even I could hear the fear in my voice.

He shook his head, and blood and spittle flecked his face as he spoke. "Get…Lau. Put him…down. Tell Tracy I'm one…of the infinite. Tell her."

"I have it, soldier," I lied without a qualm. "I got this, buddy."

His lips turned up slightly as he nodded. His eyes glazed over and locked in place. He was gone.

I didn't have the time to give him. I could hear footsteps approaching quickly, but no longer running. They would take care of Dale.

I jumped up, slipping once more in the copious amount of blood, and took off at a careful trot so I wouldn't fall on my ass again. If I had been running flat-out, I would have missed him completely.

As it was, I heard a slight chuffing sound in one of the side rooms beside me and I turned, weapon ready. Jimmy Lau had been shot, but he was still on his feet. The blood along the left side of his abdomen was minimal; he'd only been grazed. The bullet lodged in his right shoulder was more of a problem. Must have hurt like a bitch. It also made it difficult for him to move that arm to raise his gun on me.

"Falcon!" Lau chuckled. "I told Brooks it was you, not Gerard. It looks like you were both working against me. It is no matter now. Are you ready to die, my friend?"

Lau tried to raise his arm, then looked down at the gun in his hand, surprise registering on his face. His muscles had locked up, and he couldn't raise his arm to fire. For just an instant, he was alarmed; then he smiled congenially. "Or perhaps this is where you read me my rights, Special Agent?"

I smiled back. "I don't have time," I replied. I gave him half a second to digest that, and double-tapped him.

The shots were clean, even if the shooting wasn't. I didn't have a single fuck to give.

I ran past Lau's falling corpse, racing toward the sound of a chopper lifting off of a rooftop. The sound was so close! I took stairs three at a time, knowing in my gut I was, once again, too late. The bust had triggered whatever failsafe had been activated, and they had lifted off. They were taking Hope!

Hope
Chopper

I saw Callie. She was right next to me, and we were holding hands. *How sweet was that?* We hadn't held hands since high school. The pretty matching bracelets we wore were…handcuffs. My left wrist was cuffed to Callie's right. That was odd. Something about it was unsettling.

I struggled through the comfortable daze of the drug Officer Michaels had given me, fighting hard against the feeling of contented stupor threatening to overwhelm me. I'd found Callie, just like I wanted, and now we were together. *I had everything I had been searching for, so why was I upset? Why didn't I just relax and enjoy the mellow sensations racing through me?*

I was somewhere very loud…a helicopter…and I was sitting beside Callie. I wasn't seat-belted in, though, and that concerned me. It wasn't safe. I always wore my seat belt. I grappled with the unfamiliar contraption before the thought drifted away.

There was a rhythmic whumping sound and a whine. Those sounds meant danger, and somehow that penetrated even through the warmth and euphoria of whatever drug was making me feel so good. Maybe I could just rest. It felt so warm and good. I could just rest for a minute or two, is all…

The door opposite the pilot was wide open, and spotlights shone, making the rooftop as bright as a stadium. We were waiting for someone, and the pilot was becoming angry about it. He kept shouting into his headset. I didn't like that he was angry, but I wasn't sure how to reassure him. Everything would be okay; it always was.

He was cranky because of Lau, of course. Lau had been sitting in the passenger seat earlier, and he'd been such a gentleman, getting out of his seat so they could put me in behind him, smiling so warmly at me. He had left then, and the pilot had shouted for him to return. I didn't like Lau very much…but I couldn't remember why.

I was in danger, and Callie…

Callie didn't look so good. Her hair was damp and sweaty, plastered to her forehead, and her lips were lined with white. There were two girls behind us in the helicopter who also slept. *Maybe they were having good dreams?* Callie wasn't; her face was twisted in pain, just as I had seen when the cops came and told us her parents had died. She'd been only seventeen when that happened, and except for me, she had been alone in the world.

I frowned. Callie needed me. We were in danger, and I was the only one who knew it. Lau and his pilot were going to leave. They were planning to go, and to take us with them.

I promise...you don't want him to move her out of Nashville...

I slid forward in my seat, glad the cuff that held me to Callie didn't limit me as much as it would have if they had cuffed my right wrist.

The pilot screamed into his radio again, startling me and making me think he had discovered my treachery. He pulled some buttons and pressed a lever, and the whine inside the helicopter intensified. We were lifting off. That was bad.

The pilot shouted in Chinese, his words more frantic by the second. I removed the lipstick tube from my bra and twisted it clumsily, using only my right hand. I had done this a time or two in a nightclub, but, for some reason, it was much harder now. *'Drunken Application of Cosmetics' should be a required course in every High School.* The thought made me giggle, but then it slipped away. *Wait...what was I doing? I was doing something important, and I forgot.* The helicopter pitched beneath me, and I remembered.

One chance, I thought, as the *whoosh-whoosh-whoosh* of the helicopter blades grew louder, almost deafening. I felt the chopper lurch abruptly; it was lifting!

I lunged for the man's throat, slashing with the razor-sharp blade, dragging it hard across the side of his neck. Warm blood spurted generously over my hands, splashing and spraying all over the flight controls, and the pilot's Chinese screams turned to panicked gurgles. I heard gunshots booming in the cockpit of the vehicle, and the pilot jerked and spasmed, then drooped to one side.

The rooftop was full of cops now, multiple people

263

jumping onto the landing skids of the helicopter, and Eric was the first one. *Eric! I was so happy to see him!* The machine landed hard on the rooftop, and somebody killed the engine. In the sudden silence, I concentrated very carefully and put my lipstick away, tucking it as far under my right breast as it could go. Then, I rested my head against Callie's knee…but only for a second.

Hope
Recovery

The rest of what happened on the rooftop was a confused mishmash of images, sounds, and pain. At some point, the EMTs were allowed in and they swarmed the helicopter like bees returning to a hive. Callie, the two women I didn't know, and I received stabilizing treatment, and they took me to Saint Thomas Midtown, where I spent several hours with a vicious migraine, courtesy of the illicit drug I'd been given. Eric told me both Sgt. Brooks and Officer Michaels had been taken into custody; I would be expected to testify against them.

By Wednesday afternoon, I was able to visit Callie. She had been moved from ICU to a private room, but she still looked like death warmed over. I was overjoyed to see her, though, and we both sobbed hysterically while I held her, alternately telling her I loved her and threatening to kill her. We were lying on her bed together, staring up at the ceiling and talking, when Rory came into the room.

Callie broke off in mid-sentence, and there was a long, awkward moment of silence until Rory approached her bedside and pulled up a chair. He looked good—he had filled out and become a man; he was no longer the gawky teenage boy I remembered who moved like a colt, his own arms and legs seeming too long for his body. He had Callie's eyes, but his father's coloring, with a bit more olive than Callie's own Irish paleness.

"Hey, sis," he said quietly. "You look like shit."

"Yeah, I know, fuck you very much."

They grinned at each other, and the tightness in my chest loosened.

***

The three of us had been visiting for a couple of hours when Eric stepped into the room. He had been tied up in work since the chaos of the night before, and I was surprised to feel my stomach do a little flip on seeing him.

He looked spent. The light blue dress shirt he was wearing was the same one he'd had on when he'd left the hotel room. His sleeves were rolled up, and the shirt was wrinkled, as were his slacks. Mostly, though, the fatigue showed in his eyes, which found mine the moment he stepped in. He smiled at me, and a bit of the fatigue lifted.

"Hey," he said, shifting the paper bag he carried to his left hand and offering his right to Rory, then Callie. I made the introductions, feeling an absurd sense of pride and…territorialism as I did so. Rory and Callie inspected Eric, both trying to be discrete in their assessment, and

266

both failing miserably. Callie glanced at me and arched one knowing eyebrow, a small, approving smile playing on her lips.

Eric scanned Callie, too, but his inspection seemed more professional, almost clinical, as though he were going to write her description in a police report. For all I knew, he was.

"How's the clean-up going?" I asked Eric, once he'd claimed another of the visitor's chairs and brought it close.

"Right now, it's a cluster-fuck," he told us. He nodded at Rory's offer of coffee and gratefully accepted the Styrofoam cup Callie's brother handed him. "We have CIA, FBI, and the locals crawling over each other's asses. But, the evidence is coming in as fast as we can process it, so I think charges are going to stick. The entire operation is coming down."

The three of us received the news happily, and we all discussed the case for several minutes. There was a natural lull in the conversation, as each of us in the room realized just how exhausted we were. I was about to suggest leaving for the night, but Eric stood and came over to the bed beside me. His expression was serious, and…hesitation showed in his eyes. I had to look twice; it wasn't anything I'd seen with him before.

He gave me his hand to help me sit up in the hospital bed. "I've had time to think, Hope, in between busting bad guys and getting my ass reamed," he told me.

I smiled uncertainly. "That's good, I guess. And?"

"I realized last night…you're important to me. More than I knew. When I thought Lau had you, I…"

His words faded, but a flood of tenderness streamed inside me, as my eyes suddenly welled. My heart pounded in my chest, and my brain hurried to catch up

267

with his words. We weren't on the case now...this was Eric, just talking. Nothing he said to me now was because he had to.

"Me, too," I replied, almost whispering the words.

Eric's smile was pleased, and the certainty returned to his eyes. "I want to do this with your family," he said, nodding toward Rory and Callie. "At least, with your family that's here. I expect to meet your father sometime soon."

Blood rushed to my head. *Do this? With family? What in the world...*

Eric reached into the small bag, and I thought my heart was going to explode. The bag was from a jewelry store!

To my intense relief, the box he pulled out was too large to be a ring box. I was able to breathe again, but my heart still pounded with excitement.

Eric opened the box, and I looked inside. A long gold necklace lay within, a small golden charm—*handcuffs!* I noted with a laugh—on the end of the chain.

"Will you be my submissive, Hope?"

I was startled. My hand, which had been reaching out to touch the necklace, froze. *His...submissive?*

There was absolute silence in the small hospital room, and all three of them looked at me, waiting for my answer. I...didn't know what to say. I realized I wanted to be with Eric—more than I had ever wanted anything—but...*his submissive?*

Callie watched me, her eyes shining, and I could practically feel her pushing a 'yes' into my brain. Rory smiled, much more neutral. Eric waited patiently.

The only thing I could do was be honest.

"I—" The words stuck. I cleared my throat, and tried again, the words coming haltingly. "I would like to be…with you," I said, "but…I don't think…I don't think I can be in a relationship that's…unequitable."

Eric studied at me for a long moment, and I felt my heart sink. He didn't want me as a girlfriend or a lover. He wanted a submissive. I had enjoyed playing the role, but I knew I couldn't live it. Disappointment filled me, and I saw it reflected in Callie's eyes.

"It's not…completely unequitable," Eric said quietly. He reached up to his neck, and pulled a shorter gold chain out from his dress shirt. A matching charm hung at the end.

I heard Callie gasp, her eyes lighting with relief and joy. She looked at me, practically glaring a hole into my brain. That, more than anything else, told me how significant a gesture Eric was making. The necklaces matched. There was equity.

I felt my heart skyrocket, and I slowly nodded my head, smiling. Eric smiled back, and the tension in the room was gone, replaced with celebration and happiness. Eric's sense of satisfaction and happiness flowed through me, as I turned around, and he clasped the gold chain around my neck.

I turned back to him with a huge, goofy smile, then my eyes narrowed, as I looked again at Eric's necklace, already around his neck. *Cocky, much?*

I gestured to his necklace. "You have a necklace, too," I said, unnecessarily. "Does that mean you're collared to me?"

Callie burst out laughing, and even Rory grinned.

"Don't push it, girl," Eric growled, and then, he kissed me. Oh, man, did he *ever* kiss me!

Eric
Wrap Up

The next several weeks were hectic, as both the FBI and CIA worked feverishly to make as many righteous busts within Lau's organization as we could. Fibbies handled collection of the human trafficking evidence, while spooks collected evidence on the concurrent transnational narcotics trafficking. For once, our respective organizations worked together, and we made dozens of arrests as Lau's operation was dismantled. The information contained on the thumb drive Dale died to give us was invaluable, and several new investigations were opened as a result.

I was especially gratified by the arrests of Dr. Rouchard—who had provided psychological counseling both in-state and online to five of our missing women—and Dr. Albrecht Meier, a former physician, who had lost his license due to multiple malpractice suits. Dr.

Meier created and administered the narcotic cocktail that kept the women complacently stoned, and, according to information from one of Lau's staff, was planning to introduce the new designer drug to the streets of Hong Kong and Manhattan within weeks.

As for the IA investigation of my shooting...I lied. I testified under oath that Lau had raised his weapon in direct threat to my life. I couldn't explain how he'd managed it with the shattered scapula his autopsy revealed, but, to my surprise, Laurence Hairston, the lead IA officer, dropped that line of questioning after a casual mention. I knew Hairston. He was a good cop, and he was amazingly sharp. I would bet my soul he deliberately passed it over.

I let myself into Hope's apartment, the carton of Heinekens in one hand and the bag of chips, pretzels, and cookies in the other. Callie and Hope were in the living room, curled up together on the sofa, their eyes glued to the television screen. Mr. Wuzzles walked from lap to lap, nudging the distracted girls to pet him. I put the beer in the fridge and poured chips into a bowl, bringing it over and handing it to Hope. She accepted it with a quick smile, and nodded to the space beside her. I sat, and together, we watched the end of *Dirty Dancing*.

Jimmy Lau was dead, and his organization was crumbling, but I was under no illusions. Like the head of a hydra, he would merely be replaced, and the trafficking and sale of human beings would continue. Young men, women, and children would still disappear, some to be found, some to be lost in the mire of sexual slavery and drug addiction. The predators were still there, and they would still fish in the BDSM pond, because it was a well-stocked pool. But, I would be there, too, I decided, looking at Hope and Callie's clasped hands. I had innocents to protect.

I wasn't ready to hang up my whip. Not *quite* yet.

Author's Note

This novel is a work of fiction, but the issues it addresses are very real. Human sex trafficking is a global atrocity, and its victims come from all walks of life. Sex traffickers use violence, threats, lies, and coercion to compel their victims into slavery and prostitution.

In 2015, the National Human Trafficking Hotline received 24,757 reports of sex trafficking in the United States. In 2016, the National Center for Missing and Exploited Children estimated one of every six endangered runaways was likely a victim of sex trafficking. Globally, the International Labor Organization estimates 4.5 million people unwillingly involved in the sex trade.

In the U.S., if you are a victim of sex trafficking, or if you have information about a potential sex trafficking situation, please call the National Human Trafficking Resource Center at 1-888-373-7888.

Additionally: BDSM is a sexual activity performed among CONSENTING ADULTS. If there is coercion, or if minors are involved, it is *not* BDSM. In most BDSM communities, SSC (safe, sane, and consensual) practice of BDSM is the standard.

Acknowledgements

I write because I need to. The stories in my brain are too active, too desperate to be told, and too alive, to remain unwritten. That being said, there is no way I could do what I do without the help of some wonderfully supportive, helpful people.

Amanda Walker, my virtual personal assistant, has been invaluable, both as a cover artist and as a marketing assistant. The beautiful cover gracing this book was her creation. She makes my stuff look professional, clean, and crisp—she is an expert at making things pop!

Colin Rutherford is simply amazing beyond words. Working full-time as a professional caregiver and also full-time as an author, Colin still managed to find time to read and critique my novel, finding several huge, gaping plot holes, and helping me plug them. He is a colleague and he is my friend. I can't wait until July, when my husband and I will travel to Northern Ireland and Scotland to visit Colin and Heather!

Heather Osborne is also both a colleague and a friend. Not only did Heather edit this novel (any remaining mistakes are mine; I tend to be stubborn sometimes and not change the errors she points out!), she also did all of the formatting and layout. This book simply would not be, if not for Heather. Thank you SOOO much!

I'd also like to give a shout-out here to the real Todd Vogel, who is quite likely my "number one fan." Since first reading *Iron Mike,* Todd has been a supportive and enthusiastic follower, and he has become more than a fan; he's a friend.

My family must also be acknowledged, if, for nothing else, "putting up with [my] shit," as my husband so romantically declared! Kevin and Ellen are the absolute foundation of my world, and without them, I would be lost. Thank you, guys. I love you both, more than I can ever express!

Of course, the main person I write for is **you.** Yes, you! You, the awesome individual who has not only picked up and read my novel, but also managed to make it all the way through the long, boring acknowledgements page! You, dedicated reader, are the joy in my life. THANK YOU SO MUCH for wanting to read the stories I write!!

If you're interested in something completely different, but still penned by me, check out my first novel, *Iron Mike. Iron Mike,* an Amazon best-seller, is a SciFi coming-of-age story set in my tiny hometown of Shepherdsville, Kentucky. It can be found on Amazon at https://smile.amazon.com/Iron-Mike-Patricia-Rose/dp/1517286093.

I love hearing from my readers! If you would like to chat with me, please follow me on Facebook at https://www.facebook.com/AuthorPatriciaRose/ or email me at patricia_rose.author@aol.com. I also put out a newsletter (on a VERY irregular, erratic schedule, but never more than once per month). In each newsletter, there is an "offering": something I've written, either a short story, an essay, or vignette. To receive my newsletter, just drop me a quick email, and I'm on it!

Writers *LIVE* for reviews! If you enjoyed this novel (or even if you didn't), I would love to hear your feedback. Five paragraphs, one sentence, or anything in between would seriously make my day! I'm still learning how to write well, and any suggestions to help me improve my trade are invaluable.

Wishing you well,
Patricia Rose

About the Author

Patricia Rose was born a bookworm and has never outgrown it. Her love of stories started with The Bobbsey Twins when she was five and continues today with the best offerings of science fiction, urban fantasy, and paranormal romance. An avid animal lover, she shares her home with her husband, Kevin, the wife of her heart, Ellen, three dogs, four cats, and a tarantula. Technophobic to a fault, Patricia relies heavily on her friends in the Indie writing community to help her with anything more complex than Microsoft Word, this despite her husband's urgings to put down the stone knives and chisels and join the digital age! Patricia's first novel, Iron Mike, is a dystopian science fiction tale and is available on all Amazon forums. Both Hopeless and Iron Mike are available as audiobooks through www.audible.com.

29682136R00167

Printed in Great Britain
by Amazon